PRAISE

'A page turner'

—JMF

'Exciting read'

—JC

'Fascinating insight into neglected World War Two history'
   EVR-B

BEST EATEN COLD

A GRIPPING WORLD WAR TWO AND PRESENT DAY THRILLER

D M FLETCHER

Copyright © 2021 by Digby Martin Fletcher

All rights reserved.

No part of this book may be reproduced in any form or by any electronic or mechanical means, including information storage and retrieval systems, without written permission from the author, except for the use of brief quotations in a book review.

❊ Created with Vellum

For Jenny

BEST EATEN COLD

by D M Fletcher
Approx. 81000 words
stoatsnest@hotmail.co.uk
www.digbycreative.net

PROLOGUE

Gerrie came home from school at half past three. On Thursdays the boy went to *ouma* van Wiese's house. She was his father's mother. She made delicious *koeksisters*.

'*Ag seun*,' she said, 'never forget what your people have suffered. I am the only survivor of three sisters. During the *Vryheidsoorlog* the British made us sleep on wet floors. They starved us. We were given bread, but the soldiers stole it. I still remember little Gertruida crying with hunger. We buried her next to her sister Anna.'

And so it went on, Thursday after Thursday. After *ouma* died, Gerrie left the district, but forever hated the British, who had murdered his *ouma's* sisters, as well as many other innocent women and children of the *volk*.

1

Tony sipped his lukewarm tea and gazed out at the window ledge, bespattered with pigeon droppings. The shrill sound of the charity's phone recalled him to duty.

'Ello? Is that Mind over Matter?' The female voice on the end of the line had a fine sixty-a-day rasp.

'Yes ,it is,'Tony replied, pen poised.

'Look...I need help. Someone's been following me.'

'Aah...' Tony guessed where this was going.

'He's standing outside my house, right now.'

' Have you reported this to the police...Ms...?'

'Josie. My name's Josie, and yeah, course I have, but they just keep ignoring me complaints. Telling me I'm wasting police time.'

The tone of the caller's voice was sharp and aggressive, typical of many of the calls Tony received. He absorbed her anxiety and remained calm.

'Can I ask...are you on any medication?'

Josie sniffed. 'What the 'ell that got to do with it? '

'Josie, I'm here to help,'

Tony's voice was soothing, reassuring.

'We have experts here who understand your problems.'

'The only problem I got is someone following me. I ain't nuts.'

Tony sighed inwardly. 'This man – how long has he been doing this? Has anyone else seen him?' Tony trotted out the formula, trying to establish a rapport. Sometimes it worked. This time it didn't.

'You're just like Old Bill. Think I'm imagining it. Sod you. I'm not wasting any more of my time or my phone bill.' There was a click as the call ended.

Oh dear, thought Tony, didn't get far with that one, Tony mused. His experience of being abused over the telephone didn't stop him disliking it any more each time it happened. He had been about to say, as he he'd said too often on this line,

'Now, please, there's no need for obscene language...' But the phone was dead.

Tony loosened his clergyman's collar and leant back in his chair, regretting his failure. He would have liked at least to feel he'd done something to help her. So many people took out their frustration on the most immediate target. Perhaps he needed a break from this work. He would resume it when his enthusiasm returned, if ever. Perhaps he wasn't cut out to be a punchbag. He sipped his mug of insipid tea, wondering what it would be like to be stalked, particularly if you were a woman. Frightening. He'd never know, he hoped. He brought up the log on his computer screen and filled in the log: Call length, subject, outcome: 'Caller rang off'.

More calls followed. More distressed souls, but none as dramatic. Tony was able to provide some help to each, often recommending the charity's counselling service (free). By the time his two hour stint ended, he felt exhausted. He said goodbye to Beryl, his fierce unsympathetic co-worker with a personality by-pass, who had somehow wormed her way into a position of power in the organisation. Funny how charities attract such ghastly people, he thought. If anyone needed counseling, she did. He castigated himself for his unchristian thoughts as he walked down the worn wooden stairs to the street, closing the green painted door and hearing the Yale lock click its farewell. Thank God that's over for this week, he thought, as he joined the throng walking along the teeming multi-national High Street, with ornate old buildings sitting incongruously above garish modern shop fronts. Tempted by the Wetherspoons meal deal - fish and chips with a choice of drink, only £6.50 - he wandered inside the packed pub and looked around for a table. US Open tennis was showing on a big screen. He ordered his meal with an alcohol-free beer (wine was not a good idea during the working day, besides the meal deal restricted him to a few unpleasant varieties). The match was exciting and expunged the recent unpleasant experience from his mind. Half an hour later he threaded his way past the crowded tables and through the swing doors toward the ancient Whitgift Almshouse or Hospital as it was called. He followed the tram tracks, down the hill past the market and Argos towards the church, admiring the clever brickwork of more almshouses, which had escaped the town's relentless urge to turn everything into concrete blocks, at last finding his cosy semi-detached Victorian vicarage.

He did not notice the person following him.

2

Tony enjoyed his usual coffee and croissant as he sat at his study desk, hoping the caffeine would provide inspiration. It was Friday, and Friday meant preparation of Sunday's sermon. Tony was a good preacher, and often saw in the eyes of the congregation that they were actually listening. There were always a couple of dozers, people who came to church out of habit or coerced by the expectation of their families or, he thought cynically, who regarded Mother Church as a useful networking organisation. Tony found that the best way of maintaining interest was to find a relevant theme and put it across in such a way that most of them would understand how they could make life easier for their fellows. He realised that even the most inspiring sermon would only remain in their minds for half an hour or so, when they would revert to their well-trodden mental habits.

When he had been ordained and was new to the job, he'd found the task as difficult as trying to think of something for a school essay. Since his return from South Africa, Tony, a thirty-fiveish Church of England vicar, had been distracted. He'd found himself musing about his adventures there, and the affair of the bogus curate who had turned out to be a professional assassin. And there was Penny... Penny had been delightful, once he'd resigned himself to the fact that she was amoral and had no belief in God at all. Yet they'd got along fine. For some reason this adventure, when some of his behaviour would have shocked his parishioners, not to say the Bishop, had actually been a catalyst as far as his sermons were concerned. There had been a fresh awareness of life and many had remarked how the vicar seemed to get to the heart of the matter, instead of droning on about sin. The clergy was no longer held in the awe and respect of yore. There were too many stories in the newspapers of priests molesting children and generally behaving badly. One vicar, in Plymouth, had even robbed a bank.

A vibration in his pocket interrupted his reverie.

'Hello?'

'Hello sweetie, it's your long lost lover.'

'Ah, Penny... to what do I owe the pleasure?'

'Oh, nothing really, just felt like talking about old times. How're you doing Vic?'

Tony felt a glow of excitement at hearing the warm and seductive tones of Penny, his sometime lover and companion in South Africa.

'Same as usual ‑ preparing sermons, advising the confused.'

'Not fending off nubile young ladies?'

'Chance would be a fine thing.'

'Poor old you. Fancy meeting? Somewhere in London?'

'That would be nice.'

' What about next Wednesday or Thursday?'

'Thursday is fine. What had you in mind?'

' How about lunch at the Rubens, near Victoria, my treat? I'll see you at one.'

Before Tony had time to reply, Penny had gone. Tony

went back to preparing his sermon. He would preach on the dangers of temptation.

Penny's call gave new impetus to his creative thinking, after all, to him she was the essence of temptation. If he'd asked his Bishop's opinion he would have told him she was sent by God to test him. Yet there was nothing evil about Penny. Mischievous, yes. Amoral certainly. But she'd added a zest to his previously dull live and, if anything, made him better at his job, sinning or no sinning. He finished writing. His congregation would be surprised at the advice he was going to give them. Sometimes temptation could be a positive thing. He paced up and down his study reading the sermon aloud. No doubt when he actually gave it the words would change, but the message would be the same. It was dark by now, and his silhouette was clear from outside. His watcher was indifferent to the decrease in temperature. It was nippy, as September dissolved into October. The observer's only reaction to the chilly breeze was to look at their watch.

Thursday came and Tony felt a tingle of anticipation as he walked to East Croydon station, past the beggar, past the booth where the East Europeans peddled tat near the building site, whose hoarding had for the past seven years promised new but as yet unbuilt state of the art shops and offices, and into the station proper. There was the usual huddle of people anxious to get onto the Victoria train and grab a precious seat. As a man in his mid-thirties and with no disabilities, he would give his up if he saw an elderly or infirm person. He was not put to the test. At that time there were plenty of seats, and he settled down for the twenty minute journey. After Clapham Junction he saw the towers of the defunct Battersea Power Station and a minute or so later they drew into the station on the far side of the Thames.

Tony strolled through the ticket barrier and along the concourse towards the left hand exit. His stomach told him he was feeling nervous. Having fallen back into his church-man's routine, albeit with renewed vigour, he had led once more his old dull life, and the thought of meeting the alluring Penny again was overwhelming. He was scared. He found it hard to understand why a woman who, he thought, could take her pick, had chosen him, even if only for a short time.

Someone else, close behind, was wondering where he was going. It was easy to be inconspicuous in such a crowded place, and Tony had no inkling that he was being followed yet again.

Penny looked ravishing, and Tony kissed her smooth cheek. She hugged him then kissed him, softly, on the mouth.

'Lovely to see you darling. Shall we go into that bar area over there? It has a private area and I'm thirsty and famished.'

After ordering food and drinks, he said,

'O.K...so what's up?'

'Lots of things. Before we get on to them, did you know someone is following you?'

'No. Who?'

Penny sipped her G & T.

'I can't tell yet whether it's male or female, but I noticed someone coming in here behind you, and there was a certain vibe I get in these sitches. So, watch it. We can play a game when you leave, if you like. I'll wait for you to get ahead, and pretend I'm staying, and then keep you in sight. It might work if my observation isn't rumbled.'

Sitches? thought Tony. Of course, Penny abbreviated words at will.

'Thanks, I hope there's an innocent explanation, I can't think why anyone should want to follow me. Now why did you really get me here?'

Penny's hazel eyes widened.

'Just to see *you* darling, of course. Well yes that's true, I do need your help as well. I have a problem. It's my aunt.'

'I didn't know you had one, although why shouldn't you?'

'True. But this one isn't the usual cosy stereotype.'

''No, but you aren't either, so the genes must have come from somewhere.'

Penny laughed.

'Touché. This aunt has a monstrous IQ and used to work for British Intelligence. She retired a while ago to Sussex. I think she's been kidnapped or worse.'

'Why do you think that?'

'I've not heard from her, and I think there's someone else living in her house.'

'Why don't you just go down there and knock on the door?'

'If it was as simple as that, I would. However, for reasons which I can't disclose at the moment, I cannot. I was hoping you would.'

'Why me?'

'Tony sweetie, you belong to one of the best networking systems in this country. Nothing unpleasant is going to happen to you. You're a clergyman for heaven's sake. All you have to do is to make an excuse to see the local padre, volunteer to visit parishioners to get them to the church fete, and you would have the ideal excuse to visit anyone.'

The gentle violin music in the background did not quell Tony's exasperation.

'It's not so easy, I'd have to stay there for a bit, ingratiate myself and so on. I really can't afford...'

'Don't worry about the moolah. I have the funding. As for the time, don't you have holiday owing? I'd make it up to you.' She put her hand on his knee.

Tony felt stirrings. Life *was* dull at the moment.

'I'll think about it.'

Penny squeezed his thigh.

'I knew you'd help. We'll discuss the plan of action later. Now let's finish this gorgeous St Emilion.'

Tony quaffed his share; after all, this wasn't a *working* day and his head spun as Penny talked. She was attractive when he was sober, and the drink-fuelled haze made her a cross between Nicole Kidman and Helen of Troy. By the time he left he'd have agreed to do anything. The lingering kiss she gave him when he said good-bye clinched it.

Tony left the ornate 19th century hotel, managed to make his way home to the vicarage and despite his intoxicated state, to avoid being seen by anyone he knew. Penny can certainly put it away and not be affected in the slightest, he thought. No service tomorrow morning, thank the Lord.

He crawled into bed and fell unconscious, rather than slept. He awoke with a headache and crawled to the bathroom, where he swallowed some paracetamol with copious water. He dropped off again.

He was finally woken up by the intrusive sound of his mobile phone alarm. It was a horrible piercing noise like a fire engine on heat, which was why he had chosen it. His mind was in a paranoid state induced by excess alcohol. What had he agreed to? Penny was a dangerous woman, all the more so because she was so charming. Few men would be able to resist the combination of dazzling looks, soft voice...

A different noise, from the phone, this time 'Onward Christian Soldiers', interrupted his musing. It was a call.

'Hello darling, had breakfast? Don't answer, I expect you have a hangover. Is Monday too soon for you?'

'What? Now look here, Penny, I can't just up sticks and go off at your whim. Who's going to look after this place?'

'Point taken. Let's make it Monday week. I'll email you all you need to know. You are definitely being followed, by the way.'

'How do you know?'

'Followed you myself, as promised, partly because I thought you might come to mischief, the state you were in. You can't hold your liquor, can you?'

'Who is following me?'

'It's a woman. I don't think she means you immediate harm, as in your state it'd have been easy enough to bump you off. She followed you to the vicarage, and then hung about outside. I don't know how long, because I needed my sleep and left. I don't want her following you down to Sussex, so I'll have to devise a plan for throwing her off the scent.'

Despite a feeling of alarm, Tony managed to make a faint, hopeless stab at reasserting control.

'Penny, you're taking over again.'

'You love it darling. I'll ring you in a couple of days. In the meantime, get yourself a locum or whatever you do when you go away.'

The phone went dead. What have I got myself into? thought Tony. Maybe I'll be able to think clearly after a shower. He made his way to the bathroom, and as the warm water cascaded, his mood improved. Seeing Penny again made him feel he could take on the world.

3

'In the name of the Father...'

Tony made his way to the church door and greeted his parishioners as they trooped out.

'Great sermon vicar,' said a man Tony had seen fast asleep.

'Why thank you Tom, I hope I didn't put you to sleep?'

The man shuffled on without replying. Tony's thoughts on 'temptation' had reached the brains of some, but there had been no indignation afterwards. He reflected that people had reached a mental state in which nothing caused surprise and shock any more, unless he actually swore or threw something at someone. He was not yet ready for that.

There were some faces he didn't know. One, perhaps, was his stalker? He could see the vapour from his breath as he talked, cold for October, and found himself thinking, no smoke without fire. It's only condensation, you fool. Maybe I need a break. My brain's becoming addled.

He ambled back to the vicarage, a building built at the same time as the Gothic Revival church it served by an extravagant and generous benefactor, who had a penchant for alcoves containing the effigies of the heads of prominent people from bygone ages. Having decided to fall in with Penny's plan, he examined the emails from agencies that supplied locum vicars. The C.V.s' entertainment value was enormous. They read like estate agents' particulars.

Did 'well-liked by parishioners' mean 'joins them in the pub whenever he can'? Did 'focused on issues going forward' mean anything at all? He settled for the one whose C.V. was written in plain English, a man. He had been ordained relatively recently, had been a property lawyer and was available straight away. He would interview him.

He wandered over to the window of his first floor study, from which he had a good view of the street. There was a woman taking photographs. Hang on. She was photographing *him* through a long lens. He pulled down the blinds. Penny was right. He *was* being watched, but why? He decided to call a friend.

'Hello, Septimus here. How are you Tony you old scoundrel?'

'I need your advice, Septimus, I'm being stalked.'

'As your solicitor I'd say come and see me at the office on Monday, and we'll get an injunction. As your friend, are you sure?'

'Pretty sure. Can I come and see you at home?'

'I suppose so. I could do with cheering up. What's more entertaining than a vicar in trouble?'

Septimus's house was a vast mansion only half a mile from Tony's church. It was situated at the top of a small hill. Like Tony's vicarage, built by the same rich Croydonian plutocrat. There were alcoves containing heads of Roman emperors dotted along the front walls. It was an impressive building and Tony always felt intimidated by its grandeur. Septimus was only the second child, but he'd been born on the seventh of December. His father, who only ever had two sons wanted everyone to know he had a degree in Classics, so used Latin as often as he could, enjoying explaining that 'Septimus' meant 'seventh'. The house was in a prime residential area and the plot was big enough to contain a tidy block of flats. But Septimus had resisted the blandishments of developers and lived as his grandfather had, minus the servants. His possessions were for the most part inherited, and the walls of his house were crowded with paintings of ugly relatives and knick-knacks equally ugly but no doubt valuable. The overall effect was comforting in an odd way, like being in an antique shop. On the top floor there was a model railway system of enormous complexity, with junctions, sidings, points, level crossings and stations, and even a model of the famous 'Mallard' engine.

Septimus himself was a man from some earlier time, Edwardian perhaps, with hairs sprouting from ears, nose and chin. He always wore a bow tie, and his views would not have offended his grandfather, also a man of law. His brain was a repository of human experience. Shocking behaviour had become so commonplace to him that he had almost lost the capacity for surprise. Eccentric human behaviour was almost a norm. He had met murderers, rapists, fraudsters, the children of monks, even a bank robbing vicar. He was sometimes bored with the bizarre, so accustomed was he to it. Tony knew him as a good friend.

Tony knocked on the ornate brass knocker. His friend would not countenance an electric bell. The door opened and the tall figure of Septimus stood smiling before him.

'Hello, my ecclesiastical comrade, come in.'

Tony wondered how Septimus's late wife had put up with the paraphernalia. Septimus once told him she'd been a ferociously tidy woman. Every day with Septimus must have been a trial. She had died ten years ago, before Tony had met Septimus, who rarely mentioned her, not even having a photograph on display.

Now he had a girlfriend whom he had met at a Morris dancing society he had joined. It seemed an odd way to meet women, but Septimus was a shrewd judge of humans. He reckoned that such a place was more likely to produce someone congenial than pubs which were anathema to him unless Victorian or older, and served types of rare ale that meant nothing to Tony. He was also shrewd enough not to cohabit or marry again, reckoning his freedom was a thing worth preserving. They moved to the capacious sitting room and sat on each side of an ancient Chesterfield.

'What can I get you, tea, alcohol?'

'Nothing now, thanks Septimus, maybe when you've given me some advice. I'm being followed, as I mentioned, and I'd be glad of your views.'

Septimus leaned back in the sofa, as if he was about to launch himself forward. He did this sporadically, but reverted to the original posture, only his head turning towards Tony.

'Any idea who it is?'

Tony was slightly exasperated by this obvious question, but answered politely,

'No, except that it seems to be a woman.'

Septimus chuckled.

'You sly dog, sure it's not a spurned lady friend?' He chuckled at his joke, shaking as he did so. 'I expect not, man of the cloth and all that. There's only one thing to do. No crime's been committed, so the police won't be interested. I know an enquiry agent who might help. He's not cheap, though. He can follow the follower. I'll email you his details. Any other problems?

'Oh, Penny's back, wants me to get involved in some shenanigans.'

'I'd like to meet this Penny, she sounds alluring.'

'She'd give you a heart seizure at your age Septimus, thought you had a new girlfriend?'

'I have, but she's a bit unexciting, I suppose, although a very sweet girl.'

'Stick to her my dear fellow. Penny's dangerous. Wants me to go down to Sussex and find out what's happened to her aunt. There's bound to be a lot more to it, I bet.'

Septimus leaned forward. Wish he'd sit in one position, thought Tony, I'm getting dizzy.

'Now that sounds interesting, better than sitting in your vicarage compiling well-meant sermons, or for that matter, if you're me, answering tedious emails and fencing with keyboard warriors. You'll have a gin and tonic now?'

Having got his problem off his chest, Tony succumbed.

Septimus walked over to the bay window, where he kept his drinks cabinet. He peered out.

'Can't see anybody. No one's followed you here. Perhaps been scared by all the severe emperors' busts on the wall.'

The gin was Hendricks, which he and Tony preferred to all others. He poured two glasses and laced them with tonic. He wandered off and returned with some ice and a container of lemon slices. He sat down again on the Chesterfield and Tony and he took their first sips of the cheering drinks. A thought struck Tony.

'You busy, Septimus? Fancy some time off?'

'Things *are* a bit slow I suppose. Why?'

'After my previous experiences with Penny, I'd be happier with company.'

'I might be interested. I'll think about it and have a word with my partner, Harvey.'

Tony could see from the grin, which lit up the face of his friend, that Harvey would be told rather than consulted. He drank the rest of his drink and got up.

'I need to be back for evensong. Thanks for the help. I'll let you know when I'm going. Meantime I'd be grateful to have the details of the enquiry bloke.'

Tony glanced at the face of Hadrian, who was the Emperor whose face was immediately to the left of the front door and felt the eyes of his co-emperors following him as he boarded his little Citroen. By now paranoid about being followed, he looked up and down the road but detected no one.

By the time he was back he'd received an email from Septimus with the contact information of the enquiry agent, one Darren Marshall, and he emailed him,

Hi Darren

Septimus Smythe has recommended you to me. I think I'm being followed. Can you help? If so, can you come to my address (see above)

Regards

Tony

THE FOLLOWING day he received a reply:

Hi

Will 3 pm tomorrow be all right?

Darren

DARREN WAS A TALL YOUNG MAN, with a not entirely honest face. He wore jeans and a sweatshirt in the red and blue colours of Crystal Palace FC, with the words: 'Eagles for the Cup' printed on the front.

'Sorry about the gear, but I'm off to a Palace (he pronounced the word 'palliss') supporters meeting. You don't look the type, reverend.'

'Type of what?'

'To get involved with strange women.'

'I'm not involved with anyone. I'm not even sure it's a woman. All I know is that I seem to be being followed and this has been confirmed by a friend of mine who says it's a woman. Mr Smythe recommends you highly, so I look forward to your report.'

The agent listened and grinned in a nudge-nudge wink-wink way. Tony found this off-putting. If it hadn't been for the recommendation Tony wouldn't have hired him, but Septimus was better versed in these matters than he. Darren spoke in a loud nasal twang,

'I'll try to get you some info in a week. I'll be doing the work personally by the way. My charges are £150 per hour. I'll let you know when I've got to a thousand. These are my standard Terms and Conditions. Please sign here.'

He handed Tony a piece of A4 paper with tiny type all over it. Tony skimmed through the document, signed at the bottom and handed it back to Darren who said,

'I'll need £250 on account for expenses. Do you have a card?'

Darren produced a little machine and took Tony's card.

'I'll be in touch as soon as I have anything. Is there a back entrance? Don't want prying eyes to catch a gander of my good self, know what I mean?'

'Yes, there's the kitchen, you can go through there,' said Tony.

He followed Darren to the kitchen door. As he'd arrived in such a flashy car Tony saw no chance Darren's arrival had not been detected. Going out of the back entrance was futile and meant to impress him.

'Wonderful,' said Tony. Darren was not a man who was sensitive to sarcasm.

'Cheers rev,' he said, and drove off in his smart silver Beamer.

The week passed quickly, the only notable event being the interview with the locum. It had lasted ten minutes, and Tony felt sure that his parishioners would welcome him back after a dose of the human marshmallow who had dominated his study. His views were old fashioned and dull. He imagined he would drone from the pulpit and have the sinners asleep on their hard wooden seats, as the platitudes washed over them. Perhaps he was doing Rev Murgatroyd an injustice, but he thought not.

In spite of the stalker problem, Tony had been all for hopping on the train to Brighton and taking a taxi to the rural parish where Penny's aunt lived. No such luck. Penny had insisted he went into London first and take a roundabout route back to a spot within walking distance of the station.

'That'll throw her off, sweetie. Has your friend's private dick found out anything yet?'

'No, but I'm hoping. Not that optimistically, but maybe he will. If it takes a rogue to catch a rogue, then Darren's the right man for this job. Septimus may be coming with me, by the way.'

'May he indeed. Good idea, you're not safe on your own.'

'Thanks. I'll ring you when I get there, eventually.'

Septimus having, he said, obtained his partner Harvey's approval, refused to have anything to do with Tony's attempts to throw off his stalker and arranged to meet him in Brighton. The train whizzed through the countryside, and after arriving and negotiating the ticket barrier Tony was amused to see Septimus in his leisurewear. He was dressed in tweeds, with a waistcoat and deerstalker hat.

'I've been longing to wear this hat for years, and as we're sleuths, I thought it was appropriate.'

The younger man shook his head.

'I'm amazed you aren't smoking a pipe. Let's get a taxi.'

They clambered into one of the queuing cabs and after a long drive through narrow lanes approached the aunt's home village and stopped at the Duke's Head. The duke in this case was Wellington, recognisable by his beaky nose. The receptionist was an efficient blonde woman with an East European accent, who took details of Tony's debit card. Meals would be served from 6.30. The place had two rooms which were passable, and Tony left Septimus to amuse himself while he ambled towards the vicarage. The church was an ancient one and Tony, always interested in such things, was tempted to have a look inside. As he was examining a brass plaque commemorating a soldier killed aged 24 in the Crimea, he saw a man dressed in a cassock standing on the other side of the nave. He decided to own up before being accosted.

'Excuse me, I'm Tony – vicar of St Petroc's Croydon. Would you be Canon Urgle by any chance?' The Canon, with whom Tony had exchanged emails, said,

'Yes, for my sins, glad to meet you.' They shook hands. The local vicar was thin with a few strands of hair combed across his crown. He reminded Tony of a meerkat. He said,

'I'm Bill Urgle, indeed Canon Urgle formally, but please call me Bill. There are some very fine examples of pre-Reformation statues in this church - escaped the depredations of the Roundheads, Cromwell's lot gave this part of Sussex a miss I'm pleased to say. I was very pleased to get your letter. You're staying in the Duke's Head I understand. It's an old smugglers' haunt. I am doubly glad to see you. I'm in something of a fix. John Abercrombie - the neighbouring vicar from St Alfred's - was due to preach this Sunday, but unfortunately he's been taken to hospital. Heart attack, I believe. Poor chap. It does rather leave me up a gum tree, well what I was meaning to ask was, do you mind preaching this Sunday?'

'Preaching?' said Tony, 'this a bit sudden, but if it'll help out... I'd be very pleased to - any particular subject? I do a good 'Prodigal Son'. Or perhaps the Serpent in the Garden of Eden?'

'I leave it to your good judgement. I dare say the people here won't have heard any of your sermons, so you can preach your favourite, if you like. Except please steer clear of anything that smacks of Romish doctrine. Local sensitivities. Are you comfortable at the Duke's Head?'

'Yes, I'm fine. Do you have any idea where Lime Tree Cottage is? I promised to visit a friend's aunt.'

'Never heard of it, but Phyllis will have. She's a Prebendary, you know, used to sit in a special stall in the Cathedral choir, and insists on being called by her title. She lives next door. I'll introduce you.'

Phyllis was a self-important but knowledgeable woman of fiftyish who didn't believe in makeup, or, from the look of her, visiting the hairdresser either. She was very nosey about Tony's visit and he was relieved to escape after several cups of tea and tasty scones. Penny's aunt, Theresa, was apparently very secretive and Phyllis was dying to know more. She referred to 'comings and goings' and 'odd visitors', which didn't make Tony feel comfortable. She gave him precise directions in midst of the gossip before he managed to extricate himself with a promise to drop in after Sunday's church service for a sherry. He escaped to the pub, where he found Septimus. The lawyer was sitting in a comfy chair in the bar, halfway through what looked like a whisky.

'Get on all right, Tone?' he said.

'Fine, Sept. You wouldn't think tea and scones with a middle-aged woman would wear one out, but it can. I've been talking to Prebendary Phyllis, who would be a credit to the Gestapo. I understand Penny's auntie is regarded as something of an outsider. There are mysterious goings on at her place and respectable folk, namely Phyllis and the people she associates with, other churchgoers I imagine, are not happy about it.'

Septimus sipped his whisky and looked at Tony.

'So, Penny was not wrong. I hope we're not getting into something we may regret,'

'Now's the time to skedaddle, if you're worried. I daren't - I'd never be able to face Penny again. Besides, seriously, it's a matter of honour.'

'Don't worry, Tony, I'm not one to funk something just because it might be tricky. A friend is a friend and besides I'm quite looking forward to it. I was just advising you really.'

Tony smiled, 'I knew I could count on you. A large gin and tonic wouldn't go amiss though.'

'I suggest you scout around, old boy,' said Septimus. 'I'll keep an eye out from here.'

The house was a small black and white Tudor building with gnarled black beams, and there was copious ivy growing up the walls. The door was studded with thick nails and there was an iron lock. It looked nearly as old as the house. As Tony took this in, he became aware of something out of place. There were two cameras in rounded dark glass, like the eyes of an enormous fly, and they seemed to follow him as he moved. He gestured towards them and Septimus nodded.

'Looks like we're not alone,' said Septimus, 'be careful. I'll take the front and you the back.'

Tony opened a side gate, which creaked from lack of maintenance and jarred his knee against a solid object. Before he looked down, the smell gave it away. It was a bin that needed emptying. He crept further along the wall and was relieved to reach the end. He could see a garden with a shed at one side. Again, the grass was long. He crept round the side of the building, opening a gate as he did so. Keeping close to the wall, he approached the shed, aware there might be more cameras. He reached it and turning around towards the house, spotted a camera at the rear. Despite this, he decided to have a look inside the shed. There might be a light. A thick padlock denied him entry. He felt very exposed to the camera, and wondered whether it was infra-red. All was silent except for the gurgling of a stream, beyond which were trees. By now it was twilight and every minute the natural light diminished. He felt there was little further he could achieve now and made his way back, avoiding the pain inflicting bin.

'I think we should come back when it's light, Septimus,' he whispered. 'Septimus?'

His friend was not there.

4

Penny lay back in the hot spa. She'd already swum 50 lengths of the 20-metre pool, loving the feel of the warm water as she relaxed, knowing she was keeping her body in good condition., It also allowed her to think without disturbance. She wondered how Tony was doing. It was pretty harmless surely, sending him to Sussex? Vicars posed no obvious threat, and a visit by such a mild inoffensive and genuine chap would not be seen as suspicious, one would think.

Although she'd spoilt Penny, her aunt Theresa was a tough old bird. From what Penny had gleaned from her parents and odd remarks made by Theresa herself, it was clear she'd had an important job during the war, something to do with South Africa, where she had purportedly been a British secret agent. There was a garbled story about her mathematical ability and codes. Her personal life had been complicated, and there was talk of a husband or ex-husband. Of her peacetime job there was little information. Penny knew she went daily to an office in London and had sometimes met her for tea at the Ritz. She'd waited on the ground floor of a grim office building near Waterloo station while the security man had contacted her aunt and had time to read the sign showing who was on what floor. She'd noticed that one floor was occupied by the Inland Revenue, and others by organisations she'd never heard of. The significant fact was that she had not been invited to go up in the lift but had to stay where she was. Penny had been her only niece, a surrogate daughter. She recalled Aunt Theresa helping her with her maths homework and she'd even taught Penny to play chess. The impression was of an enigmatic brainy person. Some of the remarks she'd made were difficult to understand. She'd been keen to warn Penny against ever working for the government.

'I'm stuck in this job, but a girl with an active mind needs to stay out of it. The place is full of jobsworths, arse lickers, greasy pole climbers and clock watchers. Mediocrity is rewarded and, except during a war, independent thinking causes offence. A bright girl like you should go into something else. I don't recommend the law, as I understand it's a lot of stress. You'll have to find something you like. I shall be leaving everything to you, and I hope you make good use of it. I wouldn't dream of doing so if I thought you'd be idle. As for the government, they'll let you down Penny. I work for them because I have to, but if I wasn't useful, they'd cast me off like yesterday's newspaper. The old girl (and in spite of her good looks Penny thought of her as the 'old girl') had been very generous to Penny. It was she who'd paid for trips abroad and for Penny to do her MA in journalism. She'd encouraged Penny to be cheeky and question authority. Their sense of humour was the same and, as Penny's parents sometimes went abroad for extended periods, Penny often stayed with her aunt. Her own mother was a controlling, rather unmaternal soul, and was only too relieved that her sister took the rather wild and unruly daughter off her hands. The bond grew and Penny confided in her aunt in a way she never did her mother. Theresa was an elder, pleasant and exciting sister to her. The 'agent' part of her life she rarely alluded to and when Penny asked her about it she usually became vague and changed the subject. Penny, as her aunt told her parents, was 'all there and a bit more' and thought possibly her aunt was still an agent. When her aunt disappeared, not responding to letters or picking up her phone, she had not wanted to go down to Sussex herself, because she was known in certain quarters, and had felt she would attract attention.

As the shower water cascaded down her body, she heard a muffled noise from her locker. Must be that blasted phone, she thought. No need to panic, I'll pick up the voicemail when I'm ready. Fifteen minutes later she sat in her car, an old MG. She had scrolled down the calls and the name 'Tony' had come up. She pressed the recall button.

After the disembodied instructions she heard Tony's voice,

'Penny, you have to get down here. Septimus has disappeared and I think things are bad. I'm at the Duke's Head.'

Oh shit, thought Penny, can't leave him for a moment. She texted him,

'I'll be down in a couple of hours'.

The journey from Richmond to Sussex took two hours, as Penny wrestled with the dense south London traffic and numerous red lights before hitting the M3, the appalling M25, with its gargantuan lorries driven by sleepy and sometimes dangerous drivers, and finally the M23. She loathed driving on the motorway. Her MG was lovely on winding country roads, but the noise of the air as she sat in her lane on the M23 was deafening, and the ride monotonous, made nerve wracking by the constant watch for big lorries. One had once changed lane without looking and sent her little car into a spin, nearly killing her. Somehow she'd emerged from the crash with only psychological damage, a fear of big lorries, especially those whose non-British number plates showed they were left hand drive. She developed a habit of overtaking them quickly, on the basis she was invisible to them.

The mellifluous tones of her SATNAV directed her from the motorway. I don't know where the fuck I am, she thought. Instead of leading her into a field or river, as she'd imagined, she heard 'You have reached your destination' and parked behind the pub, noting the beaky nosed caricature of the great Duke. At least I can have a drink, she thought, and marched into the building with that in mind. On second thoughts she'd better find poor Tony first, he must be beside himself, poor nervous unworldly man of the cloth. She peeked into the bar and made for the oldest person she could see.

She asked the pub owner (for it was he), face red and puffy from years of drink and exposure to the Sussex weather, as he leered at her, whether a Reverend Tony ---- was resident. He said,

'Up the stairs on the left, darling, I think the gentleman's expecting you.'

Shaking off her immediate dislike of her informant, Penny trudged up the steep old stairs, built long before Health and Safety was ever thought of, each step requiring an enormous stride, and found a black-painted door. She knocked. There was the rattling of a bolt being drawn and Tony's pale face peered out at her.

'Thank goodness it's you, Penny, come in.'

'So, what's been happening darling? How on earth has your fossilised friend got lost?'

'Sit down and I'll explain.'

They sat on the bed, and Tony said,

'Like a cup of instant coffee or tea?'

'No thanks sweetie, I hate those little plastic milk things. I wouldn't be surprised if they weren't cancerous.'

'I think you mean carcinogenic. Please yourself. A glass of water, perhaps?'

'Yes, thank you.' She sipped the glass he proffered, saying,

'Now please tell me exactly what you've been doing, leaving out nothing.'

Tony told her. Penny's face wore a resigned but tolerant expression. She felt guilty but was always ready to solve problems. She said,

'I'm reluctant to involve the police, but I suppose we'll have to if your mate doesn't turn up soon. If he's been snatched, it could be by anybody. I have this feeling auntie has been snatched too. Oh dear, what a mess. Poor old Septimus. Are you game for looking for him?'

'We could have a go, but don't you think we'd better wait till tomorrow, as I think it'd be hopeless in the dark.'

'Very wise. I'd better kip in here. If Septimus does come back tonight he'll be scared witless to find me in his bed.'

'He'd think it was Christmas, more like,' said Tony. 'He's a lecherous old thing.'

'Well so are you, but at least we're acquainted. You go on the sofa. I'm not in the mood for hanky-panky. I'd better get my case from the car and square things with the old lobster behind the bar. I expect he'll want more money.' She disappeared for a few minutes leaving Tony feeling relieved. Usually Penny's proximity made his hormones go into overdrive, but his anxiety about Septimus kept them in check. He was just pleased to have her capable presence.

Penny returned.

'I've sorted him out, the bill will be thirty quid bigger but at least I'll get breakfast. Now you'd better make yourself at home on the couch.'

'Yes ma'am.'

Tony had a nervy night, dreaming of his old curate, Smitham, the professional assassin. Smitham didn't do anything - just followed him. He didn't bother to hide, just walked a few paces behind. Tony heard himself say,

'Would you mind going away?'

The spectre of his curate ignored him, staying in his wake. He woke up relieved to find he had been dreaming. He stumbled to the bathroom. After he'd had a drink of Sussex tap water, he sat on the edge of the couch, afraid to go to sleep again; the terror of the dream had been so intense, he was wet with sweat, and toweled himself down. His room was on the first floor, and he opened the window.

He looked out at the swaying trees, and thought he saw the brush beneath them move. A fox or badger perhaps. Again it moved, this time the movement was too violent to have come from a small animal, and he realised it must be a human. Now awake, he put on his dressing gown, saw that Penny was asleep, as she breathed regularly, and trod as quietly as he could manage down the stairs. The proprietor had given him keys to the lock of the main door and minutes later he was outside. He had brought a torch, which he shone into the bushes. In spite of flashing it back and forth he found nothing. Perhaps whoever he'd seen had gone. As he trudged back to the building he heard a rustling from behind him, and a faint groaning as he approached.

He shone his torch at the sound and discerned a shape next to a giant tree. It moved. The groan was familiar, and soon the torchlight revealed the sideburns and full beard of his legal friend.

'Septimus?' he whispered.

'Help me up can't you Tony, it's uncomfortable lying on wet leaves.'

Tony puffed as he hauled the corpulent lawyer to his feet.

'Wherever you've been you've not starved. Where *have* you been?'

'I'll tell you everything in the morning. I want to go to bed.'

They walked to the front door which Tony had left unlocked and crept into the building and up the stairs. They found Septimus's room to which he still had the key and Septimus flopped onto his bed, snoring almost before Tony had left.

Next morning the three of them sat at the breakfast table, Septimus tucking in to his full English. As he smeared marmalade onto his thick brown toast, Septimus at last began talking,

'When you went off to the back of the property, I heard a car engine idling. I walked down the track and saw one of those four-by-four gas-guzzlers with an old woman at the wheel. I approached and she hissed at me to get in. She then drove off despite my protests that I'd left you.'

'Who was this woman?' said Tony.

'Penny's aunt, Mata Hari herself. Pardon me Penny, but she is a mysterious woman,' replied Septimus. She's frightened.'

Penny gazed at Septimus.

'Poor auntie. Did she explain anything?'

'In a desultory way - I didn't understand a lot of it. She talks very quickly and seems to have some sort of speech impediment.'

'Ah, that's since she had a stroke. It doesn't affect her in other ways, but it is sometimes hard to understand her. She's managed to keep it from DVLA though, if she's still driving.' Penny's face was anxious, and her fingers tapped on the table as she spoke. She closed her eyes for a moment and staring hard at Septimus, said,

'What sort of solicitor are you?'

'Average,' said Septimus.

'Ha ha. I mean, what type of law do you deal with?'

'Court work, Probate, wills, this and that.'

'Just about everything then. Hmm, you might be useful. Defended any criminals?'

'Innumerable.'

'Now, why is my aunt frightened and why is she not living at her house?'

'She wouldn't tell me at first. We drove miles to another house. She wanted to know why Tony (whom she seemed to be aware of) and I were snooping around. She's been keeping an eye on her house. I told her we were emissaries from your good self, and she relaxed. She wanted to know where you were and to warn you that you, and 'her friend the vicar' were in grave danger. When I asked for more details she said that part of it was to do with her and your relationship with her and that both you and Tony had upset some unpleasant people. She herself feared for her life but did not think it was of much consequence. She said 'I too have upset dangerous people in the past and I'm still here'. I pressed her for more details. She said you were a 'capable girl' and to send you her love, she said she would be in touch, and left me a mile or so from this pub. She apologised but said she'd taken a risk going near her house and it was pointless taking another one. She thought I was safe enough, but to be careful. She did go on a bit, but I wasn't really listening properly as I was in a bit of a state. I expect it'll come back to me.'

'You managed to walk here, but why were you lying on the ground?' said Tony.

'You try walking through trees in the dark. I fell over something, probably a tree root.'

'Does my aunt want to see me?' said Penny.

'Don't think so, she wants you to avoid danger as much as possible and seeing her might put you at risk. She didn't actually say,' said Septimus. 'She definitely thinks someone wants to kill her though, and that they'll succeed sooner or later.'

Penny sat back in her chair and sipped her coffee. She shrugged her shoulders:

'The intention was to find out what sort of a pickle Auntie was in and now we have some idea. We either go back home, or have another decko,' said Penny. 'Now I'm here we might as well have a look. You game, Tony?'

'Yes, I'll come.'

'I'll pass,' said the bearded lawyer. 'I've had enough excitement. See you in a couple of hours. I'll potter about the village.'

Penny and Tony walked the mile to the cottage. When they were a few hundred yards away, Penny said,

'I'm going to disable the cameras. I don't want to be filmed.'

She took a thin object out of her bag.

'What's that?'

'A laser pointer. They're made for peep giving presentations. If the camera has an infra-red faculty, this will disable it.'

Penny pointed the device at each camera, then said,

'Run!' They did so and reached the house. She took another device from her bag.

'This is a bump key,' she said. 'Watch.'

She took what looked like a Yale key and after some dexterous maneuvering, opened the lock.

'Good thing you're not a burglar,' said Tony.

They entered the house. The place was furnished in cottagey style on the ground floor, and apart from a layer of dust, looked normal. They went upstairs. Again, all looked normal.

'Does your aunt smoke?' said Tony.

'Not to my knowledge, she's very health conscious. I can see what you mean though. This room stinks of cigarettes. Let's turn this computer on. I'll download the contents of the hard disk, so we can examine them.'

She took yet more devices from her bag, plugged them into the computer and they waited as the lights flashed while data was transferred.

'OK sweetie, now let's get out of here.' On the way out she again disabled the cameras with her laser pointer, and they were soon walking back to the village.

'Now we've got to get out of this place, whoever looks at that computer will have pictures of you and Perry Mason from yesterday's excursion. I need to get an expert onto this data.'

She kissed him on the cheek and walked off to her car.

Tony walked back to the Duke's Head and found Septimus sipping an early lunchtime pint.

'I'll have to tell the local vicar I've been called back,' said Tony. 'I was quite looking forward to thundering at these sleepy bumpkins from the pulpit, or even at some dangerous spies. Penny says it's not safe for us to stay here, as they'll have our faces on computer from the surveillance cameras.'

'O.K. old boy, you're the boss.' said Septimus. 'Am I allowed to finish my pint?'

They packed, paid the bill and took a taxi to Croydon. A short distance behind them drove another car, just out of sight.

Tony had a few days of holiday left but decided he might as well spend it at home, and let the locum do the church work, as he was already committed to paying her. His answering machine light was flashing.

There were a couple of messages from parishioners, which would keep. One remained, left yesterday at noon:

'Hello reverend, this is Darren Marshall. Sorry not to have come back to you earlier. I've found out a lot. I'll ring you again tomorrow. In the meantime, be careful, lock your doors. You are in danger.'

5

The lawyer's office was in a Victorian building in the centre of the town. At ground level there was a travel agent, and the name of the legal firm could be discerned by careful examination of the faded gold lettering on the first and second floor windows, The front of the building was shaped like a wedding cake which had been left untouched for decades, its beauty showing still in the discoloured stone, which shone gold in the sunlight.

Entry was by means of a buzzer, the sound of which would bring forth a request for identity. Another buzz would denote the release of the lock, and a climb up wooden stairs revealed a reception desk.

To see the Senior Partner required an appointment, and his concession to modernity was a computer in which he kept his appointment diary. Clients were conducted into his large chamber; its walls lined with ancient law books going back far into the 18th century.

He had kept his father's desk, and it was clear of paper, except for the files of his current client. Like his father, he never dialled a phone number himself, at least in the office.

'Get me Darren Marshall, please Vera.'

While he was waiting, he flipped through his emails. He was surprised Darren had been so slow. It was a simple job. Following the vicar would make the stalker conspicuous, and identifying the follower couldn't be too difficult for an experienced sleuth like Darren

'Sorry Septimus, there's no reply, but have you read the paper?'

'No, why? What's in it?'

'I'll bring it in.'

Septimus did not need to scan the whole of the Advertiser. The headlines told him all,

'PRIVATE EYE SLAUGHTERED IN PUB CAR PARK'

'Darren Marshall the popular local enquiry agent was found dead at the wheel of his BMW in the car park of the Lamb and Bullock in South Croydon. Police are...'

Hardened as he was to death and crime, having been a criminal practitioner in the crime-ridden town for many years, the lawyer was shocked. Marshall had been a decent person, for a private eye, although who knew what mysteries lurked away from the public gaze?

Poor old Tony was no doubt still being stalked. He decided to make a call. What was the point of being a superannuated solicitor if you didn't have contacts?

'Get me Inspector Kenny please, Vera.'

He tried to do some work as he waited for the call but was unable to concentrate. At last his phone rang.

'Hello Tom, how are you, you old scoundrel?'

'Hello Sept, what can I do for you?'

'Wondered if you knew anything about Darren Marshall. I'd just recommended him for a job. Thought I might be able to help. '

'All information is gratefully received. Fancy a pint at the Swan and Sugarloaf?'

'Not my favourite, but if that's all you're offering...I'll see you at one.'

'One o' clock it is then,' said the Inspector.

His intercom buzzed.

'Reverend Tony is in the office, Septimus. Says he knows he doesn't have an appointment, but it's important.'

'Show him in please Vera.'

Tony's pale face wore an expression of concern as he sat down opposite his friend.

'You've read the news about Mr Marshall?'

'Indeed,' replied the lawyer. 'I was wondering why we hadn't heard from him. I suppose we'll have to find ourselves another private dick. I'm having an off the record chat with a policeman pal, so I'll be able to tell you more this afternoon.'

'I had a message from him on the answering machine while we were away. I've brought the tape and machine to play it.'

Septimus played the message.

'Poor old Darren, I really hope I haven't indirectly brought about his death,' said the lawyer, turning the machine off. Do you mind if I play this to my fellow from the fuzz?'

'Not at all. He thought *I* was in danger. I'll have a word with Penny too, as she's a useful person to have on one's side. His message said he'd found something out and I was in danger - I wonder whether it's tied up with all this Penny's auntie business.'

'By all means do talk to her. I'd find any excuse to be near someone so delicious. You are a dark horse.'

Tony did not reply, but smiled as he waved, and Septimus heard his footsteps fading down the stairs. It was well past noon, time to go to the Swan. He went to a cupboard in the reception area and took out his fold-up bicycle. It would only take him ten minutes.

People took little notice of the bearded man riding a bicycle too small for him as commonplace. He pedalled down the bus lane till he reached the pub, tethered the machine to a post and entered the saloon bar.

The inspector, a nondescript looking ferret of a man in his fifties, was already half way through his pint.

'Your usual is it, Septimus? Now what have you got to tell me?' he said.

'A pint of Worthington please. I have something which may help you with the private eye murder, it's an answering machine tape,' said the lawyer, handing over the tape. 'Darren was helping a friend of mine. He was being stalked.'

'The timing of this call, you have it?'

'Indeed I do. It was seven o'clock yesterday evening. When was he killed?'

'We'd tied it down to between six and eight. Now it's between seven and eight. Mind if I take this back to the station?'

'Not at all. Anything you can give me?'

'The victim was seen talking to a young woman at the Lamb and Bullock at about 5.30 p.m., then he was on his own for a bit, presumably finishing his drink. He left and was not seen again. The landlord discovered his body in the car park round the back. The victim was sitting in the driver's seat of his car, and from a distance he thought he was asleep, but when he opened the door there was blood everywhere. He'd been whacked with an axe, which was lying on the back seat. My current theory is that he was murdered outside, then placed in the car, so an observer wouldn't notice anything unusual.'

'What time was that?'

'Midnight.'

'Any ID on the young woman?'

'None at all. Landlord says he's never seen her before. No source of DNA in the pub, so many customers have sat in the same place.'

'And in Darren's car?'

'The Crime Scene Manager is in charge of that. No doubt we'll find out.'

'We'll keep each other informed?'

'Can't promise too much,' said the inspector. 'Regulations...I'll do my best.'

'Me too,' said the lawyer. Cagey bastard, he thought. 'Is that the time? Must be getting back to the office.'

'Saw the bicycle; going green, I see. I'm off too, work to do.'

The lawyer cycled back along the bus lane leading to the centre of town. At the end of the lane he negotiated the crowded road and pushed his bike along the pavement when he came to his own street, wary of the trams coming from the station.

He folded the bike and trudged up the stairs, depressed by the way events were going.

'Septimus! I've got Reverend Tony on the phone. Says it's important.' Septimus's trudge turned into a run and he panted his way to the phone in his room.

'Hello Tony,' said Septimus, as he sunk into his leather chair. 'What's up?'

'Rather not talk on the phone. Can you come over here now?'

Septimus groaned, I must get fitter, he thought, as he unfolded then pushed the trusty bike out of the door.

The vicarage was a ten minute spin away, and the be-suited lawyer pedalled his way down the hill towards the church and its attendant vicarage. He entered the old house to find an agitated vicar.

'Sorry to interrupt your busy day, Sept, but I had to show you this.' He thrust a piece of scruffy piece of paper towards his friend. On it was written,

You won't escape me holy one, ask the dead dick.

'Did you see anyone?'

'Not at all.'

'You have to get away from here. Has your attractive friend any ideas?'

'Don't know. Think I should call her? She seems to bring trouble. I'd be getting mixed up with missing aunts and all sorts of skullduggery.'

'You already are. This may even be something to do with it, might as well meet it head on. I daren't instruct any more enquiry agents, as they may meet unfortunate ends.'

'Kick the buck, as Penny would say.'

There was a buzzing sound, and Tony fished his mobile from his pocket.

'It's her,' he hissed, holding his hand over the instrument. He turned on the speaker.

'Sweetie, I must see you. It's auntie - she's dead.'

6

Penny stroked the longhaired cat as she talked. It purred as she did so, stretching occasionally.

'Good heavens above! What next! How did she die?' asked Tony

'Her body was found in the churchyard of her village. Discovered by your friend the vicar. She was strangled. There'll have to be a post mortem. Woe is.'

'Yes, I fear so. You must be distraught. What do you think of this?' said Tony, giving her his note.

'Mysterious. The "dead dick" is the deceased Darren. I wonder whether all this is tied up in some way. Auntie warned Septimus we are all in danger. She was right. Forgive me for being practical, but does your mate do dead people's estates? I'm auntie's executor and will need help with the paperwork. I know how lawyers love lolly. She had plenty.'

'Back to the note please Penny; yes, I'm sure he'll help you. What do you think?'

'I think you get out of your house fast and come and help me. You still have your locum. Don't bring old Perry Mason though. He can stay here and look after things. I doubt any baddies would care about him.'

'So where are we going?'

'Right now? Back to the cottage in Sussex. It's my responsibility now and I'm going to change the locks. Find out if your locum will stay longer. I'll foot the bill, now I'm an heiress. Apart from the obvious danger to us I'd like to nail whoever killed auntie.'

Next morning found them on the M23, exceeding the speed limit in Penny's MG. Tony grasped his hat and was glad of his warm clothing. Penny had phoned a local locksmith, who met them outside the cottage. It looked much as before except...

'Tony, have you noticed anything?'

'Yes, no cameras, as the golfer once said.' The flies' bulging eyes had disappeared.

The locksmith, who had insisted on some form of authority, accepted a letter on Septimus's notepaper, which he'd faxed directly to him. He managed to open the stout old door without too much damage. They entered. Penny took command.

'I'll go upstairs; I'm dying to get at that computer again. You have a root around, see if there's any clue as to what has been going on. Start in the sitting room, I'll be busy above you,' said Penny.

Tony opened drawers and cupboards, lifted carpets, moved everything that could possibly cover anything interesting and even went through the garden lifting flowerpots. Penny returned from her activities upstairs.

'Now let's see what you've got. I'm going to get the computer looked at by an expert, downloading bits and pieces is a waste of time, as I discovered from my last download. Everything was encrypted. There are no doubt deletions and hidden files. I know a bloke who regards that sort of thing as a big treat. Have you found anything interesting? There's something sad about looking at someone's life. Did you notice all the Angela Brazil schoolgirl books?' Tony said,

'I imagine they were popular in the thirties or forties when she was young. Remember, there might be something helpful in a book. Super spies hollow them out, don't they?'

'True. You've just found yourself another job.'

Although it was cold Tony found himself sweating, and he wiped his face often. Aunt Theresa was a widely read woman, judging by her reading tastes. Amongst the novels, biographies and books by people he'd never heard of, he noticed a volume bound with leather. The words 'Charles Letts, Improved Diary' with a price in the bottom right hand corner, '3/-' were embossed on the faded blue cover. The year '1944' was in the centre.

He eased it out of the bookcase, flicking through the yellowing pages. The writing was rounded and legible, written with a broad-nibbed fountain pen, by the look of it. Perhaps Penny would like to read it, he thought

'Found anything your reverence?' shouted Penny, who had gone back upstairs.

'Maybe,' shouted Tony, whose quick steps up the steep stairs betrayed his excitement. 'Look at this.'

He found her opening the loft hatch and about to climb the ladder which slid down from the large aperture.

He waved the old volume.

'Pooh, that smells musty, what is it?' said Penny.

'Your aunt's war diary, if you look at the date. She has legible handwriting - intriguing, but no doubt of no use to us.'

'Go on, if it's so unimportant why did you run up the stairs? Of course, we, or rather you, should read it. I'm desperate for anything helpful.'

'Where are we sleeping?' said Tony.

'Definitely not here. The place gives me the creeps.

Besides, until all this nonsense is cleared up I don't think it's safe. I've booked us a hotel room near Gatwick airport. It's safer if we're together. Twin beds though. '

Tony sighed. His church seemed far away and ever since he'd been in Penny's company he could not dismiss the strong pull of her sexuality. The woman's presence made him think of little else but renewing their relationship. However, she was one of those people who made up their own minds about such things, and it was a waste of time making advances, even if he'd known how to go about it. He could only sit in silent frustration as she carried on in her own charming way. Moreover, they were in danger and did need to take precautions. Perhaps, as he'd read somewhere, danger was an aphrodisiac, but he didn't think he needed one. As she drove her two seater, he contented himself with a glimpse of smooth-skin as her skirt rode up.

They kept to country roads and emerged into the car park of a large hotel. It was one of those concrete brutes so favoured by architects of a certain era. The receptionists spoke with the attractive vowels, which betrayed their origin in an eastern European country that Tony guessed was Lithuania or Poland. They waited for the Priority Platinum customers to check in and at last received attention.

'Room 331. Would you like a paper?' Penny's credit card was the Open Sesame, and the lift whisked them up to the seventh floor.

'I wonder if your stalker is even now whooshing up behind us with a knowing sneer,' said Penny, as they tramped through a number of doorways towards their room.

'Could be,' said Tony.

Shall we ensnare her?' said Penny.

'How?'

'One of us goes to the room, the other waits in the stair part, and keeps an eye on the lift.'

'You'd better watch Penny, I'm hopeless,' said Tony.'

'True,' said Penny. Here's the key card, off you go Sir Galahad.'

Tony hurried to the room, was able to get the key card to work at the third thrust, and unpacked, feeling sure that Penny would be along shortly. He took off his jacket, placing it on a theft-deterrent hanger which he managed to fit into its slot, and lay on one of the twin beds perusing the room service menu as he waited.

Ten minutes later he decided enough was enough, and slid from the bed, making for the door. As he reached it there was a polite knocking. He opened the door to see a young man in the red hotel uniform, who proffered him an envelope.

'The lady said I was to give you this, sir.'

Oh no, Penny's at it again, thought Tony, and took the envelope.

'Back later. Read the diary.

P'

Tony groaned and rang room service, ordering himself a steak and a bottle of wine at an exorbitant price.

He looked for the diary, which Penny had left in her case, and found it under various feminine accoutrements. A musty smell still emanated from it, and Tony wondered if the pages would crumble when he turned them.

The first page was written in the rounded hand he had remarked on when he'd found the book. By now he was quite sleepy from the wine and it was late; he'd just take a peek before he went to sleep.

7

1 st January
   The heat of the Cape January reminds me of Cyprus.
I loved it there, and still pine for the view of the castle next
to the sea in Kyrenia. Now I look at a different bay, from the
stoep of a house on the slopes of Signal Hill, below the small
round peak known as Lion's Head, junior partner to the
massive flat-topped Table Mountain.

It is hard to work in the heat, and I'm tempted to take the
bus to Camps Bay and sit on the rocks with my feet in the
water. They say there are sharks there, but I've never seen
one, just a few seals, which they eat.

My name in these parts is Theresa, I'm English, evacuated
from Cyprus, where I lived briefly with my husband. I've
been here for three years, and I'm not supposed to keep this
diary.

They chose me because I knew the codes and am good
with maths and Morse code. They even found a husband for
me. He's dead now. Lost at sea. In this war death is as
common as breakfast.

I work for a publisher in Cape Town. John has a little

office in a back street. Business life is difficult as before the war he was agent for a lot of English publishers, now he has to publish local writers - good for them, but not so good for profits, certainly not enough to make ends meet, but he manages well. I know how. Payments from Cape importers reach his bank account on the same day every month, and they're not for services he claims to provide. He's Our Man in Cape Town, and the money comes from His Majesty. Cape Town is still an important sea route to the east although the Suez Canal is back in action. The sea off the coast is riddled with submarines, mostly heading up the coast for Durban and Moçambique waters. I intercept their signals and decode them. We can't rely on the locals. The government is on our side, but many of the personnel are covert members of the *Ossewabrandwag*, a bunch of Nazi sympathisers. If they knew about us, I wouldn't give tuppence for our lives.

Today is my 'day off', hence the musing. I'm going to meet a chap from HMS Grantham, a cruiser that's just docked at Simonstown. Ostensibly it's social, but in this war nothing is as it seems. I'm not the sort of girl who runs after sailors. He has brought the new codes. I use one of those machines that look like a typewriter, and lately I've been getting gobbledy-gook, as Mr John calls it.

I have to catch the bus into town, and then take the train.

2nd January

Gosh, that was some trip. The naval officer turned out to be sex mad. It must be those lonely nights at sea.

We met as arranged in the Sailor's Rest, the pseudo English pub in the main street. He was easy to recognise, as he was carrying the agreed bunch of lilies.

'Lieutenant Green?' I said.

'You must be Theresa; these are for you.'

'What lovely flowers. You shouldn't have.'

He smirked.

'Beautiful flowers for a beautiful young lady, I think you'll find they're what you need.'

So, the codes are in there, I thought. Good. I'll have to talk to this twit for a while, as this is supposed to be an assignation. This chap is not my cup of tea. Weak chin, mouth like a crack in a pie.

'How do you like the Cape?' I enquired.

'Very pretty, like you.' He smirked again.

'Any chance of a drink?'

'Depends what you have in mind. I should tell you, I have rather a large penis.'

Now, I've had some crude propositions in this war, but anatomical information of this sort makes me lose the will to live.

'Really. Don't know whether I should congratulate you or commiserate,' I replied.

He scowled.

'I can see I'm wasting my time. Where is the local red light district?'

'Just wait till night time. No doubt a man with your attributes knows what to look for. Your uniform will be like a beacon to the pros anyhow. I warn you though. You're as likely to have your throat slit or be robbed as get much pleasure out of it. If you have a lot of money to waste, go to the Grand Hotel in Cape Town. I expect they'll fix you up there.'

'Humph,' he replied, got up and stalked out, leaving me with my flowers.

I stayed at the table for a few minutes, smoking a cigarette. Which one, or more than one, of these people was a German spy? Did they know who I was? I hoped not, and went out into the street, where the bright light of a Cape summer's day dispelled my fears for the moment.

I caught the train back, and as usual, my breath was taken away by the closeness of the shimmering sea and the exotic seabirds going about their business. Mindful of my current task, I took a good look at my fellow passengers. There were few and none seemed to take an interest in me. I had taken the precaution of posting the codes to myself before I left. They are too important to risk. One of these indifferent fellow passengers could be anything but.

After stopping at the stations, some of whose names are imprinted on my mind like a tune that won't go away - Claremont, Newlands, Rondebosch, Rosebank, Mowbray, the scenery changed from the enchanting views of the ocean to suburban and industrial buildings which warned of my impending arrival in the metropolis of Cape Town, the final sign being the tattiness of Woodstock telling me I was now one station away. I clutched the lilies to my breast and walked along the platform. I felt a bump in my back, and fell over, the flowers jerked from my hand as my elbows hit the ground. A smartly dressed man picked them up.

'So sorry *mevrou*, that *ou* was obviously in a hurry. Here are your flowers.'

'*Dankie meneer*,' I said. As he disappeared past the barrier I looked at the flowers. The little envelope formerly containing the codes was missing. I had replaced them with a card and loving message to myself.

Ha ha, I thought. Now I'm sure I'm being followed, and they're not sure whether I am who they think I am. I went to the office where I work, to report to my boss. I took a taxi, but not the one at the head of the queue - I pretended to be about to enter this and then changed my mind so it had to take someone else. I went back into the station for a minute then took another one. I had a profound fear of being kidnapped, unlikely as this was I know. The taxi took me safely to the office in Buitenkant Street, and I was relieved to press the buzzer on the dingy door marked 'Empire Publications'. Ludio, the assistant, opened it with a grin. I followed him up the stairs to John's office.

'You've got the codes then, young lady. Good. The Jerry subs are playing havoc with our merchant ships. I'm hoping these will help us track their movements. We need to know where they are. They're sinking thousands of tons of shipping still and we need to find them so our Catalina flying boats can get at them.'

'The codes will come in the post tomorrow and I'll bring them in, but it may be better if Ludio accompanies me - I think I'm being followed,' I said. 'Someone knocked me over at the main station and took the envelope with the flowers.'

'I see. Well we can't have that; I'll get Ludio to shadow you home. He'll find out who it is, and then we'll deal with them.'

I took the bus to High Level Road and climbed the steep avenue where I live in Fresnaye, in the last house before the mountain begins. It's called Lambazi, named after a rocky place on the eastern Cape Coast where sailors were drowned many years ago. I knew Ludio, a man of mixed race, was there somewhere, watching me, although I couldn't see him.

Walking up the avenue every day has made me quite fit.

10th January

The new codes arrived and are top-hole. We now know there are three subs hovering about, two just down from western Africa. John thinks that they are coming down here because things are too hot for them in the north Atlantic, probably on the way to the Far East. The Cape isn't as impor-tant as it was a year or two ago, but we still get a lot of ship-ping. Most of that which doesn't survive is sunk further up the coast around Durban. If I can save even one life it's worth it. Our Catalina Flying Boat pilots have become quite good at spotting and sinking the sinister things.

4th February

I had dinner at the City Club with John. A Meneer Van Rensburg, who says he publishes educational books in Afrikaans, among other things, accosted us. He marched up to our table all smiles and said,

'Hello John, you must introduce me to your lovely companion.'

He had a big moustache and an oily smile.

'This is Theresa, more than my right hand woman.'

I held out my hand. He grasped it and his lips felt like a wet piece of rubber.

'Enchanted,' he said. I hope to see you again. Now if you will excuse me, I have a pressing appointment.'

'Don't trust him,' I said.

'Oh, he's all right, been very helpful to us,' said John. 'Has some excellent contacts.'

'Still don't trust him. He's got an unctuous manner.'

'You'll need to work with him, he's useful.'

I'm hoping John didn't mean it. I don't want to have anything to do with that man.

26th February

The creep van Rensburg has been ringing me. He says we must have dinner. How many times does one have to say 'No'?

5th March

John insists I see van Rensburg.

10th March

I compromised and had a drink with van Rensburg this lunch time at the club. He was trying to ply me with wine, but I stuck to orange juice. He has a farm near Franschhoek to which he's invited me. I fobbed him off.

21st March

The days are getting shorter, but I like March. It's not so hot now. John has persuaded me to go to van Rensburg's farm. He says he suspects he is an OB man trying to rumble us, and

I'm to flush him out. I won't be alone, whatever that means. I've agreed to go on Saturday.

27th March

I'm still here, alive. Franschhoek is lovely and you can see what attracted the Huguenots to the district – it's all mountains and vines. Van Rensburg's farm takes in some of them. He had a driver pick me up from Fresnaye in a car fit for a general. The drive was very pleasant and we picked up a young captain wearing his smart uniform in Somerset West.

'*Aangename kennis, mevr*ou,' he said, as he plonked himself down beside me in the back seat.

'*Ek praat net 'n bietjje Afrikaans meneer*,' I sand he

'Oh, I'll speak in English then. I'm Captain Jannie van Rensburg. Hendrik is my uncle. I understand you work for Empire Publications?'

'Yes, I'm secretary to John Powell. Are you on leave for long?'

'Only this weekend, then it's back on duty.'

I noticed his wrists were covered with fine dark hair, and his hands were broad,

'I can't ask you where, but I can guess.'

'Really? Not playing this game, mevrou. I won't even tell my *oom* where I'm going.'

'Good for you Captain. The war is safe in your hands,' I said.

'Now you're laughing at me. I'm only a small cog in a very big wheel.'

'And your uncle, is he also a cog, or is he just a big wheel?'

He looked at me hard, and his eyes were an intense brown.

'Yes, he is a big wheel. He's one of the biggest wheels in this country.'

I was interested now. Had this man revealed something more than he should? I decided to back off a bit.

A wooden portico made from tree trunks guarded *Oom's* farm. At the top was a sign 'van Rensburg'. The road had two ruts made by car wheels, and the car bumped along it at a slow pace. I saw a couple of ostriches, but no other life. It was baking in the car, and I was relieved to arrive at the large Cape Dutch house with its distinctive gables. In contrast to the arid surroundings, there was a manicured lawn watered by sprinklers.

Van Rensburg was waiting for us. He was dressed informally, wearing shorts, which revealed thin legs, brown from the sun, like most white South African men,

'Ah my dear, at last the mountain has come to Mohammed, you must be in need of refreshment, please follow me.'

He showed us into a magnificent room furnished in Cape Dutch style. The dark heavy wooden furniture was intricately carved.

Lunch was served by a black man in a white jacket. Except for his colour he could have been Jeeves. I sat opposite the nephew, and next to van Rensburg. Soon I felt a hand on my knee. I removed it. I was relieved when, for the moment, he desisted from further adventures. However, he'd made his intentions plain. Was he just a lecherous middle-aged man or was there something more to it? Perhaps there *was* something more to it *and* he was lecherous.

'Have you heard of Koffiefontein?' asked van Rensburg.

'Isn't it the place where the *Ossewabrandwag* gentlemen are interned?' I said.

'It's where Italians, Germans and some South African patriots are imprisoned, yes.'

Van Rensburg had the tanned and lined face of a man who had spent a lot of time outdoors in the veld.

'You think unjustly?' I said.

'Undoubtedly. I was hoping you thought that way too.' He

stared at me. The man's mad, I thought, he knows I'm English and am likely to be hostile to the people who are interned, but I'd better play along if I want to get out of here.

'I am English you know, but I do have some sympathy for them. Not the Germans, but the South Africans. My grandmother was an Afrikaner sympathiser during the Anglo Boer War.' I lied. It was part of my cover story agreed with John, and I'd learnt it by heart.

'Really?' He looked interested. 'Who was she?'

'Her name was Wilhelmina Scheepers. She married my grandfather, a Major Brown, in Graaff-Reinet. She went back to Britain with him after the war, but her heart was here.

'Scheepers? Was she related to Gideon Scheepers, the *commando* leader?'

'I believe so. He was hanged in any event by the *khakis*. I suppose that is why I have mixed feelings about the English.'

'A good reason. Yet your accent is very English. Do you not see their point of view?'

'My mother told me about the concentration camps and how they suffered so much. I think they should never have gone to war against the Afrikaners.'

Van Rensburg stroked his moustache and looked at his nephew, whose face was expressionless.

'Wat dink jy van hierdie vrou? Is sy vertroubaar?'

The younger man said,

'Miskien. Pasop oom.'

Van Rensburg had asked his nephew whether I was trustworthy. The nephew had said, 'Perhaps' but also 'Beware'

'Apologies, we sometimes break into Afrikaans. Although your sympathies are with us, I presume you are not familiar with the language?'

I didn't like to let on I was fluent in German and had some basic Afrikaans.

'Oh, I have a smattering but no more. Perhaps you could teach me?'

Van Rensburg chuckled.

'That would be a pleasure. It would give me an excuse to enjoy your company. Jannie, how about showing this young lady over the farm?'

'*Ja*, I will be glad to,' said Jannie.

Rows of green grapes shimmered on the vines and the mountains were blue in the distance, yet something spoilt the beauty for me.

'We lose 15% of our grapes to baboons, you know.'

'Is that why you're carrying that shot gun?' I said.

''Partly, but baboons are not the only predators round here. *Oom* has enemies.'

'Really? I have a feeling that the Garden of Eden was here.'

'There was a snake in Eden. Here there are many, real ones and maybe a human one too.'

I looked at his face as he said this. His eyes were serious.

'What do you think about the Nazis? Will they win the war?' I said.

'I doubt it, but there are many of my people who wish they would. They think that then they will be free from the English.'

'Your *oom* being one of them?'

'You've worked that out at least. You may well realise this, but he is testing you. You say you are sympathetic to us, but you are very English.'

'And you, you have been fighting for the Allies, yet you get on very well with your uncle.'

'I've known him so long. He thinks that when I come back home I'll turn into a dutiful Afrikaner, going to the *kerk* every Sunday and voting for the right party.'

'Maybe you will,' I said.

'You're very beautiful,' he said.

'*Meneer* van Rensburg, first your uncle, now you, what is it with your family?'

He smiled. 'Don't put us in the same bracket. He's a womaniser, whereas I...'

'You're not I suppose. We must be getting back to the house. I think I've seen enough of this farm for the moment.'

Oom, as I now called him in my mind, was waiting at the door.

'I hope you were impressed by my farm, now I'd like to talk business. Jannie has to go and do something over at *Meneer* De Wet's place, don't you Jannie?'

'*Ja oom*, if you say so, although I'm damned if I can remember what it is. No doubt Koos de Wet will tell me.'

The younger man drove off with a crunch of tyres on the gravel.

'Please sit down. I've taken the liberty of pouring you a glass of the same white wine you enjoyed so much at lunch. I will be blunt about what I want. I want your help.'

I sat down and took a sip of the wine. My price would be higher than that.

'I know this war will soon be over. You are not what you seem. I feel you must have a price; you may have noticed also that I bear the same surname as the head of the *Osse-wabrandwag*. I am his cousin. You have a choice; you can stay and listen, or go now. If you choose to stay, you have also chosen to help us. You will be rewarded, but I warn you any disloyalty will mean you will not live long. Stay for great reward or leave forthwith, while you know nothing of value.'

Had I been who I pretended to be, I'd have been out of there. But then I'm not. I hesitated for a few seconds. I smiled.

'Of course I'm staying.'

'Good. Now there are things I need to show you. '

He led me up the yellowwood stairs to a room with a desk.

'Do sit down.'

He went to a portrait of a man with a bushy beard and slouch hat and took it from the wall, placing it on the desk. Behind it was a safe. He manipulated it for about half a minute, and then it opened. He removed a large brown envelope

'In here I have information which at best is embarrassing, and at worst will cost some prominent people their lives, if it were to get into the wrong hands. I am the guardian of these secrets. I am prepared to sell them.'

'What has this to do with me?'

'Everything. You are going to be my messenger to Mr Churchill, or at least to his underlings. I have known for some time you are a British agent. How? That need not trouble you.'

I hope my face was impassive, but my stomach wasn't. This man was a piece of work. Or was he setting a trap?

'I don't know what you're talking about,' I said.

'No of course not. I have a sample here.' He picked up a smaller envelope. 'Give this to your employer, who will also not know what I'm talking about.' He laughed. 'The games we play. Now I'm sure you'll be wanting to get back home. I can hear Jannie's car returning.' Elsewhere he calls the nephew Jannie

The drive back was through the glistening mountains and vine-covered valleys, but my mind was too full of the afternoon's events to pay much attention to it. Jannie drove me all the way back to Fresnaye, his car crawling up the steep road that led to my house.

'Would you like to have dinner with me one evening?' Jannie said, as he held the passenger door open for me.

'Certainly, ring me in the office,' I said, masking my surprise.

What a day.

A KNOCK on the door distracted Tony, who broke off from the diary. It was a dishevelled Penny.

'Wondered where you'd got to,' he said.

'I'll explain later. I could murder a bath, darling. I'll just unpack my case.'

'I've been reading your auntie's diary. She was quite a girl in her youth. It's all submarines and sinister people,' said Tony.

Penny looked glamorous even when untidy, he reflected.

'She was always part of that world, as you know. It's who killed her I'm after,' she said. 'More later.'

'What did she look like?' said Tony.

'A little old lady with white hair. When she was young she was very attractive. I've seen a photograph - short blond hair and elegant upturned nose. Her eyes had a slightly startled look. Now I must have a bath. See you in a while.'

Tony heard the bath running for a minute or two, then silence punctuated by the odd splash, a long gurgle, and then silence again.

Penny emerged enveloped in a large white towel.

'Be a darling and turn around for a minute.'

Tony did as he was told.

'Now, where have I been?' said Penny.

'I waited while you went in here. Nothing happened for a few minutes, so I was about to follow you, when I followed a hunch instead. I went to the lobby and asked the receptionist whether there were any messages for our room.

"No madam," she said in her East European English, "but that person walking towards the exit has mentioned your name. I offered to ring your room, but they said it wasn't important and said they'd call you tomorrow."

'I looked through the glass door and saw a hooded figure of indeterminate sex going into the car park. I managed to get a taxi to follow the light blue Vauxhall it climbed into. I still couldn't make out if it was a male or female. We went miles along narrow lanes and ended up at very large gates, which had already closed on my quarry. It's a place called Montmorency Manor. The taxi driver refused to wait, saying he'd either leave me or take me back here, but he had to get home. I paid him off and got out. Luckily it wasn't particularly cold last night.

The big gate was locked, so I looked around for somewhere to get in to the grounds. The place was surrounded by massive walls, but they're not in good repair, and I found a place where a lot of brickwork had broken away and squeezed through. Then I heard dogs barking and stayed where I was for a while.

When all was quiet I did a recce. I made my way through some trees and there in front of me was a very large old house, Jacobean I'd say, but old anyway. Listed I expect. There were three cars parked in front of the house - the Vauxhall I followed, a Bentley and a four by four gas-guzzler. Just the sort of vehicles one would expect at an oversized mansion. I managed to get close enough to see the registration numbers, which I've saved in my mobile phone's organiser. The dogs started barking, and I thought, I'm off, and waded through trees and brambles to the wall. Not a moment too soon as I could almost hear the dogs panting.'

'How did you get back here?' asked Tony.

'Walked, then hitched a lift, thankfully with a very sweet lorry driver who kept telling me off for hitching, saying that a "pretty girl like you" was in danger, as "there are so many perverts about". Didn't tell him I carry a gun. ? Would she be able to get hold of a gun? Would have made him turn inside out, I dare say, and how. I'm here now and I'm knackered. Got to look up those numbers though.'

She walked over to the dressing table, picked up her cell phone and dabbed at the screen

'Very strange, it looks as if one of these cars is owned by a man with a South African Afrikaans name,' she said. 'I'll get my policeman friend to run the numbers through the police computer to see if they've been up to anything illegal.'

'Isn't that illegal, Penny?' said Tony.

'Sweetie, we could be murdered. If I'm dead I don't want adherence to some petty rules to be the reason. I have contacts who appreciate I wouldn't call in a favour unless it was necessary. Now I'd better put some clothes on.'

Tony listened bemused. Penny was alien to his cosy religious world with its ceremony and earnestness. Since he'd met her he'd had cause to wonder whether he was a suitable person to be a priest. He remembered the first time they'd met, at a church conference, how she'd come to see him soon afterwards, and seduced him in his own vicarage. There'd been a murder and he realised he must have been vulnerable, as everything was so unreal at that time. He'd gone off to South Africa with her, to find the murderer of his curate, who turned out not to have been what he seemed. It had all been very complicated, but thrilling. Now he was back in fantasyland, where nothing was like his safe Croydon existence.

Life was cheap and women, at least this one, were different.

Penny shouted from the bathroom, 'Order me some breakfast will you sweetie? Then I'm off. You could do worse than reading more of auntie's diary. It's a long shot, but who knows, it might contain a clue, and we're desperate for clues at this moment in time, as they say.'

'I've nothing else to do. You sure the Mossad or their

English equivalent won't come in with your breakfast and suffocate us?' said Tony.

Penny emerged from the bathroom, now fully dressed

'No, I'm not sure, but I think the blokes they hit are slightly more important than our good selves. I'll keep my little handgun near just in case, if that helps?'

'You're back on form,' said Tony, and rang room service.

An impassive waiter placed the tray on the table. It contained a 'full English' and just looking at it made Tony hungry.

'Hmm, scrumptious,' said Penny. 'Almost worth staying in this plastic and concrete palace for.'

'Indeed, said Tony. 'I usually have a quick muesli at the vicarage, but I'm going to order one of those when you're gone. May I have a piece of that toast meanwhile? I promise I'll get on and read more of this diary. She was an interesting girl, your aunt.'

'Help yourself to the rest of this. I'm off,' said Penny, as she kissed him on the cheek and left.

8

'Your aunt was quite wealthy, but the Inland Revenue are going to get a fair slice of her estate,' said Septimus, peering at Penny over his spectacles. 'You'll need to sign here, and I'll arrange for another lawyer over the road to witness your swearing to your signature on the Oath for Executors. It'll cost you seven pounds in cash to swear the oath. The house was valued at £500,000 alone, and there are investments in all sorts of places, including South Africa.'

Penny smiled at the lawyer.

'You are a darling to do all this so quickly. Solicitors have a reputation for being very slow.'

Septimus beamed at the compliment. 'It's not often I get a client as pretty as you. Seriously, any friend of Tony gets special treatment. Any more shenanigans in Sussex?'

'Yes. I'll tell you about it after I've done the swearing. What about the reading of the will?'

'That only happens in films. You've read it anyway by now. After all, you obtained it from Messrs Antrobus.'

'Yes, but I was hoping for some drama. Bang goes another illusion.'

Septimus led Penny down the steep old stairs, built before the days of Health and Safety, and they crossed the tramlines, passed the garish window with its overpriced computer games, stopped at an art deco building on the corner, buzzed below the sign denoting solicitors with good old English names, requested entry, and on hearing a further buzz, walked through two sets of glass doors.

'Goodness me, they've got a lift,' said Penny. 'What kind of solicitors are they?'

'Quite normal, I assure you,' said Septimus. The oath taking ceremony was undertaken by a man in his sixties with bushy eyebrows and an attractive smile, Penny thought. Perhaps a bit past any potential for hanky panky. Unaware that he was being assessed, the venerable solicitor took the cash proffered by Septimus, and may well have sighed as he watched the unusually attractive woman disappear, or so Penny thought as she stepped into the lift.

On the way back to Septimus's office Penny mused. How much should she tell him? He was trustworthy, she had no doubt, but was it right to drag this sexagenarian into what might be dangerous for him.

'You're wondering whether I'm up to it,' said Septimus, as he settled into his leather chair.

'No, I mean yes. I mean I want to be fair to you.'

''I'm not that old. Sixty is the new fifty and all that clap-trap. There's still lead in my pencil.'

'Pardon?' said Penny, as an unsettling image sprang into her mind, Septimus aroused.

'I'm sure there is. It's just I seem to get Tony into trouble...'

'Why shouldn't I have some too?' interjected the bewhiskered lawyer. 'It can be very dull, dealing with property and tax and so on.'

'I expect it can. Do you know many judges?'

'A few. What has that to do with anything?'

'I followed a car the other night and ended up at a country pile. I've traced the owner. His name is Van Wiese; he's a judge of some sort.'

'Hmm, not heard of him, I'll look him up for you.'

Penny leaned forward, giving Septimus a glimpse of her cleavage.

'Would you?' she said.

Septimus swallowed.

'No trouble at all.'

'I have to go now. Say we meet tomorrow, somewhere a bit less formal. Say the bar of a nice local hostelry. You decide. Ring me.'

She left the lawyer sitting trancelike in his chair, as he eyed her going out of the door. He wiped his wet brow. It was hot.

He had an idea - why not find out where the judge in question was sitting, and see him in action?

9

'And so, members of the jury, I submit to you that the prosecution have proved beyond reasonable doubt that the Defendant is guilty of armed robbery. I ask you to ignore the fact that he is a consecrated priest. The evidence is clear. He has been identified not only by CCTV, but by the taxi driver who drove him from the bank to the bus station. Both on the screen and in the driver's recollection there is one common factor – he was wearing half a moustache. The other half you have heard was picked up from the floor of the bank by the police officer who gave such compelling evidence, DC Brown. DNA tests have shown that the likelihood of the piece of moustache belonging to anyone other than the Defendant is six million to one.'

The bewigged prosecuting barrister, a handsome young woman with a formidable nose, sat down. A few members of the jury sniggered.

'Silence in court,' said the judge, a man whose age was made uncertain by his off-white wig, a relic of the late seventeenth and eighteenth centuries, aping the fashionable dress of 'gentlemen' of the time. 'I will not have my court turned into a circus.'

Attaboy, thought Septimus, who'd heard this very sentence many times, as he watched from the visitors' gallery, sitting next to the smartly dressed Penny and Tony, who for some reason wore a cardigan.

The jury, whose chairman was a boy who did not look older than 19, suppressed its guffaws and looked down. The Defence barrister rose.

'Members of the jury,' he began, 'I am here before you as a representative of British justice. A man is innocent, I repeat innocent, until proven, beyond reasonable doubt, to be guilty. What do the prosecution have?' He walked to where the exhibits were displayed. 'This!' He flourished a limp piece of hairy matter about two inches wide over his head. 'A theatrical moustache. Do you propose to send my client, a man of unblemished character, a man you have heard spent three years, three years members of the jury, amongst the malaria ridden people of Tanzania, to prison for at least fifteen years over a mangy piece of theatrical costumery like this?

You have heard that my client has a hobby. A very inno- cent hobby - amateur dramatics. You have heard that he has a part which requires him to wear a moustache. You have heard he is a customer of this bank. You have heard from his own mouth that he was carrying his costume with him when he last visited the bank in question. What more natural than, as he told you, he dropped it then?' The barrister's voice rose to a high pitch as he hurled the last word at the jury, defying them not to believe his client, who was after all, an ordained priest. He assaulted the jury with more verbiage of this type, ending with his customary 'My client is an innocent man!' his eyes blazing with simulated sincerity.

Judge Van Wiese began his summing up. His English was

precise, but a vowel here and there betrayed his South African origins. After going through the law on the subject, he concluded with,

'And so, members of the jury, it is you who are judges of the facts. After hearing all the evidence, you must be sure the Defendant is guilty if you are to convict. At this stage I expect you all to agree. If you cannot all agree I will issue further directions.'

As the jury filed out Septimus, Penny and Tony looked on from their place in the spectators' gallery.

'Let's have a cup of coffee in the canteen,' hissed Septimus.

'Roger,' said Penny.

The canteen was an unimpressive chamber with the usual accoutrements of such places. It was divided into booths with uncomfortable benches instead of chairs. Luckily Septimus had come prepared with coins, as no humans were available that day to serve, so the three sleuths sipped their unappetising machine-made drinks.

'Oh, this is revolting, sweeties. How on earth do you put up with these ghastly drinks, Septimus?' said Penny.

'I rarely visit the Crown Court,' said Septimus, 'I usually send a clerk. I admit he did tell me to bring coins.'

'I must agree with Penny,' said Tony, 'this coffee is what one would imagine they drank during the war, when it was made of unspeakable things, like acorns.'

'Enough, it's better than nothing, even if you don't think so,' said Septimus. 'What do you think of His Honour?'

'Seems a judgish sort of chap. Sonorous voice, self-important air, looked impressively bored occasionally. Interesting how different judges sound compared with the higher clergy, no exaggerated articulation. I suppose they have to exude authority, whilst the clergy are deferring to God. He put the boot in to the poor old padre while preserving a veneer of evenhandedness,' said Penny. 'I wonder what lurks beneath that inscrutable exterior though. What has he, or someone who lives in his house, got to do with us, or my deceased aunt?'

'That's for us to find out. Well, at least we know what he looks like and how he speaks. I doubt we'll find out anything further in this place. We're more likely than not to get into trouble if we approach him, security being what it is', said Septimus,

'What, you're suggesting we toddle off without knowing whether Tony's spiritual brother, the great amateur dramatician, is guilty or not?' said Penny.

'Dramatician? You do abuse the English language, I'm sure he's innocent,' said Tony. 'I used to play bridge with him at the East Binstead Bridge Society. Don't recall his saying anything about a hobby. He was keen on betting on horses, but that doesn't make him a criminal.'

'For goodness sake Tony, they've got him bang to rights,' said Septimus. 'The DNA evidence is conclusive. You don't believe all that claptrap about his dropping bits of moustache when he was depositing money do you? The man's a scoundrel,' said Septimus.

'He does have shifty eyes,' said Penny,' and I didn't like the way he was eyeing me up. If he's a man of God he's a lecherous one.' Necessary??

Tony and Septimus both reddened. Necessary??

'We'd better wait for the verdict then,' said Septimus, 'I feel like one of those people that liked to watch hangings.'

They returned to the courtroom.

'Silence in court! Please rise for His Honour.' All rose and the judge came in looking disagreeable.

The jury earlier filed into their seats. The callow foreman said,

'We find the Defendant guilty,'

'And is that the verdict of you all?' said Judge van Wiese.

'It is,' said the youth.

'Very well, I shall adjourn this matter for reports, including psychiatric ones. I make it clear I am considering a custodial sentence. Daniel Reedham, you are remanded in custody until 25th June.'

'Court rise,' said the usher. The bewigged and robed judge walked out of a side door from his position on the dais. As soon as he had gone people started to chatter and the inquisitive trio walked out through the swing doors.

'Where to now?' said Tony.

'You go back to the hotel and read more of the diary. I want you to write down the names of everyone she names and the dates she sees them, as well as a brief summary of who they are, what they do etc. I expect you, Septimus, have your practice to attend to. Any dirt on the judge would be appreciated.' Penny stepped into a taxi, which was waiting for her. 'See you later boys.'

Septimus gazed at the disappearing taxi.

'She's quite a girl. Feel like a pint before we do our homework?'

'I certainly do. There's a respectable looking hotel near the station. Shall we go there?'

'No. I hope my idea is better. The house Penny mentioned to you, the one where the Vauxhall ended up. Where is it?'

'I believe Penny mentioned Hurst Heath. It's a village about ten miles from here.'

'Let's drive over there, there's bound to be a hostelry nearby. We might find out a bit more about His Honour. If not, I expect the beer will be all right.'

'Septimus, this business appears to have gripped you. Either that or you want to impress Penny. It may all seem to be a bit of a lark, but there's already a dead enquiry agent and for that matter an aunt. Why don't we just let her get on with it?'

'You unchivalrous wimp, Tony. I'm bored; I'll soon be past it. It's different for you; you're still a young man. You appear to have enjoyed the sight and soft texture of those marvellous breasts and more. Even the thought of them makes me sweat. I want a piece of the action.'

"There are some good novels I can recommend. They're much safer,' said Tony.

'Shut up. Let's be going.' replied the lawyer.

Hurst Heath was one of those Sussex villages with one road going through it, dotted with a few quaint old houses and a couple of pubs. The sort of thing that featured in TV programmes, where a couple who lived in a cramped box in Croydon demanded an enormous kitchen and enough land to keep goats and grow vegetables.

'Let's try The Swan,' said Septimus. It looks up market - the sort of place I imagine a judge would hang out when he's thirsty.

The pub, a beamy 18th century or earlier building, was empty except for two men watching football on a large flat wall mounted TV. There were no bar staff to be seen, so Septimus rang a bell on the bar counter, which had a note attached, 'Please ring for service'.

A bearded man shuffled into sight from around the corner.

'Sorry gents, been serving in the Public Bar, what can I get you?'

'A pint of Doom Bar and a large gin and tonic please,' said Septimus.

'Any preference for the type of gin? You can see them up there.' He gestured to a shelf behind him.

'A Hendricks please,' said Tony who was not a beer drinker like Septimus.

They sipped their drinks, the football on TV making conversation difficult.

Just as they were finishing and about to leave, Septimus whispered,

'Look who's here.'

It was the judge himself. A familiar voice rose above the irritating sports commentary.

'Evening George, my usual please.' Standing, Van Wiese revealed himself to be a diminutive man with a bald head flanked by remnants of reddish grey hair as he waited to be served. Tony shut his eyes. That afternoon that bald pate had been concealed by a wig. Septimus's wink confirmed his recognition.

'Do you think he'll remember us?' he whispered.

Septimus shook his head. 'Let's wait a bit.'

The pocket-sized guardian of justice sat down at a table in the corner, adjacent to a series of horse brasses. He looked at his watch. He and our pair waited. Tony sipped a fresh Hendricks and tonic.

A young short-haired woman wearing jeans entered the pub through a swing door. She glanced around, saw the judge, and walked up to the bar. The barman poured her a vodka and orange. She took it to the judge's table and sat down. They talked.

'Ooh, he's got a bit of crumpet,' said Septimus.

'Really Septimus, you tend to cast people in your own mould. Let's wait and see,' said Tony.

'Fancy a game of darts?' said Septimus.

'I was the Theological College champion, I warn you,' said Tony.

'Good, at least I'll get a decent game.'

As Tony prepared to throw his dart, Septimus sidled towards the judge and his companion.

'It'll cost a great deal,' he heard the woman say.

'Money's not important. There are other things at stake.'

Tony interrupted Septimus:

'Your turn, Sept.'

'Just coming.'

'You weren't joking about being a champ, Tony. I'm going to have to keep my mind on the game,' said Septimus, as he took a dart in his hand and prepared to throw.

The missile hit the edge of the board and dropped onto the floor.

'When did you last play?'

Septimus grunted and threw again. It was a treble twenty.

'Your game is a curate's egg.'

'Ha ha,' said Septimus. 'Only the parson in your case is pretty much an expert.'

They went on playing for several minutes. In between points Septimus approached as near as he dared to the seated pair, although he did not speak to them. They seemed oblivious to him.

'Hard luck,' said Tony to the defeated Septimus, picking up the darts. 'Not bad for someone who doesn't know one end of a dart from another. We must get on.'

Van Wiese and his companion were still seated at their table talking as Tony and Septimus walked to the small car park.

They sat for a while in Septimus's old Jaguar, registration number FKU 23.

Septimus took out a notebook and wrote down the numbers of the other four cars in the car park. He started his Jag, whose engine emitted a satisfying roar, and they drove off towards Surrey.

As it disappeared, the judge moved back from the window.

'They've gone,' he said to the seated woman and dialled a number on his cell phone.

10

His Honour Judge Geraldus ('Gerrie' to his friends) Van Wiese drove his Range Rover down the drive to his Jacobean house, having first activated the electric gates. The trip to the local pub had been illuminating. The woman from the escort agency had more than her sexual talents to offer. She was also a contact with his friends in South Africa and a not very scrupulous enquiry agent. The appearance of the clergyman and the man with the copious whiskers would not have alarmed him, had he not noticed them in the spectators' gallery in court. Zelda, the agency woman, had said she was taking care of it, so for the moment he would leave it at that.

He was greeted at the door by an exuberant Doberman.

'Down Ziki, down.' He patted the lithe animal and made for the antique mahogany drinks cabinet. Later, a glass of his favourite Vergelegen Chardonnay in hand he was watching tennis on the satellite TV, just in time to catch the South African player's match. He liked Sussex and his venerable mansion, but missed his homeland, especially in winter. Thoughts of the sun and sea of the Cape, particularly the hazy blue of the mountains, which were so prevalent, filled him with a longing to return. Rugby or cricket at Newlands, as well as the familiar guttural sound of his native language, Afrikaans, made him homesick. He knew he'd made good in England but sometimes thought of his entire life here as a sacrifice, endured so he could fulfil a mission. He'd mingled with the English of the Bar and often thought many must be the great grandsons of the khaki-clad English officers who had sneered at his bearded Boer ancestors as they sent their wives and children to the concentration camps so reviled by his *ouma*.

After the match was over, he walked over to his study and looked at a framed black and white photo on the window cill. There were five people in it, people from an earlier time. One was a beautiful woman with short fair hair. One down, more to go, he thought. In the background were the Helderberg Mountains of the Cape, so beautiful and so reminiscent of home. He raised his glass to himself and to his ancestors.

Tony, back in Croydon now, was reflecting on the events of the past few days. The Diary, he thought. May as well read more, if only to avert Penny's wrath, although he had to admit curiosity about the adventurous British woman.

2ND APRIL

Dinner with Jannie was interesting. I had thought that this would be another part of his uncle's plan to use me but ended the evening hoping not.

He fetched me in a 1930s Austin, and we drove down through Sea Point. It was still light and I could see Robben Island as I got into the car. There is a secret radio establishment there. The sea was its perennial azure, and a large ship was at anchor beyond the island.

'Let me open the door for you,'

I sat on the faded leather seat.

'Where are we going?'

'It's a surprise,' he said. I smelt his aftershave and saw the outline of his face in silhouette. He was handsome, in a dark, brooding sort of way, and I felt a warmth I had not had for some time in the lower regions ????. I'd better watch myself, I thought. I am on duty at all times. Then I noticed the black hairs on his wrist as he as he clasped the steering wheel. You're only young once.

The lovemaking was, well, as good as I expected, and I can't remember much else about the evening, except what he said to me as he dropped me home as the sun was rising over the hill behind my house.

'Don't trust *oom*.'

I reported the details of my encounter with *Meneer* van Rensburg the elder to my boss but did not mention intercourse with the younger man.

'We can't miss an opportunity like this. I don't trust them though,' he said.

I nearly said, 'That makes three of us', but forbore. I didn't think he'd like me fraternising with and particularly fucking the enemy's relative.

'Let him know we will deal with him. Anything that might shorten this war is important. How will you contact him?'

'Through his nephew. He gave me a lift to the farm and back.'

'Hmm, he's the glamour boy of Sea Point, I hear. I expect he'll break a few hearts before he goes back on duty. I hear he's very close to the Justice Minister's daughter. Now if I were a younger man...'

'We all know what you're like. I expect she's blonde and buxom.'

'Very good. They say you can hear the men panting as she walks past. She'd be a very good catch for him. The van Deventers are very rich. They have a big house in

Constantia near that mansion owned by the millionaire Hugh Nevis.'

I thought he would never shut up. Pangs of emotion, I admit jealousy was the dominant one, ran through me.

'Fascinating. My only concern with this Casanova is to communicate with his uncle. I'll let you know how I get on.'

I left.

As I drove I pondered my new lover's reputation. With his looks it was likely to be justified. In wartime no one knows whether they'll be alive next week, especially soldiers. I couldn't blame him. Yet I resent my own weakness. I have resolved to go on playing the game, but jealousy is out.

10th April

Jan has promised to pass on a message to his uncle, but he doesn't like it.

'Watch yourself *meisie',* he said, as I played with hairs on his chest. *Oom* is one tricky *ou.* I know he's my flesh and blood, but my mother never liked him. He's one of those people who looks out for himself. The rest of us are there to be used.'

Thought took a back seat as he caressed my nipples and a finger explored me lower down.

'Please,' I remember saying. 'Please.'

I felt his cock hard inside me and the wetness of his sweat. I love the way he breathes so hard.

'Can you ask your uncle to give me a ring please?' I said as we lay back exhausted.

'Sure,' he said, 'but it's your funeral.'

14th April

The days are getting shorter. It's warm and bright till about half past six and then suddenly blackness.

Van Rensburg (the *oom*) has arranged to hand over *'papiere'* to me. We are to meet at a place called the Navigator's Den. It's a seedy nightclub near the docks. It's not a place for respectable people, and I have arranged to be watched. I don't want a knife through my ribs.

What worries me most is that van Rensburg is betraying his own people. What if they know and follow him to bump him off, and deal with me in the same manner?

20th April

The Navvies was the dive I'd expected, with ultra violet light making people's teeth luminous. I didn't want to be mistaken for a prostitute, so I'd insisted he came dead on eight. I sat waiting till five past, and thought, right, I'm off, when a man with a beard sat next to me.

'I think you've dropped something under the table.'

I looked down and saw a package wrapped in brown paper. I put it in my bag before I sat up. I turned to thank the man. He'd gone. I nodded to my minder, Ludio, who followed me out, with me yet not with me.

At the bottom of the dark stairs the doorman said,

'Going so soon, madam?'

'Just remembered something. I'll be back later.'

I made sure I stood in the light of a street lamp until I saw my minder, then hurried around the corner, keeping him in sight till I saw my car. As I got in I looked round to see him go and sat in the driver's seat. I heard a low voice,

'Don't look round. Drive on.'

I turned the key and pressed the starter button.

'Why go to all that trouble in the nightclub if you were going to meet me in my own car, *oom*?'

'Just keeping everyone guessing, I find that pays. Never be predictable if you want to stay alive. You'll find that package contains newspaper cuttings. I have here with me a list of our sympathisers in the government, civil service and Defence Force. I have given a potted history of each, their rank in the OB and date of joining. I'll be checking my bank account in England in a week. If I've been followed we're both in trouble. Drop me at the corner of Long Street.'

I stopped next to a traffic light and saw a figure with a raincoat drawn up around his face shuffle off. I accelerated away and soon picked up my minder's car in the rear view mirror.

I was conscious of every pedestrian as I drove up the High Level Road, but there were few of them. I expected something nasty to happen every moment, and it was a raddled me that turned into Avenue Drelingcourt. The engine roared with the strain of the climb to my house, the last before the mountainside scrub.

Later I wondered what made me stay in the car, but I realise now it was anxiety. I parked away from the street lamp and sat still, straining to see. I imagined a figure lurking there, waiting to kill me.

A loud crack and tinkle of my window breaking told me I was right, and I fell to the floor, praying to the deity. More cracks followed, then silence. There was a knock on my car door. I opened it, my small automatic ready. I saw the grinning face of my minder.

'One less enemy of his majesty, *inkosikaas*,' said Ludio, a grin on his brown face. 'My boys will be along to clean up the mess.'

That's what they did. In wartime things are hushed up in a way which is quite abnormal.

18th April

I had a long talk with my boss today. He wants me to kill someone.

'Are you mad?' I said.

'If you don't kill them they'll kill you.'

'Who?'

'A person on that list van Rensburg gave you. You've read it.'

'You mean...'

'Yes, van Rensburg, the OB traitor's nephew, Jan. Your contact, the Don Juan.'

'I'm not a murderer; you have people who do this sort of thing. I'm just a person who decodes messages and does a little espionage on the side. This is insane, loony, ridiculous, unfair and bloody stupid. What have you been drinking?'

'Only some pretty revolting tea. There's a war on, you know.'

'Really.'

'You're quite right, in a way. '

'I'm right in every way. I'm not killing anyone. It's not my job.'

'I would not ask you if it was not the only way. Either you lead him into a trap for Ludio or another one of our men to dispose of, or you do it yourself.'

'I cannot believe that you are being serious. Now I have work to do. See you tomorrow.' I would have said anything to get out of that room.

He looked at me from behind his yellow-wood desk, his eyes those of a dead fish.

'What's he to you, anyway?'

I closed the door. I was still shaking with anger half an hour later, when I arrived home.

The thought of meting out death to anyone was abhorrent. Helping another to do it was even more abhorrent. Perhaps the codes I'd deciphered had led to many deaths. But it was like eating meat or chicken. I couldn't see myself slaughtering an ox or wringing a chicken's neck, yet I ate meat and chicken killed by someone else where I could not see it being done. It was the same with the submarines. Perhaps a decoded message from me had led to upwards of forty young men drowning, and even worse, realising it as the noise of the sea rushing into their vessel meant they only had minutes or seconds to live.

Now I was being asked, told, to kill someone whom I would see alive, smiling perhaps, not knowing that soon the smiling would stop and the tears of his loved ones replace the smiles. I had not been to many funerals, but did recall one when I was a child, in Wales. Gloomy men standing in a freezing graveyard, and the service in the church. The hymn "How Great thou Art". Now I was to be the messenger of death and his angel's wings, flapping silently like those of an owl, would be hovering around my victim, and if he could see truly, the pretty fair haired charming woman in his bed was a skeleton with a sickle, grinning.

Would it be a gun, a knife, poison? Or would I finger him for a confederate to execute? He was my lover!

I'm going to bed, but I shall not sleep well.

11

Tony, shaken by what he'd read, also finding sitting in the drab hotel room claustrophobic, went down to the hotel lobby. He saw a bar with some comfortable leather chairs and picked one that had a view of the lobby. He settled down to read a newspaper. Bored and restless, after half an hour he tried Penny's number. The message,

'The phone is switched off,' droned in his ears. It was on a par with 'unwanted item in the bagging area', which irritated him so much at supermarkets.

That woman, he thought, what's she up to now?

I must go for a walk, I'm sick of this hotel. Like living in a boarding school.

The hotel had its own car park, rows of vehicles whose owners had left them there while they flew off to Turkey, Corfu and other sunny places. The unattractive airport concrete combined with the asphalt of the road added to the depressing aspect.

He wished Penny had picked a charming Jacobean pile with gardens and the odd statue and fountain. They were expensive, but she was flush with her poor aunt's money, and if one had to hole up, why not hole up somewhere pleasant?

As it was, he might as well have been in a motorway service area. They usually had those coffee places. Coffee. That would pass ten minutes. He returned to the bar.

'May I have a cup of coffee?' he said.

'Certainly sir, cappuccino, espresso, filter...?' said the receptionist, the 'r' pronounced in a way that was reminiscent of Poland, Lithuania or another eastern European country. Not France though, thought Tony. It was fun to guess a speaker's native language from the way they pronounced English. French was distinctive.

What he said was, 'espresso please.' Maybe it'd wake him up.

Sipping the bitter liquid, he ruminated over the events of the past few weeks. Since he'd met Penny he seemed to be at the vortex of a whirlpool with as much power to act on his own as a water molecule. True, he'd had a rest after the South African episode, but she'd drawn him into her chaotic life again.

He wondered how one would describe their relationship. He knew he was attracted to her, and he pictured her breasts the last time he'd seen them, all too long ago. He knew she'd used him, but there was, he hoped, genuine affection there. He wasn't exactly SAS material, although he was vain about his MENSA membership, lapsed now it was true, owing to his not bothering to pay the annual membership fee. Yet she must think he had some use.

As he finished his coffee he had a good view of the hotel's revolving door. The humanity that came through it was the same as one might see walking the pedestrianised streets at the centre of Croydon. There were short people, fat people (lots), people with children and even those with the rigid faces that betrayed cosmetic operations. What fools to advertise their insecurity without actually improving their appearance.

At last a person with a purpose he thought, as a smart girl went to the desk. Her manner was different from that of the holiday crowd. She had not noticed him. Something in that purposeful manner alarmed him, and he got up and stood behind a pillar before she noticed him. Perhaps the good Lord was looking after him, he reflected later. As he went out of her view she looked at the very spot where he had been sipping his strong coffee. That short hair, those jeans...she was the woman he'd seen in the pub with the judge.

After the lift door had closed on her, he strolled to reception.

"Oh dear, I've missed her,' he said. 'My sister, where did she go?'

'Don't worry sir; she's gone to your room. She said she was your wife actually, so I gave her your room number.'

'Such a sense of humour,' said Tony.

Aghast, Tony's first thought was to order a taxi and flee. Then he thought, are you a man or a mouse? He entered the other lift and pressed the button for the floor below his.

He watched the numbers light up-1-2-3-4-5. The lift stopped, and after a few seconds the door opened. He looked to see the way was clear, and then went up the staircase. As he reached the sixth floor, he hesitated. What was he, the Reverend Jean Claude van Tony, veteran of South African daring exploits, going to do?

Creep along the corridor, he decided, and watch. He rounded the corner to reach the small passage where his room was, and saw the woman fiddling with the lock. Indignation ousted timidity and he marched towards her.

'Excuse me madam, can I help you,' he said.

For a moment he saw a pair of startled brown eyes, then she ran down the corridor. Tony did not chase her. What was she after, him? The diary? Before he had time to think any more about it, his mobile phone let out a loud noise of greeting, that of its new ring tone, the Hallelujah Chorus. It was a voicemail message from Penny.

'Hello sweetie, can you make it to my London flat straight away?'

Tony, with his suitcase containing the diary, took a taxi to Gatwick airport, caught the Gatwick Express to Victoria and another taxi to Penny's flat in Bloomsbury. He was honoured to be invited there, and decided she was a lot wealthier than he'd realised. The flat was in a Georgian row but had a lift. It made him think of the sort of place Bertie Wooster would have lived in. Penny answered the door dressed in a towel.

'Give me five minutes to put something on, darling, and help yourself to a drink from the cabinet.' Soon she emerged, dressed in tight fitting trousers and a pink top.

'How are you doing with auntie's diary, sweetie?'

Tony hesitated. The diary's sexual content had made him even more receptive than usual to Penny's appeal. It was not just her beauty, but the way she looked at him and touched him which made him feel like an animal.

'I'm making progress. She was quite a girl.'

'So's her niece. I've become friendly with Judge van Wiese's nephew, he's a barrister.'

'How on earth...?'

'Your pal Septimus fixed it. Something to do with "instructing his chambers in numerous matters". You know the lawyerly jargon. He's acting for me in a minor dispute over the service charges relating to this flat. I've used my stage name-don't ask - I was an aspiring actress for a short time.'

'Clever Septimus. I've been spied on by his Honour's pal in the pub.'

'This is getting out of hand. Perhaps you were followed here.'

'This friend of the judge's may be my long time stalker. None of this makes sense. What have I or you to do with Judge van Wiese or any of his friends?'

Penny took his hand.

'I have a feeling it's auntie again. These peep have something to do with her, I suspect. Do you have the diary with you?'

'Yes I do, Penny, but I don't understand what relevance it has. We know your aunt was a spy, but that would give numerous people motives to kill her, most of them dead. Could be some ancient grudge passed down the family, I suppose. One thing more, the woman we saw with the judge in the pub after leaving you was trying to get into my room at the hotel.'

Tony sipped his gin and tonic. They both sat in unaccustomed silence, as Penny absorbed the news. Tony was relieved that the mental puzzle had quelled his lust.

At length he asked,

'Just how friendly are you with the judge's nephew?'

'He's asked me out to dinner. I'm thinking about it.'

'Is he attractive?'

'Oh yes, very, in a tall dark handsome sort of way.'

'Oh,' said Tony.

'No need to be jealous sweetie. It's all a job as far as I'm concerned. I can't stand supercilious self-important types anyway. I'm hoping to find out about his uncle.'

'Penny, I...'

'Don't say anything. You are my favourite person and will remain so.'

Outside, in the dark wet London street, the woman from the hotel waited. The rain dripped off her umbrella as she cursed herself for ever having taken this job.

12

2 0th April
There is a rumour that a man spoke German to a shop assistant in Garlicks, the big department store in Cape Town. If it was a member of a U-boat crew, then it was very stupid. We know the U-boats are here, because we've destroyed a few and they've sunk a fair number of our ships. My friend Jerry, who flies Catalinas with 262 Squadron, says they sunk an Italian U-boat in March. I didn't tell him I radioed its co-ordinates to his bosses. The Bletchley Park people are on to most things. It will win the war for us.

My lover keeps talking about radar and how we find U-boats. He tells me things I know already. If he weren't such an obvious patriot I'd think he was trying to get me to say something. I don't love him, but I'm fond of him and he fulfils my needs. It's good I don't love him, as I'm supposed to be killing him. Why?

Today I went for a walk along the beachfront at Sea Point. The sun lasts so much longer this side of Table Mountain. You can see it gradually reach the horizon as it sets. I saw a whale a few hundred yards out to sea. It must have been a hump back and was breaching the sea with its enormous bulk as if it was only ten foot long, instead of fifty foot. I believe there was also a calf there, but I'm not sure. The tails are remarkable. The minesweepers were further out and a reminder of war, but the sea and mountains are so beautiful it is difficult to believe that death stalks us beneath the waves. I wouldn't be surprised to see a periscope. Many have. Or at least say they have. Could be rusty pipes, seals?

I needed a part for my transmitter and found it at the radio/record shop on Beach Road. The owner thought nothing of it, as it is common in a normal valve radio. He is a Scot who wears khaki overalls and likes to exchange pleasantries. I think he fancies me, but I'm spoken for at present. He made me laugh when I asked him if he had That Old Feeling. He said, 'No, but I get it sometimes.' Then he produced the record from the back and winked at me. Mmm.

My lover wants to visit me this evening. I yearn to see him, but there is an important message coming through from London tonight, so have put him off. I am arguing with my boss about the proposed killing. Why me? I've never killed before but would be an obvious suspect. I'm not even sure why he needs to be killed. I'm not exactly an expert and if he needs things like this done he has, I'm sure, several who would do it. I shall go on resisting. I know There's A War On, but it'll be over in a year or two and I'm not a murderer.

Tony broke off from his reading. He was sitting in Penny's lounge while she was working on her computer.

'Did you realise that part of your late aunt's job was assassination? She's been ordered to bump off her lover.'

Penny looked up.

'No sweetie I didn't. She didn't tell me anything. My father, her much younger brother-in-law, was in the army and presumably saw lots of horrors, but neither he nor my mother ever mentioned her war work except in the vaguest terms.

Keep reading, we're desperate for facts, and that diary is the one place we're maybe going to find them. We've run out of tea.'

'I need a bit of fresh air and you have run out of tea - isn't there a little shop - Tesco or Sainsbury's - near here?' said Tony.

'Go out of the side door, past the Thames Bargeman and it's just there. It's a Co-Op. Please get Twinings. I don't like the other stuff.'

Tony put on his coat and took an umbrella from a stand near the door.

'See you shortly,' he said.

'Watch your back. Take the *side* exit. You're being stalked, remember?'

Tony made a face and went to the lift. The side entrance faced the Thames Bargeman and once out, he stood opposite the hostelry. Its lights were sirens beckoning him. Perhaps a half of lager? Penny wouldn't mind waiting for her tea.

He crossed the road as his umbrella turned inside out and was almost blown from his hands. He pushed the swing doors of the pub.

It was one of those small Victorian survivals, with the only concession to modernity being the flashing fruit machine.

'Half a lager, please,' he murmured to the fiftyish woman behind the bar. There was an air about her that denoted proprietorship.

'And some of those crisps,' he said.

'Certainly sir. Sun dried tomato, salt and rosemary?'

'Plain please.'

'That'll be five pounds fifty six.'

Tony took his expensive provender to a small table as far from the fruit machine as he could find and nibbled his crisps.

His fellow drinkers were an old man who looked as if he'd
been a smoker and drinker, with his marinated skin, and two
women near the window, whose mouths moved continuously,
as if they were trying to outdo each other in relating momen-
tous gossip which had to be imparted straight away. Although
both seemed to be talking simultaneously, they looked happy
enough.

Outside, the woman who had been following him shivered. Tony almost knocked her over as he came out of the
pub and rushed towards the shop. She stared at him in her
confusion, and then drew her hood further over her head.

Tony did not think about the encounter until he was back
in Penny's flat.

'I nearly knocked a woman over coming out of the pub,'
he said.

'Woman? Pub? Typical. You C of E vicars are worse than
the RC priests in your way. I thought you'd been to the shop.'

'I have, but the lights of the pub tempted me out of the
miserable street for a few minutes. I only had a small lager
and crisps. Back to the woman, I've seen her before, at the
hotel and the pub with the sinister judge. Her face was lit by
the street lamp and she looked shocked at my sudden appearance, before she covered her head with her hood.'

'Ah hah! So perhaps she's been your stalker, all along and
now she knows where I live. After what happened to auntie
and that poor private dick it may not be safe here.'

There was a buzz from the entry phone.

Penny answered,' Who is it?'

'Delivery for Miss Duchesne.'

'Ring the porter and leave it with him, please.'

'It needs signing for.'

'He'll do it.'

There was silence.

'We'll give it fifteen minutes, then go and see whether

anything's been left for me,' said Penny. She sank back on the leather couch.

'Either this parcel is from Amazon or it's something more sinister. I'm seeing intrigue everywhere presently.'

They waited for twenty minutes, then Penny led the way to the porter's office.

It was a small room on the ground floor. The porter, a grizzled man in his fifties, was watching football on the television.

'Nah, don't know nothing about anything left for you Miss Dookezny. Nobody's come into the building in the last hour. Did hear the outside buzzer, but as no one operated the door lock I thought it must be a mistake.'

It was a thoughtful pair who went back to Penny's flat.

'Someone checking I live here. Time to take action,' said Penny. 'I suggest you get your things together. We're getting out.'

They slipped from a back entrance to the building, hoping not to be noticed.

13

2 1st April
It took me an hour to fix my radio. The part I bought in Sea Point was fine, but for some reason the damn thing wouldn't work. All the right lights were on, but the signal was almost inaudible. I traced the problem to the aerial, which had come loose in the loft.

It was ten o'clock before I was able to begin receiving. Everything is in code, so it takes me half an hour or so to decipher it, although all I have to transmit is my call sign. The answering message was disquieting.

'The fox is in the hencoop. Do not trust the farmer.'

I had been expecting co-ordinates of German submarines, not this cryptic information. The sender was not content with code but was being obscure with a purpose. Who was the fox? Who was the farmer?

I did what I always do when my brain was taxed; wrote a list of possibilities.

For 'fox' read van Rensburg senior or possibly an unknown enemy? For 'farmer' read my boss? Unlikely.

Pretty useless information really. All it told me was that I'm in danger, which I know well.

I put my equipment away in its alcove in the wall and replaced the picture, which hid it. I needed a stiff drink and poured myself a large brandy and ginger ale.

I heard knocking at the front door and made my way down the stone stairs, ensuring my tiny automatic pistol was safe in the pocket of my dressing gown. I opened the door about six inches. It was my minder, Ludio.

'Sorry madam to call at this hour, but it's important.' Ludio's dark skin glistened with sweat in the light of the porch. I could hear the sound of the crickets playing their nightly concert behind him.

'Come in please and sit down, you look all in,' I said.

I led him to the dining room but did not switch on the light.

'Is someone after you? You look as if you've been running.'

'You must come with me tonight, *Inkosikaas*.'

'Why is that, what's happening?'

'The boss has sent me. He says there is something you must see. I have the car in the next road. You are watched from the house with the American car outside, so we can't go past there.'

'So how do we get there?'

'Along the firebreak. You must follow me.'

I trust Ludio. He calls me '*Inkosikaas*' meaning 'chieftai-ness', which I think is very Rider Haggard, but who am I to argue?

We slipped out of the back door and up the steps to the fire break at the bottom of Signal Hill. There was no problem in finding our way by moonlight, as we passed the plantation of blue gum trees standing to our left and speaking for myself, hoping not to disturb a sleeping puff adder. After a few minutes we spotted the streetlights of the parallel road,

Avenue De Berrange, bisected by date palms. Ludio led me to a little black Ford, parked near the top of the road and asked me to sit in the back while he drove.

'People will think it funny if they see you sitting next to a black man,' he said.

I did as I was told. Not being a South African I did not take for granted all the racial nuances and had to be reminded.

Ludio drove down into Bantry Bay and along the coastal road through Clifton and Camps Bay towards Llandudno. Somewhere near Llandudno we stopped at a clearing at the side of the road and I followed Ludio down some steep steps. I could hear the surf crashing against rocks and in the moonlight see shining white sand and black restless sea. In that light it had the texture of jelly.

We came upon a small white house, built by someone who valued solitude, and Ludio opened the front door with a key from his pocket. He did not turn on the light. I could smell cigarette smoke.

A shape arose from a seat in the kitchen. It grew into a tall figure in what looked in the dark like a Navy uniform.

I shook a powerful large right hand.

'Hello Theresa.'

The familiar voice made me feel even more unreal. By now my eyes were becoming used to the dark and I was taken aback to see the distinctive star of a German naval officer on his sleeve.

'Martyn? How can it be you? You're dead. What are you doing here? Why are you dressed up as a German sailor?' It was my husband reported dead it seemed like decades ago, although it was actually only two years.

'Never mind for the moment. I'm not a German, that's all you have to know. I have a job to do, much like yours. Now, I want you to tell me all you can about this chap van Rensburg.'

I told my 'dead' husband all he asked about van Rensburg, assuming it was the uncle he meant, although I decided to be less than revealing about his nephew. If someone else told him, that was too bad. I felt no warmth towards him. I had married him in a hurry without knowing him too well. Wartime is like that. You don't know whether you're still going to be alive tomorrow, and you do things you'd never do in normal times. So many sexual relationships, births and hurried marriages take place. Martyn's 'death' hadn't even been much of a shock. I knew he was a submarine commander and that their expectation of life was short. When I was told his ship was lost and him with it I'd been sad, but not devastated. He was a handsome man with whom I'd spent a happy week. I could hardly remember the Registry Office wedding. I hadn't even known the two witnesses, who'd been two British sailors dragged in for the purpose.

Now he was here and wanted my help. Quite why he was dressed up like this I was about to find out.

'I'd like you to get a message to van Rensburg that I'd like to meet him. I've written the time and place on this piece of paper. I've given you a week. He will think I'm commander of the U-864. My name is Korvettenkapitän Ralf-Reimar Wolfram. He pointed to the cogwheel on his plain braid shoulder strap. Luckily we have the right uniforms.'

Now my eyes had grown accustomed to the poor light, I had a better view of the three broad stripes and a star on his arm.

'I notice there's been no "Darling, this must be a terrible shock," or 'I've missed you terribly.'

'Sorry about that sweetheart, but there is a war on,' he said. At that moment I found it difficult to remember what I'd seen in him. I'd married this cold fish, who'd been so fond of me he hadn't even had the grace to soften the introduction. Oh no, straight on to the job in hand for this one. I'd rather have my lover any day.

I did not come out loud with these thoughts.

'You're going to stay out of sight, aren't you? I know U-boat officers have reputedly been seen in the centre of Cape Town, but my guess is you'd get arrested pretty smartly.'

He laughed.

'Of course. I'm staying either here or in some other hidden location. There is no need for you to do anything other than make sure this chap gets my message.'

'Then you'll be off? I won't even know where to serve the divorce papers.'

'There'll be plenty of time for that when the war's over. Now I think you'd better be going. Your driver is looking anxious.'

He did not even kiss me on the cheek.

We drove back along the coastal road. Once again, I was conscious of the crash of the waves which matched the turmoil in my head. Parking again in an adjacent road, Ludio went with me along the mountain path until we saw my house. I turned to tell him I was all right and could find my way without him, but he had gone.

I waited on the path, checking there was nothing different about the place. In my jumpy mood I grasped the pistol in my pocket and waited till the clouds had passed from in front of the moon, then darted to the front door and unlocked it.

I made my way to bed in the dark.

I could not get to sleep, so got up and sat out on the open balcony. Luckily it's warm here, so if I hadn't been so tense, I'd have enjoyed the twinkle of the lights below, although the shimmer of the moon on the sea had replaced them, owing to the coastal blackout. How many U-boats were sitting far out there I wondered, waiting for innocent souls to slaughter?

Lights were an invitation to come in and sink boats in the harbour conveniently silhouetted as in the U.S. earlier on, when a lot were sunk because of that, but I suppose in the South Atlantic they're afraid of being hunted if they give away their presence. A flying boat could take off in ten minutes and bomb them.

22nd April

In the end I decided that the easiest way of getting the message to van Rensburg was to use Ludio.

'He must have no idea the message is from me, and it's going to be in German. Martyn has written the message on this piece of paper.'

I handed him the message Martyn had given me,

'Treffen Sie mich in Garlicks am Samstag um elf Uhr im menswear Abteilung. Heil Hitler.'

It is an invitation to meet the writer at the Garlicks Department store on Saturday at eleven a.m. The 'Heil Hitler' was overdoing it a bit. Will he take the bait?

Ludio has many friends, including one who works at the Netherlands Club, where van Rensburg has lunch every weekday. He is to pass on the message by leaving it in a pigeonhole van Rensburg has there.

As Ludio seems to be in touch with Martyn, I've told him to confirm to him he's passed the message on. Saturday is tomorrow, so there is no margin for error. On the other hand, if he's from a submarine there's no time to hang about.

Ludio has told me he'll be watching and will let me know how things go.

23RD APRIL SUNDAY

I met Ludio at the garage where he sometimes works at the petrol pumps, one of his covers, I suppose. I asked him to clean the windscreen, so I could talk to him without being noticed. I even gave him a *tikkie* as a tip.

'They met and went off together in *Meneer* van Rensburg's car,' he told me. '*Meneer* Martyn told me not to follow. He wants you to come to the Kommetjie house on Wednesday at seven in the evening.'

27th April Thursday

Ludio took me to Kommetjie again It was "near Llandudno" in the earlier encounter. We used the devious route in case a spy was looking.

As I walked down the steps I felt uneasy but put that down to anxiety. Ludio opened the white-painted wooden door. Martyn was standing, smoking, but not in uniform.

'I'm here,' I said, 'What do you want?'

Martyn smiled, but it was not a warm smile.

'I need your help. I've met Mr van Rensburg and he seems sympathetic to the cause of Germany. He's promised to lay on fuel and stores for my U-boat on Friday. And he wants me to give someone a lift to Germany.'

'A lift? Who is it?'

'He's vague. Someone who needs to go.'

'You'll need a lot of help. Do you have any German speaking sailors? They won't be expecting the Captain to be taking on stores.'

'I have that organised. I don't expect van Rensburg will be coming himself. I need you to talk to your boss. I presume you've discussed me with him?'

'Yes of course,' I lied.

'I need to meet him personally. Obviously he knows about me anyway, as he and Ludio are working for us and I presume discuss things, but I think a meeting would be better arranged by you. Can you fix that?'

'Yes, I'll tell him. Martyn, this submarine, it's not really a U-boat is it?'

'No of course not, it's one of ours.'

He turned as if dismissing me. I got up and walked away without saying anything. Why involve me? Ludio was quite capable of passing on a message. Perhaps there was an ulterior motive. I was annoyed I'd been put at risk just to act as a messenger, twice.

5th May

I have not had the energy, will or desire to write this diary for several days, but now I feel I must record the terrible events which took place.

Tony was interrupted by a jab in the ribs.

.'Come on sweetie, plenty of time for more reading soon. We've got to go.

"But we've only been here for about half an hour.'

'Leave it to me, my car's outside.'

Penny is very masterful, thought Tony. They were in yet another hotel, this time a small private place in Bloomsbury, near the British Museum.

They were soon across Hammersmith Bridge and as far as Tony could see, making their way along the South Circular towards the A3 Portsmouth Road. Penny drove as though the speed limit was an advisory minimum, and Tony expected blue lights any minute. Her MG held the road well, but you couldn't call it comfortable. It wasn't. They hit the Esher bypass and Tony wondered whether they'd pass Guildford. Penny seemed to think the outside lane was the only one to be in, and the sound of the wind against the soft top made conversation a waste of time.

Every time he went onto the Guildford bypass, which was not often, Tony thought about Mike Hawthorne, world champion racing driver, who had crashed there. As the houses on the side of the dual carriageway went past he wondered where the crash had happened, and hoped that Penny, who might well have been a frustrated racing driver, judging by the speed she was going, was not thinking of emulating the late great Mike.

As he was resigning himself to going all the way to Portsmouth, they swung off at a sign which said 'Petersfield'.

Soon they saw signs for Bordon and a lot of farmland until Tony thought, strewth, where's she dragging me off to this time.

'I expect you're thinking, "Where's she taking me now?"' said Penny, as the engine's roar subsided.

'Perhaps. But as you say, you know best.'

The sports car swung off the winding highway as a gap appeared in the hedgerows. There was no sign to indicate where they were going. The track was potholed, and the car bumped up and down. Tony felt each bump and longed for them to arrive. He would settle for anywhere as long as they could get out. He was prone to carsickness as a child, and realised that this weakness was still there if the circumstances were dire enough.

'You poor darling, you look green. It must be those crisps you had in the hotel bar. Never mind, this place is a haven.'

They had stopped at a single storey farmhouse, beside some scattered barns and a tractor with a wheel missing.

'Welcome to Hazelwood Farm,' said Septimus, who appeared from behind a barn. He was dressed in a scruffy shirt and baggy brown dungarees.

Tony looked at Septimus.

'You dark horse, what are you doing here?'

'I am the proprietor.'

'It's a weekday. Why aren't you in the office?'

'Down to two days a week old chap. I've sold out to Harvey, that smooth youngster you've seen once or twice.'

'Not that pompous twit. I never understood why you and he were partners.'

'He's good with money and I don't have to worry about it

any more. I bought this place on a whim a few years ago. I'm selling the Victorian pile in Croydon. The place has gone to the dogs now. Rows of empty shops...'

'Yes, we all know that. Some of us still live there,' interrupted Tony.

'When you boys have finished, can we go inside?' said Penny.

The interior of the house was beamy and low ceilinged, and Tony, who was pushing six foot tall, had to duck as he went into the sitting room.

The three of them sat down - Penny by the fireplace, wood piled there ready for a severe winter, Tony on an old couch which he recognised from Septimus's Croydon house and Septimus in a grand but comfortable chair, looking more like a walrus far from its natural habitat than ever.

'So. What to do?' said Septimus.

'I think the key to this imbroglio is in my auntie's diary,' said Penny.

'Trouble is,' said Tony, 'there are only a few pages left to read, as she seems to have stopped writing it around May 1944.' He sank back on the old couch, putting his hands behind his head.

'You didn't tell us that,' the other two said simultaneously.

'I didn't realise. Pages have been torn out. Things are building up to a real drama, I may say.'

'I think we're safe here for the moment,' said Penny, 'so I suggest you read what's left then we decide what to do.'

'Thanks,' said Tony. 'Any chance of something nice to eat and a glass of wine first? After that journey I'm in need of something to cheer me up and to restore my energy.'

'The wine you can have now. Red or white?' Septimus moved towards the kitchen.

'If you have a cold Chablis or Sauvignon Blanc that will be fine,' said Tony. 'I expect Penny would like one too.'

Penny smiled at Septimus, as he brought in two glasses of Chablis.

Tony opened his suitcase and brought out the diary.

6th May

I have killed someone for the first and I hope only time in my life. I am only now able to put events into order. I hardly slept in the last few days.

I was awoken in the small hours by a noise on the balcony that faces the sea. I took my small revolver from the drawer next to my bed and crept downstairs. I heard a sound of something falling to the floor and crouched at the bottom of the stairs and behind the door leading to the front room. As a shape came through I stuck out my foot and there was a crash as he or she fell over. I reached for the light and pointed my gun. To my surprise it was Ludio.

'Don't shoot *inkosikaas*! Don't shoot!' he shouted.

I could see he was unarmed.

'What's this all about, Ludio?'

'They'll be here soon *inkosikaas*, I had to come in the only way I could, to warn you.'

'Who are they?'

'Not sure. I was doing my nightly rounds, driving up High Level Road, when I saw a big Studebaker. I drove to the bottom of this road and started getting out. I drove up the next road along and parked, running here to arrive before them. Now we'd better hide or get out of here.'

'Let's hide,' I said. 'You know I have a hidden room.'

This room is between the two bedrooms upstairs, a type of South African priest's hole. John insisted on it when I moved here, to my annoyance, as the builders were obtrusive and messy. Now I was glad he did. The entrance looks like a linen cupboard. It is quite roomy though, and you can see through a generous peephole in the floor.

We crammed ourselves into the room, made for one. I

smelt Ludio's fresh body odour, spiced up by his recent exer-
tion. I reflected that it was lucky for the priests who inhab-
ited their holes in 16th century England that I assume they did
it alone. Fear kept me there this time. We heard the door
open and steps on the stairs. There was whispering and
curses. The voices were Afrikaans. I heard swearwords,
'Bliksem', and *'foei tog*!' Ludio's breathing was so hard the
sounds were obscured sometimes, but after a long time I
heard a door slam and the sound of a car's motor.

Some time later Ludio said,

'Shall we go out?'

I was on the point of not caring whether it was dangerous
or not.

'Yes', was all I could say.

We crept into the hall. I did not dare turn on the light.

'I'm going to the window, see if I can see something, stay
here.'

I obeyed.

'There's nothing,' he said.

'I can't remain in this house any longer, they may come
back.'

'There's the house at Kommetjie?' see comment above re
near Llandudno

'Too isolated. Let's go now.'

We edged out of the back door, armed. As we made for
the trees at the end of the garden I saw a shape move.
Instinctively I shot at it. It fell. We made our way to it. It was
the body of a man... I'm not writing any more of this , it's too
painful.

Tony stopped reading. The remaining pages of the diary
were blank. So much for clues.

Up to now he had hardly noticed his surroundings, being
absorbed in his reading. It was like one of those rooms he'd
seen on TV, an old room before they tarted the house up for

sale at a higher price, following advice from the relentlessly pushy presenter. It was untidy, with piles of books waiting to be placed in bookcases. Stephen King jostling with Kipling and Rider Haggard. Some biographies and a 'Manual of Modern Manual Handling Law, revised 1971'. That's Septimus, thought Tony, never throws anything away.

On the mantelpiece above the comforting fire was a photograph – Hazleworth School Boxing Team 1965. There was a slim and youthful Septimus, puffing his chest out and looking as manly as a seventeen year old could. So, he's handy with his fists, thought Tony. I'll remember that should we get into yet another scrape. Funny how you never really know people - he was now a bit portly, and years of being a solicitor had led him to acquire that slightly self-important air they have. At least he's not a judge, he reflected, he'd be even worse.

I suppose being a vicar has altered my personality, too thought Tony. You become the part and act it so much you have difficulty distinguishing what you are from what you're expected to be. Penny rescued me. Showed me I'm not just a robot in a cassock, but a red-blooded...well perhaps a shade of pink would be more accurate, but my blood's getting redder all the time.

He opened a small leaded window and looked out at the fields. There were two large deer at the other side of the adjacent one, emerging from some trees. One had small pointed antlers. Roe deer. Then the other one began to pee. He turned away, then back again. Was there a little flash, as of a reflection? The problem was that the sun was intermittent and had gone back behind a cloud. He shuddered. He thought, I'm a nervous wreck.

He decided to go downstairs and join the other two.

'The diary's finally come to an end I'm afraid. Just when it was getting really exciting,' he announced

'Oh, what a shame sweetie, I'd hoped for a magic solution to our conundrums,' said Penny, who was curled up on a couch.

'Me too, I'll admit,' said Tony. 'Any ideas, aged forensic genius?' he grinned at Septimus.

'Don't be cheeky, Tone. I am more than a lawyer. The submersion of half my personality in legal drudgery for so many years does not mean I don't have sensitivities. But in answer to your question, it is naïve to expect answers to be easily obtained. Providence has decided we should work hard, then we will deserve the solution. I think it's pretty simple really. Let's open a nice bottle of Argentinian Malbec. Then the ideas will flow.'

'What a good idea,' said Penny. 'I expect you've cases of the stuff.'

They sat drinking the rich red liquid, enjoying another of the fires Septimus had lit throughout the building, hoping that their respective subconscious minds would find painless and effort-free solutions to the mysteries that enfolded them. Each expected, or rather hoped for a sudden 'Eureka' from the other. They started a second bottle.

'Someone had better get a pen and paper,' said Penny. 'If anyone does have idea we should write it down before we pass out and forget it.'

'Got one here,' said Septimus.

'Didn't you obtain data from your aunt's computer, and what about those papers you copied at van Wiese's house, didn't they tell you anything?' said Tony.

'Regrettably they didn't help,' said Penny. 'I was hoping for great things from the computer, but the only bit that could be extracted contained a whole lot of research about something called the "Peacock Throne of the Mogul Emperors"' a jewel encrusted replica of the actual throne which disappeared in India in the late 18th century, believed stolen.

As for van Wiese's papers, they were Parish Council minutes. Deadly boring.'

They sipped and sipped. If their mental processes were whirring away in the background they did so secretly. The conversation was confined to banalities. Eventually Septimus said, 'Aah!' and wrote something down. Then he joined the other two in sleep. Had the proceedings been recorded, a loud snore would have drowned the quiet breathing of the other two.

Although they didn't know it, part of the solution was very close.

14

Even in the darkness the face and the body were all too familiar. Theresa felt a pain that that was overwhelming. It was her lover. After standing still for a while, but she controlled herself and switched from her grief to the professional mode, secreting her feelings in the internal safe she had constructed years ago, saying,

'We'd better get rid of this body.'

'I will do it.' Ludio said, 'but you need to get away from here. My car is in Avenue De Berrangé - here are the keys.'

She drove down into Sea Point and along the coastal road to Llandudno. She slept in the cottage where she'd met her 'dead' husband albeit alone.

What passed for sleep was a mixture of bad dreams and anxious wakefulness. She was relieved when daylight appeared and she was able to get up. She heard noises in the kitchen and was amazed when her reborn husband appeared with a mug of tea and a sympathetic expression.

'I hear you had a difficult evening,' he said. 'Ludio has already disposed of the body. He's a useful man. I understand the dead man was a friend. Must have been a shock.'

'It was, it is. I shot him. I don't understand what was going on. How on earth have you become involved? I thought you'd be on a U-boat or even one of our submarines in the Atlantic somewhere.'

'As arranged, I met that van Rensburg chap. Interesting. In times of war it's difficult to tell what side anyone is on. I got the impression he wasn't sure himself. He was keen to ingratiate himself with the Germans, although I suspect he does not see them as the winners. His heart is still with the Boers and the pro-Nazi ones at that. The nephew - the one you've just killed - has been a mole in our forces in North Africa, I believe. No idea why he came to your house- perhaps to warn you, may have had divided loyalties, who knows? Anyhow, van Rensburg senior thinks I really am a U-boat commander, and we made arrangements for food and other supplies to be left with a farmer along the coast near Cape Agulhas. Apparently he has a swastika painted inside a barn door which is left open and lit when provisions are avail- able. It's impossible for the South African government John- nies to police the vast coastline, so it's all worked well from their point of view. Those U-boats you track are eating fresh South African fruit and drinking some of the best South African wine. You were mixed up in this somewhere. Van Rensburg mentioned you as a contact with the British he was using, and that his nephew was keeping an eye on you.'

'I see, and why were they creeping up on me last night?'

'No idea must have decided you were dangerous, I suppose. Your boss will find you somewhere else to live. Ludio can rescue your equipment. Now if you don't mind, I must go. Ludio will look after you.'

He was out of the house in five minutes. Theresa looked round. Apart from beds in the two bedrooms and a sofa in the sitting room, it was hardly furnished at all. There were thick, drab curtains on the windows, and basic accoutrements in the kitchen, but the place had a temporariness to it that didn't surprise her. It was as if someone had found an empty cottage in an isolated place, and thought, 'This will do', and ordered basic necessities to be put there without provision for comfort.

The drabness was oppressive, and she felt hemmed in, like being in a police station or a jail cell. She wished Ludio would hurry up and rescue her. Through the front window she could see the dark blue waves turning into white foam as they crashed against the black rocks. Some of them were close and she half expected them to overwhelm the house any minute. But the place had been built just high enough to avoid that, and all that reached the house was a fine sea mist, leaving salty marks on the windows.

The sounds of the sea were so loud and her feelings of shock so profound that the knocking on the door meant nothing for a few seconds. She opened it to the welcome smiling face of Ludio.

'Why knock?' I said. 'It's not locked.'

'I do have manners, Inkosikaas. I've been told to take you to a safe place.'

'That's a relief. Have you been back to my house?'

'Not yet, but I will go there. The boss has arranged for someone to remove all essentials and take them to your new home. I'm not sure where that is, but you'll know by the end of the day.'

'The new 'home' was on the other side of Table Mountain. It was an enormous mansion in Constantia, at the top of Wynberg Hill. They were greeted by a uniformed servant who took her bags without a word. Theresa made her way through a large doorway and was intrigued to see a series of bells underneath signs denoting rooms. Room service! The carved light oak stairs lead up to a panelled gallery which overlooked a large hall. Beyond that, through a very large

leaded window, she could see a long lawn with beds of yellow
roses on either side. She was guided up small steps to her
room, or rather her suite. The luxury of the fittings was such
that although she found that now she was expected to live in
a suite of rooms, rather than have a dwelling to herself, she
did not mind. As she gazed from her window over the long
rose-flanked lawn, she saw it led to a pool with a small statue
of a naked woman on a plinth in the middle. She wondered at
the thought and money that had made this paradise. Anxiety
returned though and she feared for her life. She flung herself
onto the bed and slept. She was awoken by a knock on the
door. It was the uniformed servant, who advised her that
dinner would be served in half an hour. This gave her time to
have a shower and find some presentable clothing in her
luggage which had now been delivered. Dinner was at a long
table at the end of the hall, next to an enormous fireplace
which looked as if it had been transported whole from
England. In fact, she learned later, it had been brought in
pieces and reassembled. It had once graced Nonsuch Palace
and had been removed from there when one of Charles II's
mistresses found she needed cash. Thence it'd had gone to a
smaller manor house. Again, the owner, needing money, had
sold it to the builder of this incongruous mansion. All this
she was told at dinner by the owner himself, who spoke in (he
said) a Californian accent. To Theresa it sounded very like
any other American one, with lots of 'helluva's. His family
was very rich and he, inheriting young, had chosen Cape
Town in which to build his earthly paradise.

'I told myself this was the nearest I'd get to California and
I don't have to put up with those pesky relatives.'

The house was, Theresa realised, a headquarters
containing others working clandestinely. They had dinner at a
long table at the end of the big hall with its ornate fireplace.
Mediaeval England, Hollywood version, situated in the Cape.

The millionaire was a very tall man with bushy eyebrows and face creased from exposure to sun. His native accent was punctuated with occasional lapses into South African, using words like '*sus*' meaning something was disgusting. His living quarters were at the end of a gallery which overlooked the hall, adjacent to Theresa's suite. He knew about the war work but appeared to play no active part in it.

The house was only a dozen miles from central Cape Town and had extensive grounds. Theresa felt it was possible to live there without feeling claustrophobic. In view of the recent events she and her boss agreed it was too dangerous for her to go anywhere else, as she was a target.

'Your security is that no one knows where you are,' her boss John said, having invited himself for dinner. 'I dare say it'd be quite possible for someone to creep in here and shoot you, in spite of the guards, but as far as anyone knows this is the folly of an eccentric millionaire, with apologies to you, sir.' He looked at Mr T, as he was called by everyone, who was eating with them, Mr T shrugged, as if he was used to mild abuse.

After a week of lotus eating Theresa became bored with sitting about and doing little, so one warm morning she resolved to explore the area. At the top of the property there were woods of oak and some other trees she presumed were indigenous. She tramped up a hill and was startled to see a large animal sitting and staring at her. It was a cat of some sort, sandy coloured with pointed ears. She stopped and wondered what to do. The creature continued to sit for half a minute or so, then got up and sauntered further up the hill, eventually disappearing into some bushes. After a while she decided she was safe and entered the wood. The floor was covered in acorns and there were long ditches which seemed to be old trenches running through it. She saw something metal and bent down to pick it up. It was a small lead bullet, only slightly distorted. She examined it in the light which filtered through the trees and wondered how it had come here. Shooting practice, perhaps? While musing thus she was shocked out of her thoughts. She heard a crack and a branch near her head broke and fell next to her.

She dived down into a trench, her heart thudding.

She felt for the little revolver in her pocket, took it out and waited. She heard the rustle of branches about ten yards away and what looked like a boot. She aimed a foot above it and was about to squeeze the trigger, when she looked up to see that it was Mr T himself. She stood up.

'Nearly got me there, sir,' she said.

Mr T stared at her.

'My Gaad, ah thought you were that pesky lynx that's been eating our chickens. Aam awful sorry, Miss. I wouldn't want to shoot a human, especially a pretty lady like you.'

His red face and the look of consternation in his eyes seemed to verify that he was genuinely sorry for his mistake.

'I'm the one who should be sorry sir, I had no right to be wandering about on your land without permission.'

'Aw, call me Hugh, sir is much too formal. You can go where you like, when you like, only best to tell the guy in the uniform, Anthony, so you don't nearly get killed. Why don't we go down to the house and get better acquainted over a drink? I can show you round the grounds later?'

Theresa was very anxious to get away from the woods now and said,

'Yes, I'd love to,' in her best enthusiastic feminine trill.

They traipsed down the hill and through the house. Hugh took her to the library, which led from the hall. He pushed a button in the panelled wall and almost instantaneously the uniformed servant appeared with a tray of drinks. They talked for a while about the war and how sad it was that so many had been killed. Hugh was in his forties and had no wish to fight. He felt that providing facilities for 'British military liaison' was enough. Theresa had no idea how much he was telling her was true, but played along, maintaining that she was merely one of John's less important employees, who needed temporary accommodation. Bored as she was, she found the American interesting. He certainly drank a lot. He told his uniformed servant to leave the bottle of single malt where it was and preferred it neat, although he did have a block of ice in each glass. He talked of his time in California and of a namesake who had died young in Japan, leaving a terrible inheritance case. His grandmother had sued her infant grandson and won. The fortune was based on Wells Fargo, he said. He'd been attracted to South Africa after reading Rider Haggard stories as a boy, and found his inherited wealth went far. His wife was an invalid, requiring a warm climate, and the Cape was ideal.

There was a doctor in the area who claimed to be able to cure his wife, but he was a quack and she remained bedridden in their large suite.

Thinking about the episode later, Theresa was not sure when she became aware that Hugh was trying to seduce her. Luckily the whisky slowed him down and she was able to avoid his lunges without taking drastic action. All at once, worn out perhaps, he fell asleep in his leather chair and she crept out. It was still a warm afternoon and she told the uniformed servant she was going for another walk in the woods. Hugh and his gun were safely out of the way and the caracal, which was the correct name for Hugh's lynx, had shown no interest in her.

Once again she explored the trenches. The proximity to nature relaxed her. These woods were good for her soul.

As she reached the boundary and two enormous stones Hugh had told her were called the Hen and Chickens, she heard the sound of someone moving through the bushes. She had no wish to confront whoever it was and hid behind a tree, then dropped into a trench and crawled as far as she could along it. Just as she began to feel she was over reacting she felt something hard blocking her way. It was a man's foot. She looked further and found herself looking at a body. The man was clothed in a smart suit. There was dried blood just above his right ear and a hole where he'd been shot. She did not recognise him. He was young with blond hair. Fearful that the killer might be near, she climbed out of the trench in such a way as she hoped would not to be visible and lay in the midst of undergrowth for quarter of an hour, not daring to move. At last she decided it was now or never and ran out of the woods and down the path towards the house. As she panted through the back door, she could not believe she was unscathed, and climbed the stairs to her room at the end of the panelled gallery.

She locked the door and flung herself on the bed.

So, the safe house was not safe at all.

15

My brother Jan was killed in the war. How and exactly where was the subject of rumour, but a nameless woman was mentioned, along with 'patriotic work' and possible murder. I never knew him, except for his photo in the hall. He was in uniform, handsome, manly and smiling. I used to imagine how he was, and when I was making a difficult decision I used to run it past him. His advice was always sound, although he never spoke.

Jannie had fought the Germans in the desert but, in a patriotic Afrikaans family which was by no means against them, this was regarded as an aberration. He was on our side all the time, they said.

My uncle, who seemed very old when I was a little boy, was reticent about his dead nephew, By the time I was at all aware of things, our people had become the masters of the country. The Prime Minister was Dr Malan. The English and their traitor leader, Smuts, had been ousted. The blacks and the English were in their place, and we would never be pushed around again.

The photo was always there. As I grew older I became

aware of the injustices inflicted on my people. It became symbolic of their suffering. The concentration camps! My grandmother, *Ouma* van Rensburg, told me stories. She'd been a young girl when the Khakis (British) had herded the women and children into concentration camps during what we called *Die Tweede Vryheidsoorlog*, and the British the 'Boer War'.

Before, we had lived like kings on the *plaas* with our servants, chosen by God to serve us.

I never asked *Ouma* why God, so all powerful and on our side, had allowed this to happen. So many had died of disease, but *Ouma*'s mother made sure she had enough to eat and kept her away from the infected. She used to say,

'Ek was 'n baie sterk meisie.' (I was a very strong little girl.)

The war against the British was lost and we went back to our farms. The traitors Smuts and Botha made up with the British and were rewarded, but the hatred and desire for freedom remained.

This hatred was passed down to us. At school there was one English *ou*, Mortimer. He was a big, powerful boy and in the rugby team. You would have thought this made him an honorary Afrikaner, rugby being our religion (after *die kerk*, of course). But he was an outsider. He could talk Afrikaans and swear with the best of us, but he was always *'die rooinek'* as we called people from England, their necks supposedly burnt red by the sun. This was a myth - there were lots of fair Afrikaners, we being of Dutch, German and French ancestry, and liable to have red necks. Perhaps *'wit bene'* or 'white legs' would have been more appropriate, as their touring rugby players did not have time to sit on beaches or just walk around in shorts in the sun like the South African white players.

We teased Mortimer. It was only safe to do so in numbers, as he was big, fierce and short tempered.

On leaving school I decided to become a lawyer, not from

any great love of that profession but rather because it seemed a well paid job. My parents liked the idea.

I went to Stellenbosch University, where the instruction was mainly in Afrikaans, and after five years got my B.A. LLB. A hard slog it was too. The thought of spending years in an office training to be an attorney did not appeal to me, so I became an Advocate, which is what South Africans call a barrister. The university was very politicised and Afrikaner nationalism was exceptionally strong. I became interested in my people's history and their struggles - firstly against the English, later against indigenous peoples such as the Xhosas and Zulus, then the English again. Now the English had been put in their place, it was the communists and the threat of the black population, who would not be under the thumb forever, or even for much longer. As I grew older Jannie, and the mystery of his death, loomed larger in my mind.

How had he died? What was he involved in? My imagination pictured him in all sorts of situations - fighting Germans in the desert, perhaps marching through minefields at the Battle of El Alamein, rifle with bayonet pointing forward, Jannie wearing shorts and one of those pudding basin helmets I'd seen in films like *Ice Cold in Alex*.

An alternative scenario was Jannie planting a bomb on a railway line in a remote part of the northern Transvaal or some other place to hamper the Allied war effort.

I could not reconcile Jannie the desert rat with the rumours about his involvement with my uncle and his *Ossewabrandwag* terrorism. Soldiers who fought in the desert fought for the British Empire, and the South African army was composed of volunteers. If you were a volunteer for one cause abroad why work against it at home? Perhaps he was a spy? The Jannie in the photo didn't look like a spy, but you never can tell.

By then my aged uncle had died and taken his secrets with

him. Where could I look? My parents and uncle were the only connection. It seemed that uncle was an OB (*Osse-wabrandwag*) high-up, not an ordinary member. I racked my brains to think of anyone who might know more about my brother. My mother now lived in a town called Somerset West, my father having died recently. As his executor I had the right to his papers but felt my mother would resist my snooping. It was worth trying, so I drove the twenty odd miles from Cape Town to the farm where she had a small cottage. She was sitting on the *stoep*.

'*Ag, seun*, why do you want all these papers? Your Pa and Oom had them locked in a deposit box at the Trust Bank and that's where they should stay.'

'Mom, I'm the executor, and it's my job to look after the Estate.'

Dear old mother, who was sitting in her ancient rocking chair from the farm, which she refused to get rid of, however worn, glowered. She clenched and unclenched her fists, her eyes angry.

'No good will come of it. Your brother died because of that uncle of yours and his *Ossewabrandwag* dealings. Jannie was a lovely boy and never harmed anyone. He came back from the war and soon it was that *skelm* inviting him up to Franschhoek, telling him stories about the past and egging him on. I was not told everything, but I do know that if Jannie had not kept seeing his uncle he'd be alive today.'

I listened to this tirade with amazement. All these years Mom had been bottling this up.

'Mom, why was I never told of this? 'I knew the answer - hush up unpleasant facts at all costs.

'Some things are better left unsaid.'

Mom turned and resumed her needlework. The conversation was over. The only sound was the thrum of a thousand crickets sheltering in the reeds of the ceiling. She did not flinch as one dropped onto her lap. It was bewildered, poor thing, so I picked it up and put it outside. When I came back I looked at her and saw her eyes had closed. The heat had made her sleepy. I picked up another cricket from her lap and took it out.

I decided to take a different tack.

I rang my father's bank. After many delays, repeating my date of birth and full names many times, I reached the correct department.

The bank was in a nondescript two storey building with a security guard standing with the air of one for whom his job was excessively tedious, just inside the entrance. He showed no interest in me as I asked for *Mejufrou* (Miss) Du Toit and gestured to the counter marked 'Customer Service'. Miss Du Toit was a small woman of mixed race who beamed a delightful smile at me. I smiled back, introduced myself and produced my passport and Probate authority. Miss du Toit gestured to a door marked 'Private' and knocked on it. A woman wearing rimless glasses appeared,

'Follow me please, *meneer*.'

She led me through a number of thick metal doors. Then we entered a lift and went down a floor to the basement. There was a short corridor to yet another thick door which my guide opened using a combination. She turned on the light and revealed a row of boxes on each side of a large room.

'*Ek het die sluitels*,' the guide said, breaking into Afrikaans and flourishing some keys. She approached a box with the number 15 inscribed on it and breaking into English, said,

'This hasn't been opened for many years.'

I watched as she withdrew several large files and envelopes from the box, all neatly labelled in old-fashioned typescript.

'I've prepared a receipt - would *meneer* please sign here.' It was an instruction rather than a request and my guide pointed to a typed piece of paper listing the contents of the box. The typescript of the list was old, and I reflected, must have been prepared many years ago when the box was lodged with the bank.

I'd brought a large lockable leather bag and put everything in it .Going back in the antiquated lift, one of those 1930s jobs with manually operated mesh doors, I tried to imagine the same journey in reverse. What thoughts had been going through my father's mind? Perhaps it was just routine, and he couldn't think of where else to put the papers? I would have a better idea when I read them.

I lugged the bag, which was heavy now, to the train station, and caught a train to Newlands. The walk from the station was not long. I passed the Cavendish shopping centre and Vineyard Hotel and soon came to Paradise Road. I crossed at the *robot* and came to my one storey house opposite the pines adjoining the steep bank of the Liesbeek River, a stream really. As I turned the key of the security gate I had my customary pang of anxiety. It was here my car had been hijacked, which was why I no longer drove, always using public transport. All was normal, so I made my way to the front door, irrationally relieved that I hadn't been robbed. Once inside I went into the former bedroom I now used as a study. I emptied the bag onto the large desk and began to examine the contents.

I rifled through the pile of files and envelopes and chose a large buff envelope; I suppose because it was the biggest. It was marked,

'Boetekaartjie van vergaderinge van die Kaapse komitee van die Ossewabrandwag 1938 aan 1945.'

The name '*Ossewabrandwag*' aroused my curiosity and some unease. The notorious organisation was what we now would call 'terrorist' in English. The words typed on the envelope read 'Minutes of meetings of the Cape committee of the

Ossewabrandwag 1938 to 1945.' A literal translation of the word '*Ossewabrandwag*' is 'Oxwagon sentinel', which is a mouthful that somehow does not carry the menace of the Afrikaans word.

The minutes for each meeting showed a list of committee members present. I flipped through to 1944.

June 21st, 1944 showed my uncle as secretary, but what intrigued me was another name - my late brother Jannie, the soldier who had fought Hitler in the desert.

The contents of the minutes were brief. Contact had been made with a British agent 'T. Jan van Rensburg was delegated to befriend her and obtain information.

The next meeting was 25th August. It referred to a separate written report by J. van Rensburg. I scoured the envelopes and files but could not find it.

In the minutes for 26th September J. Van Rensburg was not shown as present, nor indeed was his name mentioned at any of the subsequent meetings. The September report mentioned might provide a clue. I knew Jannie had died during that month in 1944, so it would give me some idea of what he was up to.

It was useless asking my mother for information directly. I knew she'd mentioned his having friends in the army. I wondered whether there was an ex-servicemen's organisation that could help me. I was his brother after all.

The 'Memorable Order of Tin Hats', known as MOTHS, was having a meeting to commemorate El Alamein. As the brother of an ex- serviceman I managed to gain an invitation. The meeting was interesting, with a talk from a former Rhodesian colonel about the civil war there.

As we sipped our post talk glasses of wine I took the opportunity of talking to the erstwhile speaker.

'I enjoyed your talk, Colonel. Tell me is there an Afrikaans equivalent?'

The Colonel smiled.

'Not exactly. But I know that the OB has an old boys outfit which meets in Buitenkant Street. I've never been, as they're not fond of us English speakers, but you'll find their details in the phone book. As an Afrikaner I'm sure you'll be welcome. We're still the enemy I'm afraid.'

The colonel was right. *Die Vry Afrikaner Beweging* was indeed the nearest I could find to a latter day *Ossewabrandwag*. As an Afrikaner myself, although very much bilingual and what used to be called a *'verligte'* and not sympathetic to its narrow views, I decided to join.

Its head office was, as indicated by the colonel, in Cape Town and it was not difficult to find. My name, van Rensburg, and the fact that my uncle had been a well known OB leader was enough to gain me entrance. I accepted an invitation to their meeting the following week.

The members were what I expected - not very bright. They were so pleased to have a genuine Advocate in their ranks that they co-opted me onto their committee. My object was to see if they had any archives from the OB which would help me find out more about my brother.

There was a lot of talk about a new state they were planning called Oranjia. This was going to be a reborn Boer republic.

I did not wish to scorn this madcap adventure, but I was bemused by the wish of all the members to return to their good old apartheid days. They regarded them with nostalgia and affection. Vested interests always resent the loss of privilege, but the recent great increase in crime and open corruption gave at least some cause for legitimate grievance. I did not join in but kept my scepticism to myself.

Many of the committee were young fellows, who romanticised the past as those who have never experienced things do. Quite ordinary men become heroes as the lustre of time enhances their memories like patina on bronze, hiding the prosaic original and its disadvantages.

A Hertzog becomes a Caesar, a Verwoerd or a Vorster a mystic figure who was wise, brave and a great leader.

No matter that these men were like boys with their fingers in the dyke, which crumbled year by year.

And my brother Jannie? What was he? What small anonymous part had he played in the prolonged tragedy that was Afrikaners in power?

While I mused the committee chattered on, as committees do. I reckoned that they expanded fifteen minutes of real business into two hours of sometimes meaningless talk. Much of what they said was in English, so accustomed had they become to that language, unconscious of the irony, and they used the modern banalities: 'blue sky thinking', 'sea change', 'going forward' and other such tiresome nonsense.

My aim was information.

I said, 'we all agree that the *volk* needs to remain in touch with its past. I would like to carry out research so that we can give our younger members a feeling for who they are and how their grandfathers struggled to preserve our heritage. I would be quite prepared to undertake this work myself.'

An old man, Kobus van Wyk, smiled at me,

'If I can be of assistance, *meneer*, I will. I have many papers dealing with the thirties and forties, which was a crucial period for us.'

'That's very kind *meneer*, when can we start?'

'Call me Kobus. Tomorrow if you like. I'm always at home.'

Kobus lived in a small town twenty miles from the centre of Cape Town. As I drove past the pine trees by the roadside, with the mountain rearing up to my right, I wondered whether I was just wasting my time.

Kobus lived in a white cottage on a road of similar

dwellings. He greeted me with a warm smile. I realised he was lonely and any company was welcome.

His *voorkamer* was large with its walls lined with books.

'Coffee?'

'*Dankie* Kobus, with milk, please.'

'I knew your brother, you know.'

'My brother?'

'*Ja*, Jannie. We were at school together. Paarl Gim. We were rugby mad. He was a centre and I was in the scrum. He was very quick and could have been a Springbok, in my opinion, if it hadn't been for the war.'

I chuckled.

'Why do South Africans always think of people in terms of rugby?'

Kobus shrugged.

'Yes, it's true. I assume your interest in history has something to do with Jannie? I'm not stupid. I can help you though.'

His blue eyes and sun-wrinkled face turned towards me meaningfully as he spoke, but his expression was not hostile.

'I was an OB man too. In those days we believed the English were the devils and the Germans, well the Germans were against the English, so "my enemy's enemy is my friend". The idea that Jannie should join the army was his uncle's. He was *baie slim*, that man, but a bit of a snake.

His plan was that Jannie would gain the trust of the English and the *hensoppers*, so he could be of use to us. That man was playing so many games I'm surprised he knew what side he was on himself. The risk for Jannie was that he'd be killed up there in north Africa. There was no danger he'd be found out, as he was what they call a sleeper and knew the right things to say.

It was when he came back here on leave that things hotted up. His uncle was keen he formed a relationship with an English woman. I think her name was Theresa or Tessa or something. Jannie met this woman and one thing led to another. Apparently she was very attractive. What young people now call a 'hot number', so Jannie had no difficulty obeying orders. It was the other part of it he didn't like. The double dealing. You see, he became fond of her, more than that, he was really in love with her.'

Kobus sighed.

'I'm very tired and all this is painful. I need to go and lie down. Would you mind coming back another time?'

I did mind, but what could I do? Kobus was very old, well into his eighties, I'd say. I saw myself out.

As I walked down the garden path to my car past a banana tree and to the raucous sound of a hadeda ibis flying overhead I was in a state of frustrated excitement. A link to my brother had fallen in my lap. Yet why had Kobus stopped, on the brink of what I was sure was a revelation which might end my search? I drove past the shopping mall onto the N2 double carriageway, past the shanty dwellings.

As my car slipped down Paradise Road in Newlands and I signalled right to reach the network of roads approaching my home I began to feel uneasy. By the time I had a gin and tonic in hand and was sitting in my lounge facing the pine trees and the mountain, I was inclined to dismiss my fears. I had made remarkable progress. I didn't need any more documents – I had a knowledgeable informant.

The next meeting of *Die Vry Afrikaner Beweging* was held at a different place. This time it was in a meeting room of a firm of attorneys. I wasn't sure why we'd moved but attended at seven pm sharp, anxious to renew my acquaintance with Kobus.

I was disappointed. Disappointment became alarm when the chairman stated that he had a preliminary announcement to make,

'Brethren, I have sad news to impart. Our oldest member and last link with the glorious years of our struggle has passed away. Kobus van Wyk was tragically killed in a car accident last Thursday. As I understand it a car which was out of control hit him when he was out walking his dog. The police have the matter in hand so they say but suspect a drunk driver.'

There were exclamations of shock throughout the room, not least from me. Poor old man. The rest of the meeting was a blur. As I was going, the attorney whose office it was stopped me.

'*Ekskies meneer*, is your name van Rensburg?'

'*Ja meneer.*'

'I have a packet for you. For some reason it was addressed to you PRIVATE AND CONFIDENTIAL, care of this practice. Luckily the envelope refers to the *Beweging*, which led me to keep it aside for you. Here it is.'

He handed me an A4 size envelope with expanding sides.

16

The letter said (translated into English):
'Dear Jannie's brother,

It was both a surprise and a pleasure to meet you. You look very like Jannie, older, but the genes are there. My friendship with him is something I've treasured, even though it ended in tragedy.

With this letter you will find a report I wrote to the OB about his death. Once you read it you will understand why your family have kept silent about it. However, many things have changed, including the government. I fear there is still danger in this knowledge. Indeed, I feel that it is only my silence that has kept me alive all these years.

Now you've come to see me and we've been seen talking, I don't think I have long to live. Do not think that you are safe in the *Beweging*. Most of them are good fellows, but not all. Use the knowledge carefully and watch your back.

Regards
Kobus van Wyk'

. . .

THE REPORT WAS five pages of typescript and was a carbon copy on thin paper with blue type from the carbon paper.

It was headed '*Geheime Verslag* – J. van Rensburg'

According to the report, the agent, referred to as 'J', had been given the task of forming an association with a suspected British agent, 'T'. J had reported that things were going well but he had not fully won the trust of T.

J suspected that T was quite likely regarding him as a target for her own schemes. We arranged for T to be followed and kept a watch on her house. This was difficult because it backed onto the mountainside of Signal Hill, the slopes of the mountain known as Lion's Head. This meant that T could slip out without being noticed. There were a number of places further along the mountainside with access to roads. We tried placing men on a couple, but there were too many to cover all the roads . The relationship between J and T appeared to be going well. J's uncle, V, had conversed with T to sound her out, and with the committee's authority stated he wanted to betray the OB. At this time contact was made with a U-boat captain. This was not unusual, as several U-boat personnel had landed for supplies and to make contact with us. The agent Leibbrandt was brought from Germany in a U-boat.

The report ended with the distressing news that the body of J had been washed up on a local beach. He had been shot and had been missing for several days. T was suspected, but there was no direct evidence. He had been last seen going to T's house. T had disappeared.

So now I knew at least part of the story. Who was the mysterious 'T'? If she was still alive, she didn't live here any more for sure. The OB would have been out to get her. The answer must be elsewhere, perhaps in Britain, as she was a British agent.

At this time my attention to the Jannie mystery was diverted by grief at my mother's death. Although she was not an easy woman I had been very fond of her, and in her odd way she had loved me, her only remaining child.

I was phoned by her neighbour who said she'd been taken to hospital with a stroke. I arrived ten minutes after she'd gone. She lay back in her bed with her mouth open. A pang of sorrow went through me, and it took me months to recover.

Death is a strange business. There are the feeders on it - the department of government that provides death certificates, the funeral directors. Where did I want the funeral to be? Could I provide her best clothes for the occasion? It was paid for in advance, so all that would be charged were extras. It was similar to booking a plane journey with a travel agent, it was so matter of fact.

The funeral was held in a Dutch Reformed Church. I didn't know my mother knew so many people. Possibly it was because she still went to church every Sunday and knew the *dominee*. Outside the church I stood next to him shaking the hands of strangers, although the odd face was familiar. The wake was held in the church hall and I had ordered wine and food for the throng.

Dealing with my mother's many friends was exhausting, but I thought, I've only got one mother. The sun shone through the windows of the hall and I wondered at the happy air of everyone. As my mother had been old, her death, or 'passing away' as everyone called it, was part of the natural rhythm of life.

I was surprised to find that she had been a shrewd and obsessive investor. She had owned her house and a number of shares besides. I realised I would not need ever to work again if that was what I wanted. My mother's death gave me a freedom to do whatever suited me.

I spent some days going through her papers. I found letters there from a Judge van Wiese in England. Van Wiese appeared to be an OB sympathiser. He had discovered the mysterious 'T' and there was a very unfriendly feeling towards her. My mother's letters weren't there, but it was clear from Van Wiese's letters that she wanted her dead. So all that fuss she'd made was just to put me off. She knew just about everything, certainly a lot more than I did.

'T' stood for Theresa. Van Wiese had discovered she had a niece, a Penelope someone. She was marked as DANGEROUS in capitals in Van Wiese's letters . Van Wiese was a thoroughgoing OB man, and although well embedded in the English legal system, was no friend of theirs. He seemed to despise them, especially his colleagues. He viewed them as a snobbish, blinkered fraternity, xenophobic with a veneer of tolerance and civilisation. I decided to visit him.

Travel from Cape Town to London has become very easy. With my new affluence I decided that First Class travel was justifiable. The thought of being stuffed into cramped seats with no room to move for twelve hours was distasteful, especially as I no longer had it as my only choice.

It was a sunny day in Cape Town when I embarked and a cloudy one in Heathrow when I arrived. My spirits immediately became depressed. How did the British stand it? I took an expensive taxi to a hotel in central London and sat down to go through my mother's letters again. I knew how one track minded she was and I decided to find out all I could about 'Theresa' and her 'dangerous' niece. The obvious way was to use a website dealing with voters' rolls. I had no idea what Theresa's or Penelope's surnames were, so that was a dead end. The only address I had was that of the judge. I decided that paying him a visit was the only option. I could tell him my late mother had mentioned him. I decided not to talk about the letters, as that might lead to trouble.

My South African driving licence was accepted by the car hire company and I insisted on a luxury car with Satnav. They gave me a smart Lexus at great price. I thought I might as well impress the judge. I did not have his phone number, so had to write to him c/o the Ministry of Justice. I was pleased to receive a quick response inviting me to his home in Sussex at the weekend.

I wasn't ready for the mansion in which Van Wiese lived. At a guess I'd say it was 17th century. It was set in acres of woods and surrounded by a wall.

I parked my car on the gravel and it locked itself as cars do these days. The ancient door had a bell pull arrangement that struck me as old fashioned if in keeping with the building. The door was answered by a tall man of African origin. His fine straight nose and elegant figure had him down for a Senegalese, which guess was reinforced by his French accent. In contrast to his ebony Jeeves, the man himself was small, round and had an almost bald head, relieved only by a fringe of grey hair covering the back of his dome, like the edging at the bottom of a sofa. His glasses glinted in the sun which shone through the large windows and magnified his eyes, so momentarily he gave the impression of a fish habituated to very deep water.

'Welcome *Meneer* van Rensburg. *Aangename kennis*. I haven't forgotten my native Afrikaans.'

'Very pleased to meet you, your Honour.'

'Oh please, we're both citizens of the Republic, call me Gerry.' He pronounced the 'G' softly, as if he was clearing his throat.

'Ronald will take your luggage – I presume it's in the car. I must say it's wonderful to hear a voice from home. Your room is on the first floor. I'm looking forward to talking to you, but you'll want to make yourself comfortable first.'

I ascended the carved massive stairs, following Ronald.

My bedroom was a large ornate room with a fireplace and basin.

'The bathroom's along the corridor sir. Dinner is at seven.'

Left to myself I pondered my plans. Van Wiese, urbane and outwardly respectable, was a dangerous man. If he thought I was thirsting for revenge I was sure he'd give me assistance. I would have to be careful not to question his plans. My idea was to find out how and why Jannie died and then decide what to do. I was not a latter day OB assassin.

At dinner I met Van Wiese's wife Rochelle, a middle aged woman with a strong Afrikaans accent and even stronger views. She was a woman who lived in the world of her childhood. She regarded black people as inferiors, except Ronald.

'He's quite different you know. If they were all like Ronald there would be no problem. I feel uncomfortable travelling on the trains here, you know, so many blacks.'

As a South African I'd heard all this before - back home. But things had changed there, and the views of younger people were much less prejudiced. Rochelle's isolation from progress in her own country had left her with fossilised views.

I decided just to listen and smile. Van Wiese noticed this. After the meal was over and his wife had departed for her bridge club he said,

'I noticed you didn't say much at dinner. Rochelle has a habit of saying what the rest of us are thinking, but I do have to warn her to be careful. This sort of talk amongst the wrong people would cost me my job. Luckily she realises that. As you are a van Rensburg she felt she had a sympathetic ear. Her father was high up in the OB.'

At this point he looked at me expecting me to be impressed.

'Oh really, so it's natural that she would be a strong believer in our cause.'

Van Wiese looked relieved when I said this. He was nervous in case I should turn out to be what they called a 'pink liberal'.

'We will talk in depth tomorrow,' he said.

17

Tony awoke from his wine induced doze on Septimus's couch. Penny was asleep in a chair opposite him. He was reflecting on her beauty, when she spoke,

'Penny for them Rev. You look as if you're contemplating a Michelin meal.'

'Really? I'm pretty dozy. I expect it was a dream I was having.'

'Must have been a pleasant one. I was hoping you'd have some ideas.'

'Well I do have one, actually,' said Tony, reaching for his half full wine glass.

'Spit it out man,' said Septimus, who had entered the room. 'We need something, as I for one am flummoxed.'

'What if Penny's the target? Auntie has sadly been killed, so one would have thought whatever old scores there are have been settled, but what if there's someone who, like God in Exodus, wants to punish the children for the sins of the parents to the third and fourth generation?'

'That's for idolatry', said Septimus, 'but you may have a point.'

'These biblical quotations pass me by,' said Penny, 'I'm not even auntie's daughter, if you get my meaning.'

'You know mad people only need the vaguest religious justification for homicidal ideas. You only have to look around you at the slaughter taking place as we speak,' said Tony, polishing off the remnants of his glass of wine.

'So I'm the bait?' said Penny.

'That's a way of looking at it, 'said Septimus,' if you accept Tony's biblical premise and insert the word 'surrogate' before daughter. Perhaps we ought to for the moment. How do you explain Tony being stalked and the murder of Darren the enquiry agent?'

'We can't. They could be unrelated.'

'Well chaps, we can just sit here, drinking wine, talking and let the world go by or do something.' Penny said, as she sat back in her armchair, looking from one of her champions to the other.

'Decisive pair, aren't you?'

'The only lead we have at all is that judge with the South African name who was presiding at the trial we went to. I feel if we are to find out anything we'll need to do it ourselves. Darren must have found out something alarming and he's dead.' Septimus had a way of stating the obvious.

'The diary,' said Tony. 'We're forgetting the diary.'

'No we're not,' said Penny, 'but we need a break somewhere. I'm going back to look at that judge's house. I shall pose as a devotee of Grade 1 listed buildings and ask if I can look around. I'll do it during the day, so he won't be around. You never know, he might have a naive servant.'

'If you were a man I'd say you had some balls...'

'That's enough Septimus with that rough talk, just let's say I'm more enterprising than you two...men on the Clapham Omnibus?'

'Touché Penny, we are a pair of fuddy duddies,' said Tony.

'Don't be so hard on yourself, you have your moments, boys, I know. It's my neck we're talking about, so I'd rather die doing something than sitting here sipping a G &T or asleep or whatever. Tomorrow I'm off.'

The 'boys' sat back and looked at her in admiration. What a woman.

Nine o'clock the following morning saw Penny drinking strong coffee and eating a croissant. She was dressed smartly, not too glamorous, businesslike.

'This kitchen could do with a makeover, Sept, it looks like something that was last decorated in 1935.'

'That's harsh Penny,' said Septimus, 'To be honest, it's need for refurbishment was why I was able to buy it cheaply. I bought it from my grandfather's Estate. My grandmother was so disgruntled about the state of the kitchen she threatened to leave him for a Canadian airman.'

'Did she stay?'

'Oh yes, she was just bluffing. She was fed up with drabness and rationing, so she took it out on him, the poor chap. He'd been fighting everywhere and deserved a bit more consideration, in my opinion. But you know what women are like.'

'Yes I do, we're sensible and have innumerable other desirable qualities. Don't we Tony?'

Tony was hiding behind a newspaper.

'Pardon, I didn't catch that.'

'One of your charms is that you never listen to anything I say, sweetie. Means I never offend you. I was just ranting on about the superiority of women.'

'Ah, yes, quite right,' said Tony. 'Did you know my great aunt was the secretary of the votes for women movement in Croydon in 1909? She was succeeded by another great aunt, whose name was Maud.'

'Really? How interesting. I expect you have some

powerful genes,' said Penny. 'Now the President of the Little Fetcham branch is off in her car to the lair of the Big Bad Wolf. Wish me luck.' She blew them both a kiss and left through the ancient back door.

'Do you think we should follow at a safe distance, to keep an eye on her?' said Septimus.

'Septimus, we are but babes compared to that woman. Let her go,' said Tony.

Penny hurtled down the narrow Sussex lanes in her MG, having narrow escapes in places and enjoying the fabulous cornering ability of her sports car with its wide tyres. Soon she came within sight of the ancient manor house and drove up the long drive as if it was her daily habit.

There was a long rod to pull and she tugged it with both hands. The sound of the bell was loud enough to make her wish she'd tempered her enthusiasm. She waited. At length she heard steps and the door opened slowly. Standing before her was a tall, very handsome African man.

'Can I help you?' he said.

Hmm, that's a French accent, thought Penny. How charming - and such a lovely smile.

'I hope so. My name is Toni Brown. I'm on a tour of Grade 1 listed buildings and I was hoping to ask the owner if I might look around.'

'Listed buildings? I'm only an employee, my name's Ronald, but I'm sure Judge van Wiese wouldn't mind if I showed you a few of its features.' The accent was French but not native French. At that moment Petrus van Rensburg joined Ronald.

'This lady is from the Listed Buildings organisation and wishes to inspect the building. I do not expect the Judge will mind,' said Ronald.

'I'll show you round if you like,' said Petrus van Rensburg.

What luck thought Penny. I'm in. I expect I look respectable, possibly even attractive.

The truth is Petrus was bored, and the thought of the company of this ravishing auburn haired woman for half an hour was more than he could resist. They moved into a large hall.

'I'm told these panels were bought from a royal palace when they demolished it. One of Charles II's mistresses owned it and decided she could make money by breaking it up. That's a *trompe l'oeil*,' he said, pointing to a panel which gave the illusion of a long passage. So clever, these old artists. In South Africa the designer John Jacob uses the technique at Vergelegen – an old manor house near Cape Town.' Saying this Petrus turned, 'I'm so sorry, I quite forgot to ask your name, you must think me very rude. I'm Petrus van Rensburg.'

'Not at all. I'm Toni Brown, I work freelance for a number of local councils, but I'm writing a book at the moment. I'm going to call it Manor Houses in Surrey Sussex and Hampshire.' Penny gave what she hoped was a sincere smile.

'Would you like to see some more rooms? The library is particularly fine.'

Penny smiled and nodded.

The library was another panelled room lined with old books, and at one end there was a pile of papers, left as if someone had not finished going through them. There was a pad with notes on it. As they looked around Penny made laudatory comments and sensed that Petrus was attracted to her. His brain is not engaged, she thought. The sound of a telephone interrupted her thoughts.

'Do excuse me for a moment, I must answer that,' said Petrus. He left the room. Penny whipped out her mobile phone and photographed every bit of paper she could as they lay on the table, being careful to replace them meticulously.

As she heard footsteps she moved away and began to examine a panel.

'Ah, I see you've found another *trompe l'oeil*. This place is full of them. I'm afraid I've been called away. Look, I hope you won't find this presumptuous but perhaps we could meet for lunch one day? This is my mobile phone number.' He scrawled figures on a pad and tore off a page. 'I do hope you've found this interesting and I'm sorry you couldn't stay longer, but I really do have to go. Call me Peter by the way, Petrus is a bit old fashioned.'

'Not at all, Peter,' Penny put out her hand and was taken aback when he stooped and kissed it.

''Sorry I don't have time to show you out. Ronald will see to it.'

Ronald appeared like a magician's assistant and guided her to the door. He even opened the car door for her with a beaming smile.

'Ronald, if you ever need a job...'

'I have one Miss, but thank you.'

He waved as she drove away.

As Ronald closed the door she thought, I don't expect Petrus or Ronald even looked at my number plates. If they do, they'll find the car's registered to the name I gave them at an address in Norfolk.

Driving back, helter-skelter, Penny wondered at her own boldness and whether it was going to help solve the problem or whether she was offering herself as Septimus's 'bait'. Her car drew up in the cottage driveway with a squeal of brakes which she knew was unnecessary and would wear them out. Why change? Renewing brake pads had always cost her excessive amounts of money. Just now she was an heiress in a minor way. Who cares?

'You look flustered Penny. What happened?' Tony, solicitous and worried, walked up to the car.

I now know what a *trompe l'oeil* is, 'she said.

Tony replied,

'We have one in our church, it's a perspective device. What's that got to do with anything? Have you been to an art gallery? Let's have a G &T and you can explain.'

'How sensible, Tony, let's,' said Penny, extricating herself from the low slung car. 'I need one.'

By now Septimus had appeared, dressed in corduroys, a Harris Tweed jacket and waistcoat.

'I have three G & T's ready,' he said, 'with ice and a small portion of lime.'

Later, on their third drink, the trio, with a sense of déjà vu, reflected on Penny's activities.

'I'm going to get my photos of those papers blown up and printed. Thank God for these new scanning apps and my new phone. I admit there was a certain increase in tension in case Petrus 'call me Peter' walked in. He didn't seem to be any kind of hoodlum. And he fancied me,'

'Everyone fancies you,' said Tony.

'Which is helpful. I got the feeling he was a guest in the manor. He seemed to know the historical bits but related them as if he's been told them, word for word, like a guide. There was no air of ownership. Very definitely an Afrikaner. I met enough of those when Tony and I were gadding about South Africa last year. When he said "yes" it sounded like "yis", and he pronounced "off" as "orf", like the Queen. As he definitely was not a toff, he must be an Afrikaans speaking South African. This whole business is related to auntie's war time activities, I'm sure. As they're all dead now it doesn't make sense.'

'Perhaps the sins of the fathers...' said Tony.

'Or even the mothers,' boomed Septimus.

'Indeed,' said Tony. 'I thought you were asleep.'

'No, I'm like one of those judges. I can think with my eyes closed.'

'What a talented chap you are Septimus,' said Penny. 'Doesn't the sound of your snoring interfere with your thought processes?'

Septimus's face pinkened.

'I do apologise. I didn't realise...'

'Don't worry, I was just pulling your leg. You were silent. Any more inspiration darling? Auntie wasn't a mother, but I'm the nearest she had to a child.'

Unaccustomed to Penny's speech habits, the endearment made Septimus's face go even redder.

'I'm thinking,' he said, by now thoroughly pleased with himself.

18

Theresa was now afraid to go to the window. Her enemies knew she was here, unless the shot at her had merely been a reaction. Best to assume the worst. In whom could she confide? Hugh appeared friendly but behind that avuncular exterior he might very well not be. Paranoia was her shield. She slumped onto the bed and lay staring at the elaborately decorated ceiling with its scenes of mediaeval figures and, in spite of her anxiety, fell asleep.

When she awoke it was to a soft knocking on the door, and it was dark. She reached for her little weapon and went to the door.

'Who is it?'

'It's Ludio.'

It sounded like him, but you never knew. She opened the door and stepped back, gun behind her back, turning the light on just before she did so.

'*Ag inkosikaas*,' said Ludio, 'you took a long time to answer.'

'I was asleep. Also, I didn't know who it was. I'm afraid someone knows I'm here and wants to kill me.'

'It's a dangerous job you're doing. Any idea of who?'

'None. I was in the woods and someone took a shot at me.'

'*Allemagtig* ! That's serious. I'll report to the boss. But in the meantime, we need to get you out of here quick, tonight. I have to make plans and find somewhere for you to hide. You'd best stay in this room with the door locked. To show it's me I'll knock slowly three times. I don't want my head shot off. I know you've got that little gun. He grinned: 'See you later.'

Relieved to have an ally, Theresa reflected on her position. She knew Ludio was right. She was only fifteen miles or so from Fresnaye, and once her presence in Constantia was rumbled her life was not worth tuppence. She shut the door and locked it. She packed everything essential in a small bag she'd brought with her, preparing for the impending moonlight flit. She tried to go to sleep but all she could do was imagine unpleasant fates for herself. She even thought they might try garrotting her as that would make little noise. She felt her slim neck and shuddered.

It could not have been more than a couple of hours, but it seemed like several days before she heard three soft knocks on the door. Still fearful in spite of knowing it must be Ludio, she fingered her little gun as she opened the door. She needn't have worried.

'Better bring your bag. We're going out the back way.'

They crept along the gallery and around the corner into a long passageway, every creak sounding like a gunshot, till they reached the stairs. The creaks became more frequent. At last the big oak front door was in front of them, but Ludio motioned to the right.

A voice boomed out. 'Who's there?'

Ludio hissed, 'Quick, through the kitchen.' They nipped through the door to their right and closed it. A light showed beneath the door and the sound of footsteps rang out as someone with a heavy tread walked down the stairs.

'Here!' whispered Ludio, and pulled Theresa behind a large stove, where they froze. The door opened and Mr T's shape filled the doorway. He was carrying a large shotgun. Just then the biggest rat Theresa had ever seen scurried across the floor.

'The bugger,' said Hugh. 'So that's what it was.' Theresa concentrated on breathing slowly. From Ludio there came no sound, but Theresa's heart thumped against her chest like a frenzied drumbeat, and she felt Mr T must hear it. He flashed a torch around the vast kitchen., but luckily did not switch on the main light.

Mr T sighed, mumbled to himself, turned and they heard the door shut. There was silence for a while, then a metronomic creaking from the stairs. The hidden pair remained where they were for several minutes, terrified he'd return, in Theresa's case. At last Ludio tapped Theresa's arm,

'I think it's OK now. He's gone back up the stairs.

The creaking, which had worried her so much when she had caused it, had brought relief at Mr T's departure and she said,

'What now?'

'There's a way out of here, follow me.'

They negotiated various large shapes - cookers and the like - until they came to a door with a Yale lock, no doubt where deliveries were made. Opening it, they were now on the gravel outside. Ludio put his forefinger to his lips and demonstrated slow careful steps. In spite of this the gravel gave a crunching sound and Theresa was relieved when they reached the grass and trekked down through the gardens to a hole in the hedge. They walked for several minutes along a rough path. After one hundred yards they reached a road straddled with tall trees, which looked like enormous sentries in the moonlight. Once they reached the road Theresa followed Ludio until they came to a small black Ford, parked round a bend and hidden until you were almost on it. The road was a cul-de-sac and there were other cars in front of it, their size and expensive appearance suggesting they belonged to the owners of nearby opulent houses. Ludio opened the passenger door with a key from his pocket.

'Your carriage awaits, madam,' he said, before going round to the driver's side and letting himself in. The joke, although tired, made Theresa laugh. Anything less like a carriage than the battered black little car she couldn't imagine. Soon they were going down Wynberg Hill at moderate speed, the high hedges ghostly as they were highlighted by the glare from the headlamps of the car. There were no street lamps. Theresa glanced backwards, expecting to see signs of someone following them. The only incident was an animal rushing across the road in front of the car, which made Ludio brake. Even the squeal of the protesting brakes set off Theresa's anxiety again, and she clutched at the door as if this would somehow save her. She felt certain the noise would awaken everyone living nearby.

'Where are we going?'

'Far, where no one will find you. It was a mistake hiding so close. These people know someone everywhere in the city. With luck they won't realise you've gone till the morning, so you could be a hundred miles away, and you will be.'

'Where *exactly* are we going?'

'Knysna.'

'That is a long way away. But what about the rest of my clothes? They'll be ages. And won't they miss us?'

'Yes, but where you're going you'll be fine. You'll be among friends. As for your clothes, we'll find some for you. As for me, I'm just one of the servants and no one notices us.

By the time dawn broke they had traversed the Helderberg mountains and passed through the small town of Worcester.

At another time she would have admired the endless mountain ranges, the rocks a shade of blue shining in the sun, interspersed with multi- coloured swathes of fynbos, the name given to the mixture of plants that grew in the region, comprising proteas and bushes which covered the soil on the slopes. The drive was monotonous for him and Ludio began to yawn.

'Don't you think you ought to rest, Ludio?' she said.

'Maybe. Swellendam is coming up soon and I have relatives there. I do need a rest it's true.'

They approached the quaint old town. Ludio was a person of mixed race and associating with a European in any capacity apart from that of servant was frowned on in these small rural towns at the time, so he dropped Theresa off at a little thatch roofed hotel with a long *stoep* at the front on which there were tables.

'I'll only be an hour or two. I'm sure they'll be glad to give you some breakfast. They're very hospitable in these dorps. I'll pick you up in an hour or two.'

'Why can't I go with you?

'I have things to organise and you can relax for a while. You won't come to any harm in a place like this. Also, a white woman with a coloured man will look strange and attract attention. You have lived here a few years and you should know that. The *Boere* rule here and expect us to know our place.'

'I see, well keep safe.'

Theresa watched him drive off down the main street and walked up the steps to the *stoep*, bedecked with three sets of tables and chairs. There was a wide open doorway leading inside where she could see more tables set with cutlery. She ventured up and through the doorway. Inside, some of the tables were occupied by people eating and drinking but no sign of anyone serving. Ahead she saw an ancient wooden counter with a bell on top which she rung. Presently a stout woman appeared, saying

'*Wil u ontbyt hê, mevr*ou?'

'I'm English,' she said, 'but yes I'd like breakfast, please. The woman motioned towards the verandah and asked,

'Would madam like tea or coffee?'

'Coffee please,' she said.

A waitress, a very small woman with the features and build of a San or bushman brought her food and soon she was tucking in. Like rural people everywhere she plied her with questions, as a strange woman on her own. Her English was halting and spoken with a strong Afrikaans accent, but after conversing with Ludio so much Theresa had no problem understanding her. She told the waitress the story she and Ludio had agreed, namely that she was joining her husband in Riviersonderend , a town further along the route to Knysna and she'd been to visit her sick mother in Cape Town. This lie satisfied the undemanding woman as she stood beaming while she poured out steaming coffee from an enormous pot. The hotel itself was a small white building with the *stoep* adjoining the main road. As the sun was warm by now she was happy to sit there and sip coffee and nibble toast. It was not a busy street and cars were few. Not having slept except for sporadic naps in the car, she began to doze off. While she slept the waitress poured her another hot cup of coffee. There were two men, both bearded and wearing khaki shorts, sitting at a table a little way from her. She couldn't hear much of what they were saying but what she could hear was in Afrikaans. They paid no attention to her at all. One was smoking a pipe and the not unpleasant smell wafted towards her, competing with the aroma of her coffee. The little waitress returned and Theresa said,

'Is there a map of the town?'

The waitress shook her head. Theresa racked her brains for some Afrikaans and came up with:

'*Het jy 'n kaart van die distrik?*'

The waitress grinned and walked off. The manageress, whom Theresa had not seen since she arrived, returned on her own.

'I understand you're looking for a map?'

'Yes, a road map, if you have one.'

'I have some printed tourist maps. I'll get you one.'

Theresa badly wanted to have some idea of where she was. Her work had been confined to Cape Town and except for coastal regions relevant to U-boat traffic, she was ignorant of the small towns of the western Cape, a sparsely populated region the size of Britain.

As she finished her coffee and last piece of toast the map arrived. Swellendam was in between Cape Town and Knysna and there was a blurb about it on the bottom of the pamphlet. Apparently it had been an independent republic at some time in the 18th century. This information caused her to reflect on the oddity of the place and indeed the whole country. Her last major panic attack had been years ago, when she was a teenager. The relative peace of the town and the sunshine should have made her relax, but the lull in activity, and for some reason, the idea that she was in some mad republic, together with a reaction to recent events triggered anxiety and she felt a dampness in her clothing that was not just due to the heat, and was increasing by the minute, and her anxiety, slipped almost into terror. She imagined a conspiracy between the men in khaki and the manageress to kill her. But the men went on talking, and their voices sounded so monotonous it was difficult to maintain any suspicious thoughts of them. The caffeine she had absorbed in the strong coffee contributed to her mood. She decided to breathe very slowly and think of something calming. She was alarmed when her thoughts turned to her sexual encounters with Jannie, and her breathing began to quicken. She was awoken from her reverie by the words,

'Would you like another cup of coffee?'

The beam on the face of the waitress dispelled her mood as if someone had waved a magic wand, and she said,

'May I have a glass of water?'

The normality of the place reasserted itself, and little was left of her tremors but the uncomfortable clinging dampness in her clothes. I haven't had a shower for ages, she thought. She imagined warm water cascading over her body and this further restored her balance. The hot sun induced a feeling of wellbeing, and the heat that had made her so uncomfortable a short time earlier was welcome. She noticed a pair of wagtails hopping along the street looking for scraps. A flock of starlings wheeled above a building with a corrugated iron roof. Nature applied its soothing balm and she almost felt bold. She rang a little bell on the table and the San waitress appeared.

'*Is daar nog water?*' she said, her new mood encouraging her to try a little more Afrikaans.

The waitress scuttled off, returning with a large bottle. Theresa actually began to enjoy the occasion and sipped the cold fresh liquid, soaking a rusk every now and again in it. The khaki men stood up and exchanged guttural farewells, placing money on the table. They were very big men with large stomachs and florid complexions. Theresa wondered whether it was the sun, drink or both.

Having paid the small bill with money she had in her bag, she began to look around for Ludio, as she realised that she must have been sitting there for over an hour. She got up and walked past the table formerly occupied by the pipe smoker and his paunchy companion, then down a few steps to the street. The car was nowhere to be seen, and she felt exposed waiting on the edge of the highway, with only one other person in sight, an old man hobbling along on the opposite side of the road. Just as she was beginning to feel really fed up the black car appeared. She had not previously paid much attention to it, and if asked to describe it could not have done so, apart from that it was a small dark car. Now she saw it was a black Ford, well chosen as a nondescript vehicle that would not attract attention. The sides were covered in brown dust from the roads and the windows had a murky unwashed look. Needs a good clean, she thought. It was worrying how much her mind was all over the place.

'Quick, get in quick.' Ludio motioned with his hand, beckoning her. She opened the door and had hardly closed it before the car sped off and they turned down a side street passing a row of little white Dutch gabled houses.

'What's happening Ludio? What's the hurry?'

'Bad people around here *inkosikaas*. Maybe they're looking for you.'

'What makes you think that? Let's stop out of sight and talk about this.'

Ludio indicated left, and the semaphore indicator popped out before the car turned down another side street and stopped alongside a row of shops. He explained that he'd taken the opportunity to look up some relatives in the town. A man of his race driving a car, even an old banger like the Ford, on his own, would be conspicuous, so he'd parked the car in the town's car park and walked.

On his return he'd noticed someone examining the car and writing down the details of the number plate. He waited until the man, who was white and dressed in a uniform, had left, before he picked up the car and fetched Theresa.

'There was no ticket, so he wasn't a traffic cop. So, you

see, people might be waiting for us when we get out of town and I don't like it.'

His brown face was shining with moisture as he spoke to her.

'We have to have transport so we can't just ditch this car. There's petrol rationing too. I say we go where no one expects us to go, after dark, and try to evade whoever it may be, and it may be nothing.'

'Where would no one expect us to go?' said Theresa.

'Cape Agulhas. It's on the coast and we have a safe house there. I hadn't thought of it before, but if we're going to be followed then they would not dream we'd go there, it's so out of the way,' said Ludio.

'It's the southernmost tip of Africa, isn't it? If you think that's best let's get on with it.'

Dusk in the Cape is a sudden affair, and having remained out of sight during the day, as soon as it was dark they took a detour north of the town, joining the main road further west, hoping to bamboozle any pursuers, who they hoped would expect them to carry on east towards George and Knysna. They drove through the night. Dawn came early, as it was the height of summer. They passed mile after mile of farmland always with the usual hazy blue mountains in the distance. Sometimes the farmland gave way to *fynbos*.

'Look out!'

Ludio had seen a huge tortoise in the middle of the road and swerved to avoid it.

'That was the biggest tortoise I've ever seen. Are there many round here?'

'*Ja inkosikaas*, he's lucky the light is so good. They're so slow a lot must get squashed.'

The image of the poor animal lying mangled in the road made Theresa shudder.

'We must be careful,' she said.

'I'm always careful. That's why we're still alive. Our enemies are like us in the car. I hope we're not slow like the tortoise, because they won't swerve.'

This comparison did not make her feel any better. The coffee which had hitherto kept her awake wore off, and she felt sleepy as the car turned off the road.

She saw a sign marked 'Bredasdorp' and 'L'Agulhas'. After passing through a *dorp* which announced that it was indeed the aforementioned Bredasdorp, they traversed yet more miles through a similar landscape. At last they saw the sea twinkling blue with little flashes of reflected sunlight. It was the confluence of the mighty Indian and Atlantic Oceans. They arrived at a small village, which had a sign informing them that it was the southernmost point of Africa. A lighthouse stood white and prominent a short distance away.

The car drew up outside a neat, white, one storey house which had a bed and breakfast sign displayed. Ludio took a key from under a flowerpot and opened the door. As they passed through the hall Theresa glanced to the left. There was what looked like a clothes dummy of a man in naval uniform.

'Ludio, who's that?'

'*Ag* it's not real. His name's Max. Just a dummy to make it look as if someone's here. Keeps burglars out. Not that you will find many in this village. It was put there by the owner of this house. She's a strange old lady who lends it to us while she goes up country to visit her son and his wife. She was very particular we leave it here just like that. He is a bit of a spook isn't he? She was in the bed and breakfast business, so we have left the sign up. If anyone comes we say we're full. This place has held more of our people than anywhere else, except the Knysna house, which is nicer. Enough of my chatter. I can see you're tired. The bed is always made up.'

He gestured to a door. The room was neat with a single

bed and floral curtains. It had a basin and glass in a ring attached to the wall. The lamp on a bedside table had a gaudy shade depicting an African with a spear chasing a buck with large rapier-like horns. She filled the glass from the basin's tap and drank the contents almost in one gulp. A powerful desire to sleep which had been present ever since they saw the sign to Cape Agulhas overcame her and she sank onto the bed. The bright light of the sun made her uncomfortable, so she staggered over to the window and drew the curtains before returning to the sanctuary of the bed. She soon fell asleep, but her slumber was a disturbed one. The dreams were vivid and unpleasant and she was relieved to wake up.

Her awakening was slow and she felt drugged. This wore off after ten minutes or so and she drew the curtains back. The bright light told her it was still daytime and she found she was in a small slightly shabby room. Even the bright sunshine did little to improve it. The bedclothes were quite damp and there was a faint musty smell . She opened a window.

She could hear the crash of nearby waves, so loud that she had a fear of being swamped. The feeling of anxiety returned, although not in all its previous terrifying intensity.

There was a polite knock on the door. It was the reassuring Ludio.

'*Inkosikaas,* I've managed to get you some things. My sister lives near and she's got these for you.' He handed her a bundle of clothing.

'They will keep you going while we're here. My sister was given them by *Mevrou* van der Merwe when her aunt died. They're a bit out of date but if you wear them you won't stand out here, which is good.'

The clothing was a relief to Theresa, as her current garments were becoming a trial to wear, with her small bag holding only the minimum, and she felt she would be able to

face the world after a bath and some supper. She looked at
Ludio.

'Is there a bathroom?'

'There's a room outside where you can have a shower. Go
through the door at the end of the passage.'

'Thank you Ludio.'

The 'bathroom' was in a separate building. While it had
probably been a luxury at the turn of the 19th century, it was a
shock to one accustomed to even Cape Town standards of
plumbing. There was a 'hot' tap, but she had to run the water
for some time before it became lukewarm. She noticed a
strange insect with large antennae crouched on the wall. As
the spray overwhelmed it, it scuttled onto the ceiling.
Theresa felt uncomfortable as there was a chance it might
land on her head. She heard the fierce sea wind outside, and
as she washed her herself using a tiny cake of red Lifebuoy
soap, notable for its familiar pungent antiseptic smell of
phenol, the defeatist in her began to think it would have been
better to have stayed in the comfort of Constantia, assassins
or no assassins.

The presence of one insect made her fear other wildlife,
and for a moment she fancied there was a snake hanging from
a hook. Looking more closely, she saw it was a rubber hose
and turning off the water, clasped the towel she'd brought
with her round her cleansed body, tucked her dirty clothes
under her arm and walked back into the house. The whole
place was a potential haven for non-humans, especially
insects.

After a lot of effort in finding clothes amongst Ludio's
bundle that both fitted and looked more recent than 1920,
Theresa finished dressing. After a supper prepared by an
unseen hand but which included eggs, toast and the ubiquitous coffee, she felt almost human, and her anxiety subsided.
She was ready to face L'Agulhas, as the village of the Cape was

called. Walking was exhilarating, if one could avoid being blown over.

Ludio had told her in the car that this was the place on earth where magnetic and true north were the same. It was a place of shipwrecks, and the howling of the wind could have been the death cry of a thousand mariners.

She thought back to her submarine tracking activities. Wasn't it near here that a farmer was rumoured to be supplying the U-boats? She decided to explore.

She walked along the coast, seeing only a man with a dog in the distance. She thought about her lover Jannie. He must have been playing her for a fool, although she had never given herself entirely to him. Being involved in these spy games one was always aware that one was but a speck in Life's Great Plan, or however one chose to express it.

Even her husband was in fancy dress and presumably still alive. The question of why she was a target bothered her. By now she was useless as an agent, so elimination would be a waste of effort. It must be personal. Perhaps it was Jannie's uncle, or the shadowy organisation which he'd said he wanted to leave. Maybe it was an affront to them that she'd shot one of theirs. Musing thus she noticed a large house set back from the sea. It had the characteristic Cape Dutch gables, so had to be at least a hundred years old, she thought. Her curiosity overcame her fear, and she decided to use the old excuse of asking for a glass of water from whoever was at home. She opened the wooden gate and walked up the gravel path to the door. This was a massive affair, with the hinges attached in ancient style, the metal reaching nearly half way across the wood, which she guessed was oak, or perhaps stinkwood. The knocker was decorated with a crest, and the functional part came out of a large lion's mouth. Unintimidated by this grandeur, she took the knocker in her hand and gave several raps. There was no need to knock again, as loud steps clumped towards her from within, the sound not reduced by the door, old and thick though it was.

'*Ja, Mevrou?*' The door was answered by a stout woman with the severe hairdo typical of rural Afrikaans people. Her lined leathery skin betrayed years of working, or perhaps sitting in the sun. Her pale blue eyes exuded authority but not suspicion.

'*Mag ek 'n glas water hê, asseblief?*' she said in what she hoped was correct Afrikaans.

'*Wag 'n bietjie,*' the woman said, and clumped back into the house, her thick stocking-clad ankles like a pair of small tree trunks as she disappeared into the gloom within. Near the door and on the walls to the left and right Theresa saw large old paintings. The one that caught her eye was of a man in what looked like 18th century costume. He was wearing a wig, and his expression wore a sternness that might have struck terror into his slaves, to whom no doubt he dispensed a severe justice, which would have included flogging and even hanging. The woman, whose face wore a similarity to that in the portrait, perhaps of her ancestor, returned with a glass of water.

'I see you're looking at *Oupa* van Rensburg,' she said, as her face broke into a smile, which gave her rugged face a kind of beauty not hitherto apparent.

'*Baie dankie vir die water,*' Theresa said. 'Yes, I was admiring him. He looks a bit fearsome. I expect that's just the portrait, and he was a kind man,' as she broke into English, the effort of even a few Afrikaans sentences being too much.

'I never knew him, he was my *oupa se oupa*. They had slaves in those days and he may have been cruel to them. Their quarters are still here on the farm. Once the English abolished slavery we started paying them, but the servants here are their great grandchildren.'

'Your English is very good,' said Theresa.

'You think so? There are a lot of English speaking people around Agulhas and Struisbaai. The van Bredas, who are quite rich, send their boys to an English boarding school in Cape Town. I like the English. My husband is not so fond of them though. He might not even approve of me giving you water. He's wary of strangers. If anyone goes near those barns he'll shoot them. He says there are thieves and *skollies* everywhere ready to take our stock .'

'I see,' said Theresa. 'Will he shoot at me?'

'Just keep to the path and away from our land and you'll be all right.' She chuckled. 'You don't look like a stock thief to me!'

'No, I wouldn't know what to do with them. I'm a townie just visiting, so he needn't worry. I wanted some fresh air and this coast is so magnificent to look at.'

'Ja, it is. It's a lonely place though. I miss my sons.'

'Where are they?' said Theresa.

'Not in the army, that's for sure. Up in the Transvaal helping their uncle.'

As the woman said this her expression altered as if the conversation was at an end and she'd said too much. The presence of a friendly female face had caused her to open up and she regretted it.

Theresa observed the change and, having drunk her water, handed the glass back. The woman extended a thick wrinkled arm, which was covered in age spots.

'I'd better be on my way; I'll remember to be careful.'

She smiled a genuine smile, as she liked the woman who had been kind to her.

The woman smiled back as she held the empty glass. Still smiling she stood watching Theresa as she walked back down the path to the gate, and Theresa felt the woman's eyes on her until she heard the door close.

. . .

THERESA STROLLED along the sand towards the sea till she
got to where the water lapped up to her feet. She stood
watching the waves crash over the rocks until they had
expended their energy and trickled to just short of her
shoes. She gazed at them, just as in England she used to stare
at the changing shapes of the fire in the front room of her
grandmother's cottage in Sussex in the middle of cold pre-
war winters. The endless movement mesmerised her. She
was about to wander back to the boarding house when
curiosity about the barns and the warning given to her by
the old woman made her determined to see what they
contained. By now she hoped that the woman, whom she
imagined to be watching her from a window, had become
tired of her sport. She saw that if she made it past the huge
rock to her left she'd no longer be visible. She ambled on to
her left past this rock, a massive monument to a prehistoric
geological event. The beach curved round and she walked
on, looking for the forbidden barns. At last she saw them in
the distance, set well back from the sea, about 400 yards
inland. There was a path from the farm, which went towards
them, wide enough to take a car or a tractor. As she
approached them she expected half expected a shout or a
shot, but the only sound was the constant moan of the wind,
which was strengthening now, augmented by the occasional
screaming of the gulls. It was not so cold inland, but she
could still feel a slight chill from the sea breeze, although it
weakened as she approached the first barn. They both had a
weathered look caused by the continuous wind and spray
from the sea. As she approached the door of the nearer,
larger one, she looked about her like she'd seen the little
birds who fed from the bird table at her parents' cottage in
Sussex, fearful of predators. She was now hidden by the

rocks as she'd hoped. She pushed at the door and it creaked open. Not much security here, she thought, or perhaps the barn's very isolation was thought to be enough. Within she saw what looked like farm machinery. Beyond it were many bales of hay, stacked several feet high. Reflecting later, she wondered what made her go further into the barn. Maybe she couldn't bear the thought that she'd bothered to take this daring action and found nothing of interest. She could hear the door flapping in the wind, its creaking saying 'oil me, oil me' in its own barn-type voice. Expecting nothing but hoping for something, anything, she groped her way forward in the dim light.

Further inside there were more bales of hay. Her enthusiasm trickled away and she felt what an idiot she'd been. What if the farmer came and accused her of being a thief?

Turning to go out she marvelled at the specks of dust chasing each other in the beam of sunlight, shining through the open door. She followed the beam and a glint caught her eye. It came from between a pair of bales at the far end of the barn. Probably some ancient piece of redundant machinery, she thought.

She walked over to the corner from where the flash had come and tried to lift up the nearest bale. Underneath was a large metal crate. It looked new. As she pushed the bale that had hidden it she saw writing stamped on it. She had some knowledge of German, but hardly needed it. Emblazoned in large letters were the bold words:

Achtung! Munition

She thought of trying to open the crate but that would give her discovery away. She tested it to see if it was full by trying to move it, but it was much too heavy. It was bound with metal tape. She replaced the bale and pushed aside some more bales. Lifting them revealed more crates.

There was enough ammunition here to start or continue a

war. The word *'Explosivstoff'* denoted the contents of some crates.

Every creak was the sound of someone who might discover her, and she peeped out of the door like one of her little Sussex birds. All she saw were the waves crashing down on the beach and some seagulls who gathered at the carcase of a dead creature. She watched as they tore pieces off the animal, which she recognised as a seal. Fearful of being seen visiting the barns by anyone from the farm, she walked on further to the left then doubled back, hoping that if anyone saw her they'd assume she'd kept to the beach. By now she was exhausted, as the wind had risen and each step was a struggle just to stay upright. She was grateful for the hat she'd stolen from the maritime dummy, which protected the skin of her face from the rays of fierce sun, magnified as they were by the sea. She had to hold it tight onto her head to stop it blowing off and along the sands.

As she passed the farmhouse on her right, she waved at her unseen friend, the farmer's wife, in case she was watching, which she hoped was in keeping with her innocent façade. She trudged along the sand till she saw the lighthouse. Exhausted, she staggered up to the house.

Ludio had given her a key and she went through the hall to her bedroom. The naval dummy looked odd without his hat and she plonked it on his head. It gave him the look of a scarecrow, so she adjusted it to a smarter angle. She flopped down on her bed and decided to await Ludio, who was due at eight o'clock, when it would be getting dark.

She slept dreamlessly, waking up feeling as if she'd been drugged. It was dark outside now, and her only company was as usual the crashing of the waves and the crying of the seagulls. A person could go mad here, she thought. She touched her skin and found she was covered with sand so decided to brave the dreadful shower again.

She undressed, put on her dressing gown and steeled herself for the ordeal ahead. Crossing the exposed passage between the house and the shower building, she pushed open the door and by candlelight saw that her insect acquaintance had either left or been evicted - perhaps Ludio had obtained a cleaner. Or maybe the clever insect whom she nicknamed 'Mab the Malevolent' was hiding in a corner. The flickering candle played games with shadows on the wall. The water came out of a type of pump. The trickle was enough to clean her, but she wished the water was hotter. As she towelled herself she thought she might as well be camping.

Back in her room she dressed and looked for Ludio. She opened door after door, but he was nowhere, so she made herself a cup of tea from the old kettle and teapot she found in the ramshackle kitchen.

There was an electric lamp in the room with the sailor dummy, so she wrote down her problems on a pad she'd found, which had been used for shopping lists:

1 Ammunition and Explosives

2 Whose ?

3 Who to tell?

4 Safe to stay?

She did not dare go out in the dark for fear of getting lost, and the noise of the wind was not encouraging.

Someone had left a booklet giving the history of the area on a little carved table and she browsed through it. There was a map and she saw that the name of the farm was that of the owner, van Rensburg. Van Rensburg was a common name and there might be nothing in it but still the name was a warning. Mevrou van Rensburg was nice enough but the fact that her husband was so sensitive to strangers meant he knew what was going on and must be involved in it. Was he a relative of her recent acquaintances? She saw that she'd been walking towards a place called Struis Bay. Apart from the farm it looked as if there were no habitations for several kilometres. It was an ideal place for landing supplies from a submarine as long as the sea was calm.

She saw herself as a hunted person, but still wanted to deal a blow against the enemy. As she was thus musing Ludio appeared.

'At last. I thought you'd abandoned me.' she said.

'*Ag* no *inkosikaas*, I wouldn't do that. I've been investigating ways for you to escape. Mr John in Cape Town thinks you ought to leave the country.'

'Good. But I have important information for him. Will he come down here? It's only a few hours' drive.'

'He's a cautious man. He might be watched.'

Ludio had sat down by now and was talking with half closed eyes, thinking.

'What is the information? This place is far from anywhere and I don't see what you could have found out apart from that it's very windy.' He smiled.

'Ludio, that's the point. It is isolated. Towards Struis Bay there's a farm. '

'*Ja*, van Rensburg's place, I've heard from my sister. She does some work for them. It's a mixed farm - goes back a hundred years. The van Rensburgs were friends of the van Bredas who founded that town we went through - Bredasdorp.'

'Are these van Rensburgs the same ones as those I've been involved with?'

'I don't know but could be. These Afrikaans families are usually related.'

'Someone's storing ammunition and explosives in a barn there.'

'How do you know that *inkosikaas*. You've seen it?'

'Yes, this afternoon.'

Ludio slapped his thigh.

'*Allemagtig*! So, the U-boats have been here. They want to overthrow the government!'

'Very likely, but we need to be cautious. I'm all for passing this on to John. What can we do?'

'We can watch. I'll ask my sister to find who comes and who goes. I expect it's those Ossewa *okies*. Maybe there are explosives there too.'

'That's true. The German word for explosives is on some crates, so there are. I'm sick of being a fugitive. Do you have a weapon?'

'*Ja, ja*. I'm not keen on acting without authority though. I'll get a message to John.'

Conscious that her visit would have been regarded as an event by the woman at the farm, Theresa felt powerless. In these rural places strangers were noticed and talked about. With luck the woman would not have thought her especially noteworthy. Her English accent was common in the Cape. British servicemen and women came to South Africa for training. She knew that the RAF, for example, trained numerous pilots in Africa's enemy-free skies and she'd met some. Her feelings of anxiety returned and she picked up the packet of Camels, took out a cigarette and began smoking, which was something she'd given up. Ludio had left the packet on a chair near the dummy and there were matches nearby. As she drew in the smoke she'd been hoping for a wave of relaxation. Instead she coughed and found the taste foul. She went to bed and was soon asleep. She woke early and dressed. After a cup of coffee, she decided she could not stand the house and the ridiculous dummy any longer and made for the door. The farm direction was unwise, so she walked towards the lighthouse, curious to see what was inside. The door at the bottom of it was ajar, and she walked in, knocking on the door as she did so. Long hours at her radio transmitter had made her very aware of the sounds that went with it, and a faint tapping of Morse code jolted her. It was coming from up the wooden stairs to her left. She was in one of her bold moods, so climbed them. The sound of her steps rung through the round building and as she got to the first floor the tapping ceased. There was no one there, so she climbed further to yet another floor. Sitting at a battered desk she saw a man in South African Navy uniform. He showed no surprise at her appearance.

Getting up, he extended a hand

'Ah, Mrs--------, I was wondering when I might meet you.'

'You know me?'

'Yes, we have a friend in common. *Mevrou* van Rensburg has told me about you.'

'Nothing uncomplimentary, I hope?'

'Not at all. She was most impressed with you. The arrival of a stranger in this part of the world is an event, you know. I'm a friend of the family. Did you enjoy your walk yesterday?

'It was quite pleasant, but the strong wind takes some getting used to. I expect many ships have been wrecked on this coast.'

'Indeed, it's notorious for storms. We maintain a small presence here to keep an eye out for ships in trouble.'

'Essential, I'd imagine,' said Theresa.

'Would you like some coffee?'

Theresa was desperate for company and the chance of a normal conversation was very attractive.

'That would be nice. With milk, no sugar.'

'This is precious in our current rationed times, but we Navy people are well supplied.' He winked.

Theresa tried to gauge the age of the navy man. His beard was black and he had dark bushy eyebrows. About forty? She thought. Against her will there was that tingle she felt very occasionally when she... She put the idea to the back of her mind. He was an unknown and could be an enemy.

There was no sign of any radio equipment, so she felt it wise not to bring the subject up.

'Are you the lighthouse keeper?' she said.

'*Ag* no, I just come here occasionally. He's got the day off today.' He gave a wintry smile.

There was something in the man's smile that Theresa did not like.

They sat and drank coffee and chatted about the wildness of the place and how remote it was. The naval officer knew a great deal about the area. He kept referring to 'we'.

'We being?' said Theresa.

'The navy. As you can see from my uniform I'm in the S.A.N.'

'Apart from that I expect nothing much happens here. Well, I'm sure you have work to do - I heard you tapping away from downstairs. I suppose you need to warn ships of bad weather coming.'

At this the naval man's expression altered.

'Yes we do. This lighthouse has saved many lives. Are you staying long in L'Agulhas?'

Theresa noticed the change of tone to sharp.

'No, I'm only dropping in on a relative. I'll be going soon.' His manner warned her not to impart any more information than she had to.

'Well thank you for talking to me.'

She turned and made her way down the stairs.

The naval man sat still for a while. Then he went to the window and watched Theresa walk away from the lighthouse. He opened the cabinet which housed his radio equipment and soon the sound of Morse Code filled the room.

Theresa found Ludio cleaning his gun.

'When do you intend to visit?' she said.

'Not sure,' he smiled. 'Always good to be ready. John

wants me to go and look at the barn again. He says to be careful.'

Theresa made herself a cup of coffee, this was becoming an addiction, she thought. As she finished it, she said,

'You sure you don't want me to come along when you visit the farm? I suppose you're going check for yourself that the crates are there.'

'You can come if you want, it might be dangerous, but I can give you a gun. I've just cleaned it,' said Ludio.

'Yes I saw you.'

Theresa thought, why not go with him? She might as well see this through.

'All right, what time shall I meet you here? Better go separately. People talk!' she said.

'Half past six would be fine. *Totsiens*. I need to make some preparations...'

As she walked back to her room she thought, what have I got myself into now?

Once she was in the room she checked the little revolver Ludio had just given her. She saw it was unloaded and hoped she wouldn't need it.

Ludio returned and caught her loading the gun.

'Hey *inkosikaas*, what you doing now?'

'You can see young man. I have a nasty feeling about that naval man in the lighthouse and I suspect he may be watching when we go to investigate the barn this evening. Why can't we leave it to the authorities?' said Theresa.

'The authorities aren't here and John thinks the crates will be gone. No one I know in the village has seen the naval *oke* before and I bet he's something to do with the crates,' said Ludio.

'Good point. He may have put them there. I thought you knew him,' She said.

'I know *meneer* van den Heever, the lighthouse keeper, but not this man,' said Ludio

'I heard him sending Morse code,' said Theresa, 'but by the time I got up there I could see nothing.'

'The way I see it; it's better to be cautious about this man. We want him where we can see him. You should go to the farm. Only I'm going to be watching you,' said Ludio.

At 6.25 pm precisely Theresa left the house. It was still light, but she knew the darkness would descend in a few minutes. As she walked along the shore she marvelled once again at the titanic waves. If material was being landed from a submarine they must have found an inlet where the sea was calmer. This sea would crush a small boat into matchsticks and scatter any cargo to wash up miles along the coast. It was notorious, 'The Cape of Storms' being only seventy or so miles to the west.

These random thoughts fled from her mind as she smelt pipe smoke. As she rounded the large rock, which obscured her path, she saw him, sitting on a small rock, in his uniform, smoking. He raised a hand in greeting, and Theresa felt a knot in her stomach.

'Hello, I see you're walking again,' he said.

She smiled weakly,

'I like the exercise.'

She could feel the revolver hard against her thigh.

'Mind if I join you?' he smiled.

'Not at all, company's always welcome.'

I wonder where Ludio is? she thought.

They made their way past the large rock and saw the white farmhouse. So pretty! thought Theresa. Further along the large barns stood like square pyramids. Theresa shuddered, whether from the cold wind or fear she didn't know.

There was something in the naval man's casual air that made Theresa think: he's been here before, loads of times.

'Ever wondered what's in those barns?' he said.

'Agricultural things, I should think. What else?' said Theresa.

'Now let's have a look,' he said, opening the door of the larger barn.

The door opened - but did not creak as before. The naval man shone a torch at the bales of hay and Theresa went to the back where she'd seen the crates, shining her own torch. She lifted them one by one. At first all she could see were more bales, then there was a glint of metal. She looked round.

The naval man, where was he? She heard a step and a sharp pain to the back of her head, then nothing...

She awoke with a sore head in darkness with her hands and feet tied tightly together.

She rolled onto her side and felt her revolver was gone. At first, panic consumed her and she felt herself shaking. As the minutes went by she calmed down. She tried to stand up but the tightness of the cord that held her ankles together made this futile.

She could just discern the shapes of the bales in the gloom. She felt cramp in her arms and legs. Despair overcame her.

19

Ludio watched as Theresa entered the barn with the navy man. After a short time, perhaps quarter of an hour, the navy man emerged. From behind the rock Ludio had a good view of him as he made his way back in the direction of the village. Instead of carrying on he stopped at the gate to the farm and walked up the path. He knocked on the door and Ludio could see the woman who let him in.

The moon provided good light and Ludio walked back to the barn. As he entered he shone his torch at the bales. A shape bigger than the rest hissed at him,

'Ludio, quick, get me out of here!'

Ludio took out his pocket knife and cut Theresa's bonds. He had to help her up and they staggered out of the barn together. Before leaving he lifted some bales ,and whistled:

'You were right. Now let's go.'

The cold air revived her and they crept along the shore, hiding behind rocks. There was a bright moon. If someone had been looking they would have seen their shadowy shapes as they flitted between the rocks.

They were not disturbed and managed to get back to the house.

'We can't stay here for long. When the navy man finds you're gone he'll be after us,' said Ludio.

Theresa, to whom a cup of hot tea imparted a new energy, said,

'We need to deal with him. He has my gun, but you must have one. Thank you by the way, for yet again saving my life. I must be a worry to you.'

Ludio grinned.

'All part of a day's work. Yes, I agree. We should set a trap for him. You must go back to the barn and lie where you were. Only you won't be tied up and I'll be hiding and knock him out.'

'Sounds simple. We'd better go. What if he's been back already?'

Ludio handed her a pistol. 'We'll both have guns and I'll be ready to shoot if necessary.'

'What if he's genuine navy? By the way, where do you get all these guns from?'

'It's wartime and there are plenty about. He shouldn't be hitting women over the head and tying them up.

'True, let's go.'

Back at the barn Theresa and Ludio took up position behind a bale. Theresa assumed her previous position as best she could. The darkness would make it difficult to see anything was amiss. After a while they heard the sound of a vehicle and steps followed. The navy man stood with his back to the light and advanced towards Theresa, who was lying where he'd left her.

He spoke. 'You're going somewhere far away, lady,' He began to haul her up. Ludio, who had crept up behind him, hit him on the back of his head with the butt of his gun. The man sank to the ground.

'Now what do we do?' said Theresa.

'First, we search him. Then we get rid of his vehicle and him.' Ludio stuffed a rag in the man's mouth and tied him up with wire he'd brought. He also blindfolded him.

'Search his pockets. I'll see what's in his vehicle,' he said.

Theresa took everything that was in the man's pockets and laid it in a pile. Ludio returned.

'It's as I thought, this man's not from the navy, he's in a civilian vehicle and it's a farm vehicle at that. Let's look at what was in his pockets.'

At this point the man groaned. Ludio took a syringe from his jacket and plunged it into an ampoule he also produced. He inserted the needle into the man's neck.

'There, he won't wake up for a while. We can leave him here and take his papers back to the house. I'll drive the vehicle beyond the rocks and make it look as if someone's parked it there. You stay here.'

Theresa obeyed orders. She was relieved just to do what she was told.

She walked to the door and watched Ludio drive the vehicle, a *bakkie*, out of sight. She turned to examine the prone body. Suddenly worried that Ludio had killed him, she knelt down and felt the man's pulse. He was alive. She looked around and searched for the crates she'd seen before. They were gone, but there was a much older one, which looked different, in the corner. Curious, she opened the lid. Moonlight caught a sparkle and she felt inside. Even in the poor light she recognised jewellery. She doubted that one man could remove everything so quickly. Others were involved. Perhaps they were miles away by now, or perhaps a few yards.

As she mused she heard footsteps. It was probably Ludio, but...

She saw a woman walking towards the barn. She was carrying what looked like a shotgun.

Theresa ducked behind the door and waited.

'*Dirk, Dirk waarom die lawaai? Waar is jy?*'

Theresa waited for her to enter the barn then stepped up behind her, prodding the gun Ludio had given her into her back.

'Mevrou van Rensburg, please drop that shotgun.'

The old lady did as she was told, then turned,

'What have you done with my son?'

'He's safe enough, *mevrou*. He won't be smuggling any more explosives though.'

'I should have realised you were up to no good. I knew Dirk was dabbling in dangerous affairs, but I don't want him hurt.' She sat on a bale and began to weep.

Theresa liked the old woman and felt sorry for her but knew Dirk would happily have made her food for the fishes. She said,

'The authorities will be here soon; you'd better tell them all you know. Where is your husband?'

'He's in Bredasdorp arranging for transport. He'll be furious,'

The lights of a vehicle appeared and motioning to the old woman to sit down out of sight, Theresa went to the door and pressed herself against the wall next to it. The door opened. She saw a uniform and as the figure passed she said,

'Hands up or I shoot,' just as she'd seen actors do in films.

'Hello Theresa, you do get about.'

The voice was one she knew well. It was that of her husband and he was dressed in German uniform. He did not turn, however, and put his hands up.

'What on earth are you doing here? Ludio will be back in a minute.'

'I know, he sent for me. I seem to be a bit late. Who are they?' He pointed at the man on the ground and the woman seated next to him.

'*Mevrou* van Rensburg and her son Dirk, who seems to be a friend of the Germans. I hope you can help to sort this out.'

Mevrou started at the German uniform.

'*Herr Kapitän*, thank God you've come, look what they've done to Dirk.'

The '*Kapitän*' spoke to *Mevrou* van Rensburg rapidly in Afrikaans and then turned to Theresa.

'Trust you to cause trouble. We were hoping to catch bigger fish here. Perhaps we still can...'

Ludio arrived in a *bakkie* and Martyn and Ludio lifted Dirk into it.

'I'm afraid we'll have to take you into custody for a short while *mevrou*. Would you mind stepping into the *bakkie*?' said Martyn.

The old lady did as she was told.

'I need to go now.' said the '*Kapitän*'. 'You and Ludio had better go back to the town. It's a short walk, so you'll be all right.' He left.

Theresa's discovery had made her think. Ludio was coming back in through the doorway.

'Ludio, there's something we need to do before all hell breaks loose. I've found some interesting objects.'

The next day, when half a dozen OB members arrived in a lorry labelled 'van Rensburg en Seun ', they were surrounded and arrested.

20

'South Africa,' said Septimus.

'Yes,' said Tony. 'And? '

'Well, I think the answer to all this lies there. I've been doing some reading while you and Penny have been chasing around. There were a number of wrecks off the coast, some of them East Indiamen. Carrying valuable cargos. There have been books written about them. I've been reading one by a Professor Addington. He was a Professor of Music at a South African university and wrote a book about the wreck of the Arniston in 1815. It was ostensibly carrying mainly troops, but Professor Addington has evidence it was also carrying a secret cargo of gold and possibly other precious things. Even the famous Peacock Throne of the Mogul Emperors, a fabulous jewel encrusted replica of the actual throne occupied by the said potentates, which is lost to history but had been received as a bribe from some sultan or other. There was an excavation in 1982 by archaeologists from the University of Cape Town, but nothing of that nature was found. However, there were previous attempts to salvage the wreck, and this is where it gets interesting. A company was formed in 1938 for the purpose. The three driving forces behind this were some wealthy Afrikaners called van Rensburg and Van Wiese, who relied on the expertise of an Englishman, one Frederick Duckham, a civil engineer.

The wreck was at a place near Cape Agulhas, the southernmost tip of Africa. The book says that the owners of the ship were too mean to buy a navigational aid called a chronometer, so the captain thought the ship was off the Cape of Good Hope, when in fact it was off Cape Agulhas, so when it changed course to the north it foundered on rocks and was wrecked. 378 people lost their lives and there were only six survivors.'

'Sounds dreadful, but what has all this got to do with auntie and our present sitch? Although I must say the Mogul business rings a bell, I'll have to think.' said Penny, looking pensive.

'I've been searching for a reason why your auntie was killed, said Septimus. 'You remember she snatched me from outside her cottage? Well at the time I didn't think it was important, but she did tell me some story about Cape Agulhas and treasure. I forgot about it till I read the book. She also mentioned the *Ossewabrandwag*. At the time I had no idea what she was talking about, but now it's beginning to make sense.'

'You mean this Judge van Wiese may be tied up with the treasure seeking Van Wiese, and the van Rensburg who appears in what we have of the diary may be too? They are common South African names,' said Penny.

'There are other names – there's a Hugh T. Nevis, an American millionaire who lived in Cape Town. Apparently he was tapped for money to finance the search.'

'Hmm,' said Tony,' it ticks a lot of boxes.'

'For God's sake Tony, you sound like one of those house-hunters on that TV programme,' said Septimus.

'I was joking,' said Tony.

'Well you asked for thoughts and you have them,' said Septimus, sitting back on the brown leather Chesterfield. 'I've thrown you a ball and am inviting you to run with it.'

'Now who's talking gibberish, you watch too much sport on telly. You have uncovered something that may be very valuable, though. We have little else. I drew a blank with the documents I copied in van Wiese's study, parish council minutes as I recall, but now I remember a mention of this throne in the computer info I downloaded from auntie's computer' said Penny.

'So, what do we do, going forward,' said Tony.

'Stop using silly expressions, you and Septimus are playing some ghastly verbal game,' said Penny. 'Seriously, I'm thinking.'

'Blue sky thinking?' said Septimus and Tony together.

'You boys shut up. This is not funny,' said Penny. The excitement is getting to you.'

'Perhaps your aunt Theresa got hold of some of that treasure. She was very wealthy,' said Septimus.

'As her Probate papers have told you, man of law. Maybe whoever killed her thinks I have the treasure now and so I'm a target.'

Both Tony and Septimus turned to look at Penny. They must have been staring, because she looked irritated.

'The penny may have dropped, boys (no pun intended), but it's rude to stare,' she said. 'So maybe Van Wiese et al are after treasure, or maybe we're just guessing. If I'm to be murdered it should at least be for something I have. She may have converted it all.'

'You would have to declare it in an amending affidavit,' said Septimus.

'For goodness sake, that's the least of our worries, whatever that revolting sounding procedure may be. Thing is, if she had it, where did she stash it?'

The two men looked blank.

At last Tony said, 'There may be a clue in the cottage. When we last visited we weren't looking for anything specific.'

'Ho hum,' said Penny. 'We'll have to go back there. I need to check on it anyway. I am armed, but it'd be safer for you two not to be. You might shoot each other or even me.'

'It's a nice day, we might as well go now,' said Tony. 'I'm sick of sitting around, charming as this house is, Septimus.'

'Very well, I suggest we go in two cars to the village and make our way as unobtrusively as we can to auntie's cottage. I have the keys here with me,' said Penny, getting up and making for the door. 'I'll drive alone and you two can follow in Septimus's impressive personalised number plated show off car. With a plate which says SEPT 7, you do announce yourself.'

'It was a whim. No one can tell how old the car is with one of those.'

'Yeah yeah,' said Tony. 'You're just trying to show off and reveal yourself as a rich chav.'

The chav and Tony sunk into the opulent seats of Septimus's old but well appointed Jag and by the time Septimus started the car Penny had already reached the main road, leaving only a cloud of dust to show she'd passed that way.

Half an hour later they had passed the Duke's Head and were parking in the little village car park.

'How long you reckon we'll be, Tone,' said Septimus.

'I'd put two pounds into the meter, shouldn't be more than two hours,' said Tony. 'And I'd prefer Tony. Just because you have a chav's number plate you don't have to talk like one.'

Penny's car was in the car park but there was no sign of her.

'No Penny. She must have gone on ahead,' said Tony. 'Let's go to Aunt Theresa's cottage. I expect she's already there.'

They plodded down the now familiar path to the cottage and found the door open. Walking into the front room they found Penny sitting on a chair looking furious.

The reason for this lay in the chaos surrounding her. Not only did the room look like someone had dropped a grenade in it, but there were long straight fissures in all the cushions, which had been taken apart.

'Good grief,' said Tony, 'the forces of Beelzebub have been busy.'

At this Penny's grim face broke into a grin.

'Ah Tony darling, trust you to bring the bible into it. Yes, the baddies have been about. But in a way that's good. We know that they think auntie has something they want. Ordinary burglars don't massacre cushions…'

'This is true,' said Septimus, who always liked to contribute. 'Burglars leave a terrible mess, but they don't cut up cushions.'

'Have you looked upstairs?' said Tony.

'Not properly, sweetie. I had a glance and it was so depping I came back down here to drown my sorrows. Can you see whether the forces of Babylon, or whomsoever you think did this, have taken the gin? I think we could all do with a stiff one.'

Tony scuttled off to the kitchen and returned. 'The fridge is open, but they've left that bottle of tonic you bought last time we were here. Let me examine the drinks cabinet.'

The ancient cabinet, which would have been a credit to any Victorian home, still contained a couple of bottles, including a half full bottle of Hendricks.

'I hope no one's slipped a Mickey Finn or worse in there,'

said Septimus, whose face wore a dazed look, like a someone who'd come to look for bodies after a night of German bombing during the Blitz.

'I don't give a shit, pardon the expression darling. I'm desperate for a drink,' said Penny.

The gin seemed untouched, Tony volunteered to taste it and gave his verdict,

'Seems OK to me.'

'Question is', said Septimus, 'did they find anything?'

'Aye there's the rub,' said Tony.

''For goodness sake talk normally sweetie,' said Penny. 'Yes, we have to consider that. But if they descended to ripping or at least lacerating cushions I would guess not. They had the big disadvantage of not knowing auntie and the way she thought. While whizzing down here I had a blinding flash of inspiration.'

Both men, by now sitting on a bedraggled couch which would never fetch a farthing on eBay, leaned forward, suddenly fascinated by the beautiful Penny's words.

'Yes, and...?' said Tony.

Penny, conscious that her friends were now all ears, could not resist hamming it up.

'Hmm, guess.'

'Penny, if you've taken till now to think of whatever it is, how do you expect us plodders to know anything?' Septimus spoke in his most exasperated tones, usually reserved for clients who were not taking his advice.

'Remember the diary, Tony? You found it sitting amongst other books in the bookcase, didn't you? I thought, given auntie's devious mind, where would she hide something? And very important, what would she hide? Then it became obvious. A key. A key to something like a safety deposit box. I have the only bunch of keys. She made sure I had them. It's what she said at the time that now

makes sense. When she said it, I thought she was just
waffling on in a geriatric way. She liked to do crosswords
you know.'

'This is all riveting,' said Tony, 'but what did the esteemed
lady say?'

'She said, 'One of these keys is to my past. Be careful as it
will unlock my death and I hope not cause yours.'

'I have to admit I thought she was being dramatic. She'd
been going on about some old boyfriend in South Africa
who'd met a tragic end, then mentioned how East Indiamen
containing all sorts of exotic things were wrecked of the
South African coast. She said many had lost their lives, but
that a few survived.'

'How many keys do you have?'

Penny opened her capacious handbag and produce a
bunch of about a dozen keys. She held them up and jangled
them in front of her.'

'Here they are. Question is, which one and what does it
open?'

'Might as well try them in the various locks we have in
this house,' said Septimus. 'I'll have a go when I've finished
my drink.'

Ten minutes later, refreshed by his libation, Septimus got
to work. Penny and Tony went outside to see what had been
happening there. The shed door was open and a broken
padlock lay on the ground. Garden tools lay scattered and
even a metal box holding harmless screws had been smashed.
There were signs of digging in one corner.

'Hoping for buried pieces of eight,' said Penny. 'What
amongst loads of other things, worries me, is that they might
be watching us and follow us. You've been followed, so some
devil's binoculars might even be trained on us as I speak.'

'True,' said Tony, but this spot is sheltered by the house
and trees, so I doubt it. Just in case I think we ought to make

a big song and dance when we leave, and also call the police, as that's what normal people would do.'

'Good thinking, Reverend. I really had overlooked that. We'll wait till Septimus has tried all the keys though, and we've made sure there are no more clues for us, although I doubt there are.'

At that moment Septimus, looking like Father Christmas out of uniform, entered the garden.

'I have only three left,' he said. 'I'll just try this small one on the padlock.' He picked up the dirty old padlock from the ground, where it had been discarded by one of the vandalous burglars.

It fitted.

'That leaves two. This padlock will never be any use again. I've been using gloves by the way, I don't want my finger-prints mixed up with those of the villains, although I expect they're professionals and haven't left any. DNA testing will no doubt not be done. You can expect a perfunctory visit from a 'specialist' and then the file will join millions of others in a black hole in some place where they keep their records. At least that's my experience of burglaries, especially as nothing's been taken, just vandalised.'

'Thank you Septimus. I expect you're right. I'll ring the police when I get inside. We should then go back to your place with these keys and decide what to do next. We'd all better stay till they arrive though, as it would look odd if some of us buggered off,' said Penny.

Tony winced at the language but did not have the energy for even a mild reprimand of his fair friend. She was in a very stressful situation after all and must be overwrought. Septimus rang the local police station on its daytime number, as 999 was inappropriate, there being no immediate emergency.

'We'll get someone round there as soon as we can,' said a

tired voice. 'Only we're shorthanded what with the aircraft crash over in Eastbourne. Probably be tomorrow.'

'That's encouraging,' said Penny. 'I'm glad we didn't ring them while the burglars were still here. I suppose we'll have to hang around till tomorrow so they can look around. I don't fancy sleeping in this house though. We should stay at that pub, the Duke's noggin. I hope they have room. We'd better drive into the village. Anything left here won't be safe.'

So it was that they found themselves sipping their various favourite tipples in the Duke's Head. The landlord greeted them like old friends. He had two rooms only - one double and one single.

'I'll take the single, please. The two gentlemen can share the double.'

Tony sighed. He had been hoping... But better this way, he thought, no complications.

'So, we have two keys,' said Septimus. 'Where do you think we'll find our answer? One place we could enquire is the deceased's bank. They may have a safety deposit box for her.'

'I do wish you wouldn't refer to auntie as "the deceased", Septimus. It sounds so sepulchral. Especially as you met her briefly, and she was lively, even at her advanced age,' Penny said.

'Sorry,' said Septimus. 'My lawyerly habits of speech betray my profession. I shall refer to your aunt as "Theresa". "Auntie" is an appellation I shall leave to you.'

'You really are a pompous old git,' said Tony. 'I suppose you can't help it.'

'Thank you, Tony. May we continue with the main conversation now that I've been put in my place?'

'Indeed, sweetie. You are a dear old thing really,' said Penny. I shall hot foot it to Coutts once we've dealt with the local plods tomorrow, taking the keys with me.'

'That's settled then,' said Tony. 'Now we can get on with

our drinks. I hadn't expected this pub to stock such a fine Chateauneuf du Pape. It really is rather delicious.'

'Well make sure you're sober enough to get up those stairs to your room, sweetie,' said Penny. You do snore when you're plastered I recall, so poor Septimus may be in for a disturbed night.'

'All this repartee is exhausting,' said Septimus. 'I'll have some of that wine, too.'

After some hours of steady drinking the two men staggered up to their room. Penny, who was an all-round smarter person, sipped plain tonic, reflecting how foolish intoxicated people appear to the sober. She needed her wits to remain sharp, and a hangover was not a good idea when engaged in work that required concentration.

After a serious breakfast for Septimus and Tony, and a light Continental for Penny, they repaired on foot to the cottage, leaving their cars in the pub car park.

The police arrived in the person of a female, PC Anstruther, who said she was a fingerprint expert. After asking a number of questions as to what was missing, she set to with her equipment and announced that Penny, as proprietor of the residence, would be hearing from her in due course. She got Penny to sign a form with various basic details on it, handing her a helpful pamphlet with advice on household security.

'Thank you so much, officer,' she said. 'Now that you've done your work, may I put the place back in order?'

'Yes of course madam. I have what fingerprints there are. I must tell you that burglars of this type usually wear gloves, so the best hope of detection is if stolen goods are found. You do say you have not identified anything missing. If you are able to do so, it would give us something to go on.'

With that she disappeared into her little police car.

'Now that's over I'd better make for the Big Smoke, or go

up to town, as auntie used to put it. The safest place for you boys is Septimus's abode. Don't forget to be vigilant.'

The 'boys' did as they were told and were soon lost in country lanes. Penny decided she needed make herself difficult to follow and drove to Gatwick Airport, parking in one of the car parks. She wandered into the departure halls and then slipped into a Ladies lavatory. Ten minutes later she emerged sporting a black wig and a complete change of clothes, large sunglasses completing the disguise. If someone was following, they would have a hard job. She got onto a train at the airport station and alighted at East Croydon. There she got out and caught a tram to George Street, whence she joined the throng of shoppers and hoi polloi who milled along the pedestrian North End, eventually making her way to West Croydon station. She caught a London Overground to Highbury and Islington, then the Victoria Line to Victoria, finally taking the tube east to the Temple. She walked up some ancient steps to Essex Street, making her way along the Strand to Coutts's branch at number 440. Just outside she removed her wig and glasses, presenting her passport and bank card to a service desk.

'I wonder if you can help me. I'm Penelope Duchesne, executor of the late Theresa Duchesne. I believe my solicitors, Armstrong's, have registered the Grant of Probate. I'd like to see Ms Duchesne's safety deposit box please.'

'We usually need people to make an appointment for that. They are not actually on this site, so we'd have to make arrangements. I presume you have a key? I'll need to check whether the deceased had such a box. Would you mind waiting?'

So ensued one of those dull days in which one is subjected to much form filling, questioning and general hassle. Eventually she was told to 'come back tomorrow'.

Penny decided to stay at the Savoy, as she was now a

woman of means, and who knows who might be watching her flat? It was a mistake. Not because of the price - almost £500 a night, but because she forgot to replace her wig and sunglasses when she left the bank.

Penny had not frequented the Savoy much. Although she'd earned a reasonable sum as a journalist, and auntie had given her some generous gifts, it was a place for the odd special dinner, not somewhere to burn twenty pound notes.

Auntie had been so well off, although she'd lived modestly in her Sussex cottage, that Penny never need work again. She did feel a bit guilty about all this wealth and intended to 'do something' with some of the money, but she hadn't decided quite what.

After making herself at home in her room she decided to have a drink at the Beaufort Bar. She smartened herself up and descended in the lift. In a place like this, home to the well-heeled, a smartly dressed woman on her own was quite acceptable. She mused on all the glitterati who must have sipped, or even drank copiously, in these surroundings. Auntie's favourite, the alcoholic actor Robert Shaw, had probably downed bottles of scotch, or even vodka.

As she mused a voice repeated,

'Miss Brown, Miss Brown.'

She looked up and saw a middle-aged quite handsome tanned man looking at her and beaming.

'You obviously don't remember. It's Peter van Rensburg. You were inspecting Montmorency Manor when we met,' he said.

Penny did a double take. Curses! It was the man who'd shown her round Judge van Wiese's pile. No wig, no dark glasses, no disguise, she was rumbled.

'Of course, I remember. You're the gentleman who was so charming when I turned up unannounced. How rude of me not to recognise you straight away.'

Petrus smiled.

'Quite natural. Now you are someone a man would never forget. It's not often one meets such an attractive woman.'

If blushing was one of her attributes, Penny would have blushed. It wasn't. She'd become used to such compliments from her teens onwards.

'You're too kind. Please join me. I could do with some company. Such a lie, she reflected, she had so hoped to remain incognito. Her life might even depend on it. Now here beaming at her was someone in the enemy camp, as far as she knew. Oh well, better bluff it out.

'What brings you to the Big Smoke,' she said, giving him her sweetest smile, enough to launch a thousand male sexual reactions.

'Business. I have things to do for my cousin the judge. The Savoy is famous, so I thought I'd find out why.'

Yes, he was attractive, thought Penny, in a colonial masculine sort of way. No sex with this one, though. Much too dangerous.

'I saw him in court once, Very impressive. Lost most of his South African accent.'

'Unlike me, but English people seem to understand me all right. Have you ever been to South Africa?'

'Yes, very recently. One of my...' Penny was about to say 'journalistic adventures', when she remembered she was supposed to be an expert in ancient buildings. 'On one of my trips to see their old buildings. The Cape has some interesting seventeenth to nineteenth century architecture. I found Vergelegen fascinating.'

'Ah yes, it's wonderful.' He looked at his watch. 'I'm afraid I must be going now; I have to meet someone and I'm late. It's been a pleasure to meet you and to see...all this.' He gestured at the opulent surroundings.

Penny was thoughtful as Petrus 'call me Peter' took his

abrupt leave, realising that her careful plans to be anonymous might just have been ruined. What if Petrus was in league with van Wiese, who was in league with…heaven knows whom? She resolved to find out whether there was a back entrance to the hotel.

After a quick snack and one further extravagant drink, she established that there was a back entrance adjacent to the river and decided she would use it wearing her rudimentary disguise - not foolproof, but better than nothing. There was a boat called the Silver something or other, which was leaving from there for Greenwich. She'd catch it and come back into the Strand by train. How tiresome.

The morning found her still cautious, even paranoid. She paid the bill as herself, then sloped back to her room and proceeded to disguise herself as best she could. The river entrance could be reached by separate stairs, and she made sure she emerged dead on 9.15, when the river boat was due to leave. She'd bought her ticket from reception and flashed it at the major domo guarding the entrance. She was relieved to see she was one of only three passengers, so only two others to worry about.

One was a small moustachioed man in his late forties, dressed in a smart pin striped suit. The other was an expensively dressed young woman with black hair, who looked as if she might be Italian or Spanish.

Both ignored her - the man was busy texting someone on his mobile phone and the woman gazed in front of her, seemingly lost in thought.

Penny nevertheless regarded both with suspicion - one never knew. Most likely they were harmless. They reached the Greenwich platform and she let her fellow passengers alight first.

She then walked to the Cutty Sark, took the DLR to Bank, walked to Cannon Street and took the tube to Charing

Cross. It was a bewigged figure in dark glasses who walked along the Strand back to Coutts.

'Yes, madam,' said the impeccably dressed bank official, 'we have your box ready for inspection. There is a fee due next month, which will be paid by direct debit as usual. Your solicitors have dealt with registration of the Grant of Probate, and the identification you provided yesterday was satisfactory. I regret having to make you go through so many formalities, but discretion in dealing with our customers' affairs...'

'Of course,' said Penny, thinking, he sounds and looks like Dennis Price playing Jeeves in an old film.

'I have a list of the items here, we provide that free of charge.'

Penny wanted to say, 'how generous', but decided playing the game was the best way of seeing what she wanted to see quickly. Humour the old buffer, 'old' in the sense of how he came across, as he wasn't a day over 45, with sleek black hair, quite probably unassisted by anything artificial.

'We have brought the box up to one of our private rooms on the first floor, if madam would be kind enough to accompany me.'

Penny, her wig disguise safely in her bag, followed the pinstriped servant of the bank up in an incongruously modern lift. Hmm, so the olde worlde stuff is just to impress the blue chip customers, she thought. I expect they have all the bells and whistles of modern technology.

The box itself was something that would have done justice to the Antiques Road Show. It was made of a dark wood and covered with carving. 18th century, thought Penny. £1000 at auction but it has sentimental value, so I won't be wanting to sell it. It's the innards I want to see.

'Here you are madam. I shall leave you to inspect the contents. I have a list.

'I shall lock the door. Security, you know.' He handed her a list, typed, it seemed, on an old fashioned manual typewriter.

Penny was only too glad to be behind a locked door. While she had no suspicions of the Jeeves-like bank official, she was feeling very unsafe.

She examined the list.

1 box, locked

1 diamond ring

1 diamond and ruby pendant

1 ruby and diamond necklace

1 envelope - sealed, marked 'to my niece'

1 small box – locked

Various medals

Penny tried the larger of the two keys she fished out of her bag. The lock turned easily and the contents were before her.

The little box intrigued her. It had a small lock of its own. The remaining key fitted. Inside was an envelope. This was a relatively new one and was sealed. On the outside was written in Theresa's distinctive neat handwriting, her own name, 'Penny'.

She ripped the envelope open and read the letter inside.

'Penny sweetheart

You are my only relative and I've been lucky to have you. Once I was young and beautiful like you. Now I'm old I need to pass on what I know. If I haven't explained how to find this, it is because they've got me at last and you're looking after my estate. Last night I met that legal friend of a friend of yours with the odd name and tried to explain some things to him. I think he was a bit bewildered but hope he took enough in to give you a clue of what to look for if I'm dead. If you read this he succeeded.

It's all to do with the War. As L.P.Hartley said, 'The past is another country' and it really is.

I was in South Africa then on secret business. My diary of some of that time is lying about in the cottage. I hope you rather than my enemies have found it.

I had a tragic love affair, and before that a typical rushed wartime marriage to someone I thought died.

In any event I was mixed up with some very dangerous people - all in the cause of His Majesty, but one thing leads to another.

I became aware quite by chance of the secret of great wealth which was recovered by some South African people inimical to the British and intended to help finance their and Germany's struggle against us.

They were smuggling arms and all sorts of wartime paraphernalia.

In amongst the arms I discovered a cache of indescribably valuable jewellery - some of it is in that box. I managed to get part of it back to England but hid the rest in South Africa, as it was too bulky. It's still there. My partner in crime was a wonderful South African man called Ludio. He was of Khoi descent. We hid it together but soon after he disappeared. He does have a grandson of the same name. His details are on a bit of paper in the box. If you do go to South Africa he will help you.

I never divulged my find to my employers - it would have been swallowed up where all our taxes go - what a waste! There are people who buy these things and as you will see I've amassed wealth. The major part remains hidden in South Africa.

For some reason it has taken years for the descendants of our foes to realise that they had been deprived of their wealth and that I possessed the secret.

During the past year I've become aware that they know and they want it.

They have sympathisers in England and one is even a judge. The whereabouts of the rest of the jewellery, including the fabled Peacock Throne of the Mogul Emperors, a treasure beyond price, is a secret, which I am going to reveal to you. In the box is a map drawn by my friend Ludio. I had thought it better you didn't know, but the problem is that they think you know, and you and your friends are in great danger. So I've changed my mind. This may explain odd things that have happened to you and your religious friend. You're close to him and I regret he is also in danger. Big money begets big evil. I'm afraid this is all I have time to say for now. If I survive a week or two longer, then I hope to tell you more. With this letter you'll find a map drawn by Ludio. Hang on to it, as it shows where we hid the treasure.

All my love darling,

Theresa'

Penny put the letter down and sat for a while, shocked. So that was where all the money came from, and these jewels! She had enemies and poor Tony had them too. All for a secret she hadn't known about. Till now.

She took the letter and other pieces of paper, including a hand drawn map but left the jewels - Septimus would make her declare them and have them valued and she would rather leave them where they were for the moment. She had quite enough money from her aunt's estate already. Maybe she'd give them to charity. That could be dealt with later. And there were even more jewels and this Peacock thingummy still hidden in South Africa - her head spun with the new information.

She pressed the buzzer next to the door and waited for Jeeves, or rather Wilkinson, which was his real name.

'Is madam going to be taking any items with her?'

'Only the envelope and a few notes. You may remove them from the list.'

He scribbled on the list. 'I've deleted them. Please sign this receipt.'

Penny did as she was told and said,

'Is there another entrance to this bank - a private one?'

Wilkinson smiled a knowing smile, no doubt one he'd used a thousand times when dealing with secretive customers.

'Indeed there is. If you be kind enough to follow me...'

Penny followed the besuited official as he padded along various corridors, leading to a fire escape. They went down some old stone stairs and emerged into a small side street. Penny turned to thank Wilkinson, but he'd gone. He made no remark about the fact she'd put on her wig and sunglasses. For a minute or so Penny was lost. Then she decided to go into a nearby Chinese Medicine shop and took out her phone from her bag. The map app showed she was now in Adelaide Street. She made for Trafalgar Square and hoped the sheer volume of people would hide her from any observer. The meeting with the South African man had made her nervous, especially as now she realised that she was assumed by her aunt's enemies to possess a valuable secret. Poor Tony! She reflected, was his stalker part of some gang after her?

She joined the underground system at Embankment and took the District line to Victoria. As she boarded the Brighton train she decided to be clever and walk through the carriages and found a cosy seat obscured from the windows, indeed from all but the most assiduous observer in the train. Still gripped by paranoia she watched the dense scruffy buildings of south London become the concrete of Croydon and past Coulsdon the countryside. All the way to Brighton was her aim. Tony and Septimus had agreed to pick her up.

21

'You realise that we'll be in danger for the rest of our lives,' said Theresa.

Ludio, who was driving, grinned. 'Yes that's true, but we'll both be rich.'

'Money isn't everything, but we've made our choice. I've got to work out how I'm going to sell this stuff. Not in this country. I will have to make sure you get your share and you're going to have to be discreet about it.'

'I don't want much, *Inkosikaas* Theresa. Just enough for a house and to be comfortable. You know we coloured people can't live where you whites live in big houses in Constantia like that Mr Nevis. I don't want to leave this country. It's my home. I just want to be more comfortable.'

'That's fine, but you're in a lot more danger here. If those people think you know where the Arniston gold and jewellery is hidden...'

'They won't find out. My main worry is how we smuggle what's in the boot to England.'

They were nearing the town of Hermanus, the blue mountains forming their familiar shimmering backdrop to their right. I love this country, thought Theresa. She said,

'I'll miss the Cape. I'm going to transport the jewellery as part of my luggage on a passenger liner when the war's over. Meantime we'll hide it.'

They sat silent as the Humber Snipe, which they had swopped for the Ford, ate up the miles. Theresa kept craning her neck as she looked obsessively to see if they were being followed.

'Ag *nkosikaas*, you'll have a sore neck if you go on doing that. If anyone is looking for you, it'll be in a Ford.'

'I can't help it Ludio. I'm getting so used to being followed I get anxious.'

'*Moenie* worry *nie*. I have an eye on the mirror and I've seen nothing. Ludio will look after you. I've done well so far.' His face lit up with one of his characteristic grins. 'This car is a make the army people often use. No one looking for you will expect you to be travelling in it.'

'Yes, you have Ludio. I'd have been dead long ago without you.' She patted his arm. 'You're a true friend.'

'And a rich one now I hope,' he said, as he swerved to avoid a small animal darting across the road. It began to climb and they were travelling up Sir Lowry's Pass. They went through an unlit tunnel, which frightened Theresa, but Ludio drove through it with aplomb. They reached the top of the pass and approached Somerset West, near where Theresa had arranged to stay. The roundup of the OB men had, she hoped, removed the immediate danger to her, at least while they were in jail. She was to stay in a house overlooking the nearby sea at a place called Strand a town adjacent to Somerset West.

Their loot they had put in a large trunk. It was only a small part of the hoard they'd found in the barn at Cape Agulhas. Ludio, resourceful as always, had helped her hide the rest in a cave he knew of, where his people, he said, had hidden from the whites during the troubled 18th century. They'd selected valuable but not heavy items to take with them, leaving behind the bulk, including a bejewelled replica of the famous Peacock Throne, in the cave, hidden by brushwood. Ludio assured Theresa he was the only living person who knew of it.

Before Ludio left, he fished a piece of paper out of his pocket,

'This is a map of the cave where we left the heavy items. You may never go back, but if you need more money they are worth millions. The OB people would kill to find it. Keep it safe.'

Theresa looked at the piece of paper. It was a well-drawn map and she could see it would lead her back to the cave if she wanted to go there.

'Thank you Ludio, I'll keep it safe. I hope I don't need it.' Theresa waved goodbye and was overcome with a feeling of sadness. She'd become fond of her companion, who reminded her of a leprechaun. Once the car had disappeared she made herself at home in the small house. She had to get back to England but did not think the risk of travel was worth it yet, as although the *U-boat* threat had diminished, it only needed one torpedo to sink a ship.

Meanwhile Ludio drove towards his home in the part of Cape Town known as District Six, where he lived with his ancient mother and father. He was thinking what he was going to do with all that money. His mother greeted him,

'Ag Ludio, you *skelm*, where've you been? I've been worried sick.'

'No need mom, I've just been doing my job, working for the publishing company.'

'So you say, but it's dangerous driving all over the place like you do. People talk...and what they say isn't nice. That

Gertruida Meintjies who works in Constantia says you've been seen with a white woman. Is this true?'

'Yes, it is, it's been my job to escort *Inkosikaas* Theresa. I was ordered to do so. She needs protection'

'Aren't you the big man now. Protecting people. Why don't you get a job at the petrol station or gardening for the City Council? It's much safer.'

'Ag mom, if it was up to you I'd be doing gardening for peanuts seven days a week. Any how I need a rest, so I'll see you later.'

He went up the stairs to his bedroom, and his snores resounded through the little old house.

Next day he reported to John, his boss.

John's office was north of the centre of town in a street of ramshackle commercial buildings. The nondescript door with peeling paint led to some wooden stairs and a booth surrounded by glass. Next to it were rows and rows of new books on shelves, for John's organisation was a legitimate importer of books.

John himself was a small handsome man with carefully combed dark hair and a fussy manner.

'Well Ludio, back at last, perhaps you can tell me what you've been up to. The valuable Miss Theresa back safe and sound?'

'Yes boss, she's in the Strand house.'

Ludio then related his adventures, leaving out any mention of the Arniston hoard.

'Well done. You've performed a valuable service to our cause. I'll see you receive financial recompense.'

'Does that mean *geld*?' said Ludio.

'Indeed it does. These OB people are a menace, and the explosives and ammunition you and Miss Theresa found would have cost many lives. I will have more work for you, but in the meantime you can have the day off.' John walked over to a safe, the front hidden by his body, and there was a clicking sound as he went through the combination. When he turned round he had a wad of banknotes in his hand, which he thrust towards Ludio.

'Here's fifty pounds. Spend it wisely.'

'Thanks boss, I will.'

Ludio made his way on foot through the narrow streets to District Six. Although an intelligent man and competent at his job, he had one weakness - drink. He gave his mother one half of the money, telling her it was a 'bonus' and then walked towards Hanover Street, where he was well known in the Rose and Crown, a typical English name for a District Six pub. The mostly 19th century buildings were dirty and what paint there was left showed itself in faded marks. But, like most inhabitants, this place was home to many 'Coloureds', descendants of Malay slaves, Khoi and Europeans who had carelessly scattered their genes amongst their slaves and servants in the past 300 years. It was a place where life was cheap and sometimes short, where anyone with money was a target. It was also a place with firm loyalties. Drink was then, as now, a common solace for those who had hardly enough to buy food.

He ordered a beer. Soon the alcohol took effect and he fell into boastful conversation with old acquaintances. The wad of notes diminished quickly as he paid for rounds of drinks for many.

'Ag Ludio, you're in the money,' said Riempies, a well-known *skollie* who prowled drinking places like a hyena, looking for victims.

'Maybe, said Ludio, 'maybe.'

'You're a big *ou* now.' The *skollie*'s pinched face wore a smile that had he been sober would have sent out warning signals to Ludio. But Ludio was no longer sober, and all the accumulated stress of the past weeks was expressing itself in yet more beer.

'Yes, bigger than you'll ever be. There are things I know...'

The *skollie* listened. This pub was a gold mine. He knew Ludio had a job that took him away from the area and he had been seen driving cars with white people in them. His instincts were roused and his animal counterpart would have felt the same way about the blood of a freshly killed buck.

'I always thought you'd come good. When we were begging as little boys in the Grand Parade you were always the smart one.'

Flattery was a trusted weapon for the *skollie*.

Through the haze of smoke and alcohol something in Ludio's mind stopped him from boasting further.

'Yes, I remember those days. I've got an honest job now, but you've grown up into a *skollie*.'

Riempies flinched at the insult. He knew what he was but didn't like to be told.

'You be fokkin careful what you say. I'm as good as you with your fancy ways. Just because you suck up to white people and they give you money doesn't make you better than me. You still live in District Six and they just use you like a servant.'

The *skollie*'s face took on a furious aspect, and the tone of his voice changed from wheedling flattery to harsh hatred.

Drunk as he was, Ludio looked at him with contempt.

'Everybody knows you're no good. It's *ous* like you who give us Coloureds a bad name. If you weren't such a titchy little *gogga* I'd knock you flat.'

The reference to Riempies' diminutive stature and comparison with an insect enraged the *skollie* further.

'You'll eat those words I promise you. You think you're the big man but one day you'll lie *vrek* in the street like a dog that's been run over.'

'So it's threats, now,' said Ludio. 'Well I wonder who's going to end up *vrek* first. You better watch your step. Ludio's anger had made his mind clearer. He went on,

'I'll *klap* you here and now if you stay here a second longer. You stink anyway.'

The menace in Ludio's eyes was a warning to Riempies. He knew he was no match for the larger and stronger Ludio. As boys they'd had scraps and Ludio had beaten him easily. He was a coward, and moved towards the door of the pub.

'OK big man, but watch your step.'

The warning was like the yap of a small dog behind a fence when confronted with a large one. Defiant, yet feeling safe behind its protection. In this case it was because he'd retreated to the door and knew Ludio was too drunk to chase after him.

Gammat, a friend of Ludio, had been listening to the discourse with interest.

'*Ag* Ludio you've made an enemy there. He's a *skelm* and will want to kill you now. Those *skollie*s want money but now he hates you.'

'He's always hated both of us Gammat. I can deal with *goggas* like him.'

'Maybe when you're sober. But you be careful on the way home. Do you want me to come with?'

Ludio blinked and eyed his friend.

'I'll be right as rain. I'm not scared of that piece of horse's dung. You want another beer?'

'Don't mind if I do,' said Gammat, to whom Ludio's sudden generosity and munificence were a compelling combination. 'Make it a pint of Castle with a chaser of brandy.'

The pair sat drinking and reminiscing for an hour or more.

Ludio found his legs did not obey the command to walk in a satisfactory way, but being a stubborn man, he was determined to traverse the few streets to his home. Gammat forgot his offer to accompany him, and indeed was in similar difficulty when it came to locomotion.

Outside, in a dark corner, Riempies waited.

Ludio staggered out towards his home. It was dark in the badly lit streets. If he had been sober he would have been alert. Indeed, he'd not have walked alone. He felt a jarring pain in his head.

JOHN LOOKED at the clock on his wall. It was an antique he'd brought with him from England when he first came to the Union, as South Africa was then referred to, a passenger on the Pretoria Castle. The clock had a picture of smiling sun in the middle, Ten o'clock. Where was Ludio? He decided to enquire at Ludio's home, as Ludio's mother did not have a telephone.

The walk to District Six was only a quarter of an hour. He walked past the quaint houses that needed a lick of paint and dodged a football kicked by a young lad playing in the street. A sheet of newspaper flapped against his leg, propelled by a gust of the South East wind, so common in Cape Town.

He knocked on the door, 15 Frere Street. It was answered by a small Khoi woman in her fifties.

'Excuse me, I'm John Powell, does Ludio live here? He works for me at the publishing company.'

The woman answered in kitchen English.

'Ja *meneer* John, he lives by here, *maar* we haven't seen the *skelm* since last night. I expect he's asleep somewhere. He likes his drink.'

'I see,' said John, 'but he's never failed to turn up for work before. I'll enquire of the Police.'

Ludio's mother gave a shrug.

'They won't be interested. Us Coloureds mean nothing to them. It's better if you wait to hear from him.'

John nodded and sighed.

'Well you know your own son. I must admit he's never been late for work or appeared to have a drink problem.' There was nothing more he could achieve here, so he turned away.

As he did so he said, 'If he turns up can you ask him to get in touch urgently? He knows where I am. He's been really useful to me and I don't want any harm to come to him.'

The woman nodded. 'I understand. I *jus* as worried as you *meneer*. It's not like him.'

John walked back along the dingy streets to his office. He reflected that they were a warren that hid all kinds of vice and crime, but there was a faded charm to the hundred year old buildings which had been created to house freed slaves, immigrants and the flotsam and jetsam of a growing 19th century city. There was no doubt there was a life about it, although the City Council already regarded it as a slum and had plans to demolish it. A shame, he reflected. With a bit of tarting up it could be an asset to the city, which he'd grown to love in his five years in Cape Town. Some buildings showed signs of former affluence. When he got back, Theresa was waiting for him.

'Hello Theresa. I knew from Ludio you'd returned with him but I didn't expect you in today. Have you heard from him? He came in yesterday but hasn't graced us with his presence today, but his mother said he didn't come home last night.'

'Ludio can look after himself. I expect he'll turn up. Now, there are things we need to discuss,' said Theresa.

'Have you met my ex-husband who masquerades as a U-boat captain?'

'No,' said John, 'I've not actually met the man, although I

know of him. He's an important agent. The marriage to you, I'm told, was a camouflage, but I expect you've worked that out. He's gone back to England now. That hoard of weapons you found near Agulhas was the last big danger from the OB, at least as far as this war is concerned. We're just the remnants of a sideshow now. Monty and the Yanks are getting near to the Rhine. I expect they'll be in Berlin by Christmas. Once the war is over I fear the Afrikaner Nationalists are going to have their way eventually. Smuts is old and his cabinet is composed of uninspiring men, in my opinion. They'll clear the English and their countrymen who get on with us out of government, the army, everything. They want power and they'll get it. I wouldn't be surprised if this country isn't a republic before another decade goes past.'

'Phew, that was quite a speech. In a roundabout way you're saying there's no job for me any more?'

'Not here, but no doubt Whitehall will need you. The next enemy will be the Soviets, and they have codes to break. A lot of us will have to find proper jobs, but I expect they'll want you.'

'Such a relief. Is it safe to travel home by ship?'

John's frowned. 'No, I wouldn't do it. You'd be taking a chance. There aren't many U-boats left but you could be unlucky. Better for you to stay here, although there is a risk of some OB maniac singling you out. They were very much after you before.'

'I think I'll go home,' said Theresa. ' I really don't feel safe here, even with Ludio around to look after me.'

'Ludio. Such an able man. I am very worried about him. If I don't hear from him by close of business I'm going to make enquiries of the police.'

'Who saw him last?' said Theresa.

'His mother said he went to a pub somewhere. He did like a drink. It was his only weakness.'

Theresa felt grave unease. In spite of her earlier throw-away comments, Ludio had kept her alive, but as is often the case with those who are good at looking after others, he may well have been bad at looking after himself.

'I feel I have to do something,' she said.

'But what can we do? The streets in District Six are notorious for crime. If you went looking for him, you'd very likely end up a corpse. A white woman on her own in that district would be asking for it.'

'The white woman needn't be on her own,' said Theresa.

So it was that the two of them scoured the streets of District Six. They found nothing.

Theresa hoped she would hear from Ludio and left an address in England with Ludio's mother.

In spite of John's warning, she decided to risk going home by sea. There were no passenger services on the lines of the pre-war Union Castle service, and Theresa found a berth aboard a cargo ship that had a few passenger berths.

Every day she stood on the deck looking at the bizarre flying fish breaching the waves and gliding for up to fifty yards at times and thinking about her past and future. There had been no further attempts on her life and she was sad to leave the Cape. Her treasure was kept with her at all times. In those days it was easy to smuggle items and being a 'special' passenger, no one questioned her.

She planned to stay with her mother, who lived in rural Sussex. She was not familiar with how one disposed of jewels, but there were ways, no doubt.

The passengers ate in a small dining room. There were six of them: An elderly couple, who'd been torpedoed off West Africa and evacuated to Cape Town, had decided to go home as they felt if they didn't they'd never see Blighty again. There was an assorted bunch of three others - another couple and an injured RAF pilot who had somehow turned up in Cape

Town. He wore a patch over his right eye and a gleam in his other.

'I say,' he said, as he sidled up to her, gazing as she was at the flying fish.

'Don't I know you from somewhere?'

Theresa looked at him. What she saw was a latter day pirate, and the patch was probably responsible for the impression.

'Perhaps in a previous life? Were you perhaps Captain Kidd and I was someone he kidnapped from a merchant ship?'

Bob, for that was the pilot's name, guffawed.

'Ho ho, perhaps indeed. I think nearer to home. Were you anywhere near Kenley in 1940? I flew Spits from there. Later went to North Africa - pranged badly, I'm afraid. Ended up in the sleepy Cape. '

Theresa ransacked her memory.

'Kenley? Isn't that near Croydon? I remember going to a pub called the Kenley Arms and it being full of rowdy RAF types. Perhaps one of them was you? I remember a chap with a handlebar moustache who was always putting his hand on my knee. Very loud and distinctive voice, said 'Good Show' frequently. He was a Squadron Leader or something.'

'Good lord, sounds like Pongo Anstruther. So you *were* at Kenley. I expect your beauty shone out like a beacon and fixed itself in my brain.'

'Hmm, I doubt it. That pub was so full of cigarette smoke that you'd have had to be sitting a few feet away to see me clearly. That squadron leader, I remember his name, Alan something. '

'I know exactly who you mean. Definitely Pongo, aka Alan Anstruther. He was after anything in a skirt. Not that I put you in that category of course, but a bit of a rum cove.

Splendid pilot. Got transferred to Biggin Hill and bought it over France, I heard.'

'That is sad,' said Theresa. So many of you those laughing cheerful chaps haven't lived to see twenty-five. You're still here though.'

'I am indeed. I must say your presence on board has cheered me up no end. I was expecting nothing but frowsty old dears creeping back home for company, not...'

'A gorgeous young woman like you.' Theresa had heard this sort of line so often during the War she couldn't resist finishing Bob's sentence.

'Spot on,' said Bob. 'I say, you wouldn't like to have a spot of gin and tonic? I managed to get some gin on the hush hush and my cabin is very comfortable. I could get some ice from the kitchen.'

''What's wrong with that little dining room?' said Theresa.' I'm all for the G and T, but I think your cabin is best occupied by you alone.'

'If you say so, just thought we might have to put up with those bores, the Jenkinsons. They'll probably ask us to join them in a game of rummy, or some other equally dull card game.'

'That's a risk you'll have to take, Bob. I certainly will. Anyway, I'm always game for rummy. I used to play with my great aunt Madge when I was a little girl.'

'Ah well, it's the dining room then. See you there in ten minutes?'

'Yes, I'd be glad to,' said Theresa. Ship life was so boring, a gin would cheer her up, and even the risk of rummy was better than being left with her thoughts. What had happened to Ludio? for example.

The dining room was indeed occupied by the Jenkinsons, who turned out to be partial to Bob's gin. However, they were not card players.

'Where did you get this, Bob?' said Mr Jenkinson, who was called Peter. For a man with an English name his accent was very guttural. No doubt he'd been living amongst Afrikaners.

'Oh, I have a friend who has a friend,' said Bob. You know how things are in this War. One knows people,'

Peter Jenkinson chuckled,

'I see, well lack of provenance won't stop me enjoying it.'

They sat sipping the coveted liquor, and Bob's face grew longer as he saw his seduction tool wasted on the old couple, for Peter Jenkinson's glass emptied quickly and Bob felt compelled to refill it. Theresa, on the other hand, on the basis that harmless as these people seemed to be, one couldn't be too careful, husbanded her own drink as if it was the only one left on earth.

'You're not drinking much, Miss Duchesne,' said the old man.

'I only drink gin rarely, 'she said. Besides, Bob's only got one bottle I presume, so it would be a shame if we were to finish it in one gulp, so to speak.'

'I consider myself admonished,' said Peter Jenkinson. Nevertheless, by the time they decided to go to their respective cabins the bottle was empty. Bob was by now pretty merry and Theresa and Mrs Jenkinson were the only sober people left.

Mrs J was a hard faced woman of about sixty, with wrinkles imposed by a Karoo or Highveld sun, Theresa guessed. Her watery blue eyes did not disguise an inner steel, and at times during the evening Theresa looked up to find the woman staring at her. Oh dear, she thought, what interests her? Perhaps the natural distaste for the old and plain for the young and pretty? She hoped so.

She soon fell asleep. Even a single gin was enough to send her off. She dreamed of Agulhas and found herself in a cave with Ludio. He was saying something to her and wagging his forefinger as if in warning. She was awoken by a loud knocking her cabin door. She staggered from her bed to open it. It was Bob, brandishing another bottle of gin, with a silly grin on his face.

'Sorry Bob, you'll have to drink it on your own. I'm tired. I'm surprised you can still walk. Please go back to your own cabin. .

She must have sounded convincing, because his face fell and he walked off without a word. He never spoke to her again.

The voyage took three weeks and the cold and fog of Liverpool was a shock after the warmth of the Cape and the sea voyage.

The next forty years were spent in the Civil Service. Ostensibly Theresa was a clerk in the Admiralty. In reality she was used for confidential missions to eastern Europe. September 1974 was spent in Prague where she was seconded to the British embassy as a very junior filing clerk. Her real job was to communicate with the Czech resistance. The Soviet invasion had shocked the West and there were many disaffected Czechs willing to sell secrets.

Theresa loved ballet, and in the interval at many performances in Prague, she bought refreshments from her contact, Kristina. Another meeting place was the zoo, and in front of cages containing hungry snarling Siberian tigers she would bend to hand spectacles to a woman who'd dropped them. The spectacles she handed over were identical, but those she received contained microfilm. On the last occasion she was aware of being followed. Luckily for both her and her contact nothing had been exchanged that day, so there was no evidence. Fraternisation was enough though, and the Czech government requested she be transferred back to Britain.

Theresa was sad about this, as she was fond of the

splendid city with its trams and ornate buildings. Even the presence of ubiquitous Soviet soldiers and a statue of a tank on a large plinth did not spoil it.

By now she was in her fifties and her controller felt it was time she confined herself to desk work.

Soon after arriving in Britain from South Africa she'd found she was pregnant. In those days illegitimate children were frowned on. The father was Jannie, dead in South Africa, so she visited a back street abortionist. The operation was botched so she became infertile.

In 1982 her sister Jenny, born a late child to her mother after the war, had a daughter Penny. Jenny was not married, but times had changed. Theresa was a generous aunt and Jenny was grateful for the many gifts her much older sister bestowed on her.

Theresa had money for school fees, and Penny went to a coeducational school for the sons and daughters of the well-heeled. Somehow she managed to get expelled. There was talk of an affair with a teacher, but the full details were hushed up. Penny was just as beautiful as her aunt, and very self-willed. They saw each other often, and Theresa bailed her out on several occasions. Penny became a freelance journalist and was very good at it. In a profession not renowned for high pay she managed to get some scoops involving 'celebrities' and pursued a wayward life.

As a member of the wartime Secret Service, Theresa had skills and experience which were useful, and she had slotted into a Civil Service life in Whitehall. In those days, before computers and the Internet, it was quite possible to be discreet about one's wealth.

The booty from Agulhas she methodically disposed of and amassed a large amount of money.

No one was interested in the fact that she was able to finance a niece at an expensive school, if they even knew about it. People had relatives and legacies, and it was their own business.

One day the past returned. Theresa had been asked to attend a secret criminal trial. The defendant was an alleged spy for the Russians and had been working at the South African embassy as a driver. In the course of his job he had won the confidence of the ambassador who'd become careless with his documents. The driver had been photographing them and the Russian embassy had received a stream of information, mostly uninteresting but some of it important. The driver was a white Afrikaner with a sense of grievance against the West for its perceived betrayal of his people and a pressing need to finance his gambling habit.

The trial was a dull affair, with bewigged barristers droning on and on. Theresa was so bored she'd asked for the teenaged Penny to be allowed to accompany her to 'take notes'. Really what she wanted was some amusing company.

The timing of the case was leisurely, ten till four with an hour for lunch. It amused the two women that the judge, who appeared to be dozing, seemed to have a clock in his head, as at five to one each day he woke up to announce that the court would adjourn, warning the witness of the moment not to discuss anything with anyone.

Although the trial was not open to the public there were sundry representatives from the South African High Commission there, of various ethnic origins. One was a senior legal advisor called van Wiese, dual qualified in South Africa, where he was a Senior Counsel, and in England where he'd made it to QC.

The case went on for three weeks. Theresa and Penny had lunch each day at a wine bar in the street of Old Bailey itself.

The jury was out to consider its verdict.

'Only one more day, sweetie,' said Theresa to her niece. 'Will you miss our lunches?"

'The lunches' yes, but the trial is pretty dull. At first I was impressed with the grandeur of it all, but gradually I've become bored. Is he going to be found guilty?'

'I expect so, dear,' said Theresa. 'They've got him bang to rights, as the fuzz say. I mean, he was stupid enough to put all that money into his bank account every month and is not able to account for it. I think he's a bit dim. The information he provided the eastern peep is pretty unexciting, but you can't just go copying an ambassador's papers and handing them over to a foreign power.'

'What'll happen to him,' said Penny.

'Oh, a spell in prison. I doubt he's important enough to get swopped for one of ours.'

The trial duly ended with a guilty verdict. Thereafter, though, Theresa began to sense she was being watched.

Odd things told her this. All of us get into a routine and see certain things and people every day. Soon after the trial the concierge at the block of flats in Chelsea where she lived asked to talk to her.

'Morning madam. I don't want to talk out of turn, but I feel you ought to know someone has been asking about you.'

'Someone? Mr Giles could you be more specific? Sorry to sound sharp, but it may be important.'

'Not at all, madam. It was a middle-aged gentleman, had an accent, sounded a bit German but maybe more South African. Said he was a relative. Asked where you worked, had you been here long. Told him that the affairs of residents are confidential, and if he wished to make enquiries he could perhaps leave you a note with his phone number. He said that wouldn't be necessary and he'd merely been passing and would drop by again.'

Theresa had been paranoid about South Africa ever since she left. Had the OB at last caught up with her?

22

The sight of Tony in his dog collar and Septimus like some attenuated walrus with his side-whiskers gave Penny a feeling of comfort. In this bold bad world, they were a rock of decency and goodwill. There was nothing glamorous about them, but they weren't boring.

'Well boys, I can see you're dying to know how I got on, so let's adjourn to a pub.'

The Electric Grape was a wine bar on the road leading to Brighton station. It was a place for students and Tony and Septimus could have been mistaken for someone's parents or, in the case of Tony, an elder brother.

'Will we be able to hear ourselves speak?' said Septimus.

'No sweetie,' said Penny. 'But the manager is a friend and she has a back room where we can talk.'

The friend was a thirty-something woman with a pretty face and slightly overweight body.

After profuse 'darlings' and hugs were exchanged between her and Penny, the woman, whose name was Sheila, led them through the bar to a room with a desk, a couple of comfortable but threadbare chairs and a wall covered with photos of assorted entertainers.

'You won't be disturbed in here, darling,' said Sheila. 'I'll have some tea brought in, unless you'd like something stronger.'

'A pint of Ruddles or that new-fangled Doom Bar wouldn't go amiss,' said Septimus.

'Do you have any Sauvignon Blanc?' said Tony.

'Of course,' said Sheila. 'And you'll be wanting a large gin and tonic?' she addressed Penny.

'Thank you sweetie, that would be lovely.'

Penny turned towards her friends. 'Right boys, no bugs here, so I can tell you what I've found.'

Penny related her discoveries at the bank and showed them Theresa's letter.

'Extraordinary,' said Tony. So, all the shenanigans in Croydon may be related to your aunt's find in South Africa. What worries me is that these folk are out there, wanting what they think you've got. I presume the map you took from the bank shows where the rest of the treasure is. No wonder your aunt was wealthy. I must confess I'm at a loss to know what to do.'

'Indeed, sweetie, with your ecclesiastical perspicacity you've hit the nail on the head. How do we protect ourselves?'

'Make them think we have no idea? I presume you just want to leave this Peacock Throne replica and so on where it is?'

'Yes, I would rather. But on the train I did come up with an idea.'

'Do tell,' said the 'boys' as one.

'We go to South Africa, find the loot. Announce it to the world and present it to some museum or other as a gracious gesture, so those after us can turn their attention to robbing that institution, as we'll be of no further use.'

'Brilliant!' said Tony. 'Only we're quite likely to be killed doing it.'

'If you have a better idea sweetie, spit it out, as they say. We're slow moving targets here in England. They may even be hovering about outside. The only reason we're not dead yet is they want the loot first, us for afters. As they say in films, "it's not personal" - well at least as far as Tony and our forensic friend are concerned. I'm not sure about me.'

'How very comforting,' said Septimus.

'Well you could butt out, Sept, you cuddly walrus you. I mean I shouldn't think they'd expect me to have told you where it is. Had no idea it even existed myself till the past 24 hours.'

'No, I suppose not. However, I don't think I'll butt out now, as you put it. For one thing I shall be intrigued to see this Peacock Throne. Since meeting you Penny, I've realised what a dull life I've led.'

'And you Tony?' said Penny.

'I'm rather stuck, aren't I?' They're not going to leave me alone. I'm guilty as far as they're concerned. I bet that judge fellow who lives in the manor house is the Moriarty figure.'

'And Penny's Holmes,' said Septimus.

'More Irene Adler I'd say,' said Tony.

'Thank you for all your sensible contributions. I suggest we travel separately on two or even three different airlines, if we're agreed. I'll be paying the bill for the tickets. I'll also need to go back to that snooty bank to retrieve the map. Then it's off to S.A. and Cape Agulhas. A week should be long enough for us to find what we're looking for, or realise we can't.'

At that moment Sheila appeared. "Can I get you more drinks, chaps?'

'No that's all right, Sheila darling, do you have a back door we can use for a surreptitious exit?'

'There's the one we use for deliveries. The alley it goes
into stinks a bit, but you're welcome to use it. Are you up to
something vitally important for the Nation? First of all, your
request for this room. Now legging it through the back door.
Will I get a visit from the police?'

'No of course not. We're just being careful that's all,' said
Penny.

'I see, you don't want to talk about it.' Sheila grinned and
made a sign that her lips were sealed. Tony's wandering eye
had marked her down as 'very attractive', but he sighed as he
thought he'd never see her voluptuous beauty again.

So it was they slipped out of the back. Penny went first,
and five minutes later Tony and Septimus scuttled down the
alley trying to look casual once they hit the street. The
woman whose job it was to follow them went into the pub.

She spoke to a woman behind the bar.

'I'm looking for some friends I promised to meet here. A
young woman and two older men. They're my cousins.'

The bar woman was aware she'd seen people of this
description but had been told not to give any information.

'Yes, perhaps they were here. But I didn't see them leave,
sorry.'

The woman turned and walked out of the pub. Duchesne
and her friends must be aware they were being followed. It
was time her boss took steps.

Penny booked tickets for Cape Town. She decided on
First Class for herself on British Airways, and the 'boys' went
via Dubai.

On reflection, separating Tony and Septimus was pointless. They might get lost.

They met at the Vergelegen restaurant in the town of
Somerset West, an expensive but charming place amongst the
vast trees and other spectacular scenery that surrounded the
old manor house, now owned by a vast mining conglomerate.

Septimus was impressed.

'Worth coming out here for this alone,' he said. 'Those mountains! I could happily have lunch here every day.'

'Yes, said Tony, but in every Garden of Eden there is a serpent.'

'Thank you for spoiling the moment,' said Septimus. 'Ah, here comes the ravishing Penny.'

Indeed it was she, clothed in a light summery outfit which barely concealed her natural attributes.

When he'd recovered his equilibrium, which took a few seconds, Tony stood up and kissed her on the cheek.

'Septimus was just saying what a wonderful place this is.'

'Yes, I know. We might as well get something out of this before we get down to business. I like your khaki shorts, Septimus, you only need some long socks and a comb tucked into them to pass for an Afrikaner. You have the beard and whiskers, although perhaps not the tan. Those white legs of yours shout 'Englishman' to everyone here.

'Thank you Penny,' said Septimus. 'I'll apply some fake tan tonight.'

'I'm not joking, I think you should,' said Penny. 'You want to blend in if we're to be incognito.'

'And I?' said Tony. Do I blend in?'

'The clergyman's collar and long trousers are your disguise. You are what you are darling. They won't know what a devil lurks within.'

Tony blushed. 'I suppose so.'

Septimus looked hard at Tony. 'Devil within? You must tell me some time.'

'Now keep your locker room talk for when you're alone, darlings, although I'd hope Tony doesn't do locker room talk. He's not aiming to become the American President.'

They ordered two bottles of the eponymous Vergelegen Sauvignon Blanc, followed by one for the road, and it was three plastered UK citizens who slumped into their beds. Penny stayed at a local hotel and the 'boys' at a 'rather nice b and b', as Septimus put it.

'We'll go in separate cars and meet at a place called Swellendam, thence we'll proceed, separately again, to Cape Agulhas.'

'Roger,' said Septimus, who was relishing the adventure after years of completing forms in his Croydon office. Tony, who felt he'd had enough excitement for three lifetimes, said nothing.

Penny soon disappeared into the distance in a BMW, while Tony and Septimus chugged along in a Toyota Corolla.

The town of Swellendam had changed since Theresa's wartime visit. The fifty or so old Dutch buildings were augmented with coffee shops and touristy eating places.

Penny chose a place near the *Drotsdy*, or old Magistrates Court, where they sat admiring the mountains and picking at platters of food.

'Why don't we just stay here and forget about our quest?' said Septimus. 'I could adapt to this life very easily, especially the tiny bills we have to pay.'

'Ah yes,' said 'Penny. 'If only. But you'd probably get bored after a while.'

Tony stirred.

'Based on my previous experience of this country, there's an awful lot going on that's not nice. We're experiencing the sweet outer coating. Inside it's not necessarily so sweet. People can be violent and we need to be on our guard. I don't know if Penny's ruse will work, but I have a feeling that those who want to harm us in England will find a way of doing it here.'

'Wise words, Tony darling. Please both restrict your-selves to one glass of wine each, as we must hit the road in the next half hour. I'll go ahead as before and you can amble along in that Corolla. Doesn't it make it difficult overtaking?'

'Depends how much overtaking you do,' said Tony. 'Sept and I tend to let other people do that sort of thing.'

'Yes,' said Septimus. 'Seen too many injured motorists in my time and defended too many careless drivers.'

'How dull,' said Penny. 'Nothing I like more than seeing the speedometer jerk upwards. Seriously, I'll get to the b & b first and be waiting for you. Here's a map and it's the house I've marked with a cross. Auntie owned it - bought it in the fifties I believe, and as you know, Septimus, I've inherited it.'

'So that's the place the South African attorney was dealing with,' said Septimus. 'I'll be interested to see it.'

'Well you will.'

After downing a cup of coffee Penny disappeared in her powerful car.

'Hope she isn't done for speeding,' said Septimus.

'She's a fast girl, never does anything slowly,' said Tony. 'Better give her twenty minutes and then we'll be off.'

The pair drove towards Cape Agulhas, guided by the signs, passing Bredasdorp and miles of open country till at last they saw the ocean.

It was such a small place that they found Penny's house quite quickly.

'What on earth is that in the window?' said Septimus. 'It looks like a sailor.'

'No idea. Didn't know anyone else would be here,' said Tony.

Penny greeted them. 'What kept you? I've been here for an hour or more.'

'You just drive fast, Penny, who's that chap in the window?' said Septimus.

'Oh, he's a thing dressed up to look like a sailor. Apparently been here forever,' said Penny. 'He's definitely not alive.'

'I see,' both the males said in unison. 'A kind of inanimate guardian of the house,' said Septimus.

'More like a pet,' said Penny. He is weird I agree, but then so is this whole place. Let me show you your respective bedrooms. I'm afraid the ablutions block is outside, so you'll have to compete with a few spiders. I'm sure that won't worry tough chaps like you.'

Later they decided a good rest was in order and they'd get on with their task of finding the cave the next day.

The morning was bright and warm enough to make them comfortable, in spite of the strong sea breeze.

They trekked for miles along the beach.

'How much further is it?' said Tony, who had taken on a bedraggled appearance, his sandy hair looking like a pile of grass that had been walked through. Septimus was brave enough to wear his shorts, and his as yet untanned legs reflected the bright sun reddening as the hours passed. Both men looked unsuited to the African environment and Penny hoped they were not conspicuous. She was wearing a pair of shorts and a white blouse. In spite of her whiteness she looked flawless as usual.

'Is that a farmhouse?' said Tony. 'I remember a farmhouse being mentioned on the map.'

'Looks like it,' said Septimus. 'One of those Dutch gabled jobs, very attractive.'

'Yes boys, we're on the right track. Should see some barns ahead if they're still here. Got some trekking to do still.'

Sure enough, they saw some barns, only there was a sign saying 'Two Oceans Holiday Cottages' with a pointer in the shape of a hand with a long finger pointing to them.

'Humph,' said Septimus. 'Converted I see.'

They walked further along the beach and saw a cluster of large rocks ahead, no more habitations were to be seen, and the rising wind added to a sense of isolation.

'Oh dear. it is getting cold,' said Tony as he shivered. 'I hope we find this place soon.'

The coast was by no means straight and they passed the rocks, reaching a sharp bend. As they rounded it there were a series of cliffs. .

'There are a number of caves hereabouts,' said Penny. 'The most famous is called *Waenhuiskrans*, or wagon house cave, because it's supposed to be big enough for a wagon. The place we're approaching is called Arniston, after the wrecked 19th century ship. The cave we're after is reached through crack in the ground. We have several hours of daylight left and I do hope we find it today. Auntie has marked a distinctive rock which is right next to it and I pray it's still there, as I don't want to go asking locals and drawing atensh to our good selves.'

After some more walking they saw what was now the village of Arniston, and a bit further on they came upon a sign saying 'CAVE GROT,' with a large arrow pointing to the sea.

'I assume your aunt's cave isn't this one?' said Tony. If so the treasure will have been taken long ago.'

'What does '*grot*' mean?' said Septimus.

'Cave,' said Tony. No need to look it up. This place is like Wales - everything translated into another language, in this case Afrikaans. The 'G' is pronounced as if you're clearing your throat of phlegm.'

'I'll remember that,' said Septimus. 'You have such good powers of description.'

'No, she wasn't stupid,' said Penny, answering Tony. 'It has a hidden entrance and I do hope no local has discovered it in the last sixty odd years. Have faith. We should take the path to the well known one though, as it's not far from here. And please try not to mention disgusting things, even if they are accurate.'

They trod down the path, the grass flattened by the feet of tourists. Penny stopped about half way, within sight of crashing waves and steps leading to the well known cave.

Penny looked for the rock.

'She said it's big, at least ten foot tall and shaped like a witch's face from a certain angle, so keep your eyes open.'

'That one over there looks likely,' said Tony. 'It looks a bit like one of my parishioners, Mrs. Murgatroyd.'

They hastened to the rock in question, which was some 400 yards away.

'Look for a fissure in the ground,' said Penny.

'It's pretty much overgrown,' said Septimus. 'We're going to find it tricky.'

'Good,' said Penny. That means no one else has been here. It's in a twenty-five yard radius of the rock, so I suggest we split up and have a look. Try to look casual so as not to attract attention.'

They sauntered about, pretending to look at the view, very comical, as they were hopeless at the deception. After quarter of an hour Tony said,

'This is hopeless. It must be the wrong rock.'

Penny, who had stopped looking and was gazing into the distance through her binoculars, said,

'Tony sweetie, you're right. There's another rock I can see which fits the bill. Only this one looks like a whole witch with a full skirt. It's a good quarter of a mile away, right near the edge of the cliff.'

They trekked in the direction pointed out by Penny.

'Good heavens,' said Septimus, 'it's another witch, although a full figured one this time. This place is a veritable coven of the creatures. Well spotted Penny.'

The rock was on the edge of the cliff and a good ten feet high. As they got closer, it became less of a witch and more a gnarled rock, covered with lichen and glistening with the spray from the sea, drops of water running down it in spasmodic rivulets.

They set to once more, combing the ground with their eyes.

There was a cry of pain from Septimus.

'Ouch! I've twisted my ankle in this hole.' He slumped on the ground as the other two ran to help him.

'Oh dear, you poor lamb, I hope you can walk,' said Penny. 'I'm not sure Tony and I could carry a big chap like you all the way back to Aghulas.'

'I'll be all right, Penny, I expect I can hobble back. This damned hole...'

Septimus rolled away from where he'd fallen and Tony helped him up. Penny came over and examined the spot where his foot had caught.

'Let me look at this hole,' she said. 'Mmm...'

She got onto her knees to look at it. 'Hey, I can feel a breeze coming up against my cheek.'

She put her hand into the hole, which was made almost invisible by tufts of grass. It disappeared and she yelled,

'This is it; I can't feel any bottom to it!'

Tony came over and said,

'Let me see,' and looked where Penny had lain down. 'See, there's a line in the grass where it's discoloured.' He ran his hand along the line.

'There's a big gap here and a plank that's rotted.' He sat down on the grass and kicked at the plank.

'I can see light. We may have cracked it.'

'I'm the smallest,' said Penny, and she wriggled through the gap Tony had created and disappeared. After half a minute her head popped up.

'There's a cave down there boys, follow me, Tony. Sept you had better stand on guard, as you won't be able to join us in your state.'

Tony followed Penny. His frame was slim, but he had to draw his breath in as he squeezed his body through the hole.

He was surprised to see how light it was, and he and Penny found themselves on a gentle ledge leading to the floor of the cave, some 30 feet below. The mouth of the cave was small and Tony walked to it to have a look. It was covered with foliage, but he found he could push this aside and an area of sand of a good twenty yards was between him and the point where the waves expired.

Penny had had the gumption to bring a torch.

'Be careful you don't make a hole in that stuff sweetie. I don't want people from outside looking in until we're well clear.'

The roof of the cave was high, about twelve feet, and it extended back well beyond where they'd come down.

'Now for the search,' said Penny. 'We'll have a hard time getting anything large we find back up through that hole, so we'll have to think of how we remove anything.'

'We need to find something first,' said Tony. 'There may be nothing.'

Penny ignored this remark and followed the beam from her torch back into the cave, looking about her as she stepped.

They could hear the roar of the sea and were having to shout to be heard. The seaweed squelched under their feet.

Penny flashed the torch up and down and right and left. The cave began to narrow and soon she was crouching. Tony was frightened that one of them would become stuck, so he hung back, ready to pull Penny out if necessary. Soon she was on her hands and knees. Tony was resigning himself to a fruit-less search when there was a loud squeal. Penny began to move backwards, as the cave where she was too narrow for her to turn around. At last there was room for her to stand up.

'I felt some sacking and there's a clink of metal. Maybe we're onto something.'

'Can you get it out?'

"Not sure. I think we need some rope. Best we come back this evening when it's dark. We need some transport. 'She pointed up and Tony followed her to the surface, where they found Septimus sitting gazing out to sea.

'Find anything?' he said.

'I think so sweetie,' said Penny. 'Only we need to come back with something to carry it in, at night, so we won't be seen. I'm going to mark the spot, so we don't spend hours searching. The rock is easy enough in daylight, but if we leave a glove next to the hole then we should find it.

'Unless some person or dog takes a fancy to it,' said Septimus. 'That white rock will show up in the dark, and I reckon you and Tony can carry it fairly easily.'

The rock weighed a few pounds and was heavy enough to stay where it was without being so heavy that they couldn't move it.

'We'd better get moving. It'll be dark in an hour or two and Sept can't walk fast in his condition,' said Tony.

They trudged back to Agulhas with Septimus doing his best to keep up.

At last they arrived back at the house and were comforted by the sight of the familiar figure in the front window, as by now the dummy had become a symbol of their temporary home.

'I could murder a shower. I'm filthy, so see you boys later. Help yourselves to a gin and tonic, whisky or whatever you want. Soft drinks are in the fridge.'

Septimus made a whisky and soda and Tony found a bottle of Chenin Blanc in the fridge. He laid a towel over his chair, as he too was filthy. Septimus did the same. It was almost dark and they took in the spectacular sunset as they sipped their drinks, silent for once.

A couple of hours later they were refreshed and ready to go, except Septimus, who was lame.

'Is there a road to this place?' said Tony. 'If we're to carry things we may as well put them in the boot. Sept will be no good walking and I presume you can drive?'

'I think so. I can wait in the car,' he said.

They drove for several miles till they came to a sign which said 'Arniston'. Under Penny's direction they parked near another sign, which pointed to the well known cave.

Penny and Tony had each brought sacks.

'Don't use your torch till you have to, 'said Penny. Odd lights are bound to attract attench.'

'All right, but finding that place again in the dark will be very difficult, said Tony.'

'Don't worry sweetie,' said Penny. 'I have an app which is allied to GPS and all we have to do is find the coordinates which I marked this afternoon. We also have the white rock we put down as a marker.'

'Good grief,' said Septimus, 'and there was I worrying about witches' rocks and how on earth we'd get the right one, and you have the answer in your phone. I feel humbled.'

'That's an achievement, that's what celebrities say when they've been awarded an OBE,' said Tony. Let's proceed.'

Tony followed Penny, who kept an eye on the little dot on the screen of her phone, which showed them where they were. At last the massive witch's rock was silhouetted against the moonlight, and the murmur of the waves had become a roar.

'Here's our marker,' she said. 'Let's see if we can feel our way down without putting the torches on. She got down onto her bottom and wriggled out of sight. Tony followed, and the cold sea air struck him as he reached the bottom.

'The light from our torches will be visible to anyone at sea, but we'll have to risk it. I'll go in and hand you whatever's there.'

Soon Penny handed Tony a large metal object, which he placed in a sack, first wrapping it in bubble wrap. It seemed as if they were there for hours, but later checking told them they were only in the cave for twenty minutes.

'You go first sweetie,' said Penny, 'and I'll hand the sack up to you.

Tony did as he was told, and they managed to get it to the surface.

'Any more?' said Tony.

'No, this is enough for now,' said Penny, as she panted to the surface.

She looked round like a wild animal anxious about predators. There was no one to be seen. They trudged back to the car and put the loot in the boot.

Septimus had dozed off, and they had to tap the driver's window to wake him. Septimus started the car and drove back through the village,

'That was quick,' he said. 'I'm dying to see what you've got.'

'I'm not quite sure darling, but it feels interesting, there's a lot more, but I think that what we've got here is enough for the moment,' said Penny.

The lights of their car were on full beam, as traffic from the opposite direction was rare, and Penny had warned Septimus to be careful lest a buck or other wild creature should cross the road. At last the lights of L'Agulhas grew brighter, and they drew up outside the house, the dummy staring at them as it was lit up by the headlights.

'I'll go and open the door and you two bring the sack in as quick as you can. I want to give anyone who may be watching as little time as possible to notice us. Are you OK to carry anything Septimus sweetie?'

'I think I can manage a few yards', said that man.

The two men took the sack out of the boot and into the house in less than half a minute, and were careful to keep it off the ground, to avoid clanking metal.

With the door safely locked, Penny said,

'Keep the sack away from the window. Let's lock it in one of these rooms and look at what we've got in the morning. I'm knackered.'

'I could do with a nightcap after all that,' said Septimus.

'All right, a brandy for each of us. I'm keeping my gun close, as anyone could have seen us, and for all we know may be lurking and waiting to pounce. This may not be Johannes-burg, but it is still South Africa.'

'I'm dying to look inside the sack,' said Septimus.

'Me too,' said Tony.

'Yes, boys yes, I understand but It's better we get some sleep and remain alert. It'll still be there in the morning.

They all went to bed.

Tony awoke and it was dark. He'd suffered from insomnia for many years and was used to these periods of wakefulness. He heard a scraping sound. What do I do? He thought. His inclination was to dismiss it and try to go back to sleep. Prob-ably an animal. But...He got up, clutching the *knobkerrie* he had kept by his bed since arriving. He knew that everyone was vulnerable to burglars and felt the need for a weapon. The sound was coming from the window. He crept towards it, hugging the wall, and waited. He heard the clunk of the window lock as it fell to the floor. The shape of a head appeared against the curtains. Man of God though he was, Tony had the spirit of a warlike priest, and hit hard down on where he thought the head was. There was a groan and he flung back the curtain. An unconscious man was slumped forward, half way through the window. Tony pulled him into the room and yelled 'break-in'. Septimus appeared and switched on the light.

'Tie him up' he said.

'With what?' said Tony.

'My tights will do for a start,' said Penny, who had followed Septimus into the room. 'And stuff your socks into his mouth. He may have accomplices nearby and we want him to keep quiet.'

Soon the intruder was trussed up and blindfolded. Penny, who seemed prepared for anything, produced some chloroform and placed it over his nose.

'There, that'll keep the bastard quiet for a while. Now what to do?'

'If we call the police we need to have our loot out of sight; we don't want to explain ourselves. We should also call the police now, as otherwise they'd wonder why we delayed,' said Septimus, ever aware of legal implications.

'Boys,' said Penny. 'I don't think the presence of the police is going to help us. This brute will never report us. I vote we dump him somewhere miles from anywhere and let him find his own way home.'

'Penny,' said Tony. 'I think that's dangerous. All he needs to do is contact his pals and we're in worse trouble.'

'I don't believe there are any police in Agulhas anyhow. Let's check the Internet on my phone. She pressed buttons on her phone. 'I see, nearest police station Struisbaai. I'll ring it if it makes you happy.'

Penny tapped in the number of the station and waited.

'It's ringing and ringing. Probably a piddly station with one man or something. Let's truss him up good and proper and lock him in a room.'

There was no opposition, and the unconscious man was tied up and left on the floor of an unused bedroom.

They slept for a few hours, but dawn found them all dressed and sipping coffee in the kitchen.

'Have you checked our visitor?' asked Tony. 'We don't want him to come to any harm.'

'He's fine,' said Septimus. 'I checked his bonds and as he was groaning gave him a small whiff of that chloroform. He's a big fellow. At least six feet. You did well to knock him out, Tony. I will never take the mickey out of your large stick again. I wouldn't give much for your chances if you hadn't nailed him. Now can we look at what we've got?'

They dragged the sack into the kitchen, now blazing with sunlight.

The sack contained one large object, which Septimus removed.

'Blimey,' he said.

Glinting arrogantly was a bejewelled object in the shape of a throne. On each side was a peacock, resplendent with rubies and a vast number of pearls. In the middle was another, larger peacock, if anything even more spectacular. The size of the object was not as much as a half metre wide or high.

'Boys, behold a model of the lost throne of the Mogul emperors, stolen by the Persians in the 18th century. I had a hunch it would be here. It's priceless. No wonder they'll kill for it.'

'It's magnificent,' said Septimus. 'It should be in a museum somewhere.'

'Yes it should,' said Penny, but I have doubts we'll get it near one with these villains after it. Just because we have one safely tied up it doesn't mean there aren't more waiting to cut our throats. I've deliberately left the rest of loot behind; the Peacock Throne was all I felt we could cope with for the moment.' said Penny.

'You know,' said Tony. 'I didn't say anything at the time,

but I agree that the safest place for the rest of that stuff is just where we've got it from. Now we've been rumbled we're very vulnerable here. Someone with a gun could just come and take it.'

'True,' said Penny, 'Far too risky. I already have a place to stash this marvellous object. I couldn't resist taking it, in spite of the difficulties it creates. It's in Cape Town. I suggest two of us stay here to report our prisoner to the police and one of us transports the Throne to Cape Town. If we leave one car here, then it'll allay the fears of anyone watching, I hope. We will put it in a suitcase and I'll place it in my boot. My car is much quicker, and you two can deal with everything here, which will mainly be seeing that the police take the burglar into custody.'

Being gentlemen, the pair saw that they were in the more dangerous position, so agreed.

Penny sped off with a squeal of tyres. She had transferred the suitcase through the back door of the garage in which her BMW was kept. She hoped that anyone watching would think she was making a local journey, as the other car remained openly at the front of the house. That would give her a start.

Tony and Septimus gazed at the disappearing car.

'Do you think she's the reincarnation of Napoleon?' said Septimus.

'Sherlock Holmes, but much more attractive,' said Tony. 'I do hope she makes it. Notice she told us no details about where she was taking the loot. Time we had another crack at ringing the *Struisbaai* police.'

The station answered and a Constable du Plooy with his colleague Constable Mtlalana arrived an hour later.

'You say you overpowered this burglar? And put him to sleep? That'll make our job easier. I'd just like to take a statement.'

The statement taking was a turgid business, and the policemen handcuffed the burglar before putting him, partially awake, into a van.

'I hope they'll put off any of his pals for a while. I expect they've cottoned on to the fact that Penny won't be coming back. Her car is conspicuous, even if fast. We might as well go back to Penny's house and await orders,' said Tony.

Meanwhile Penny, wearing a black wig, had visited the branch of the car hire company in Hermanus, returned the BMW and hired a Lexus. She had arranged this some time before, and the whole exercise took five minutes.

A furious member of the AWB, the organisation that carried the torch of the former OB, had taken off after her once he saw the police. He had his contacts in the force and the corrupt policemen who looked for the BMW could not find it.

Penny drove past Somerset West to an address in Bishopscourt, an expensive suburb of Cape Town, where she parked in the garage attached to a large house formerly owned by the CEO of an insurance company. She'd bought it in the name of an offshore Trust before leaving England and the Lexus slid into the cavernous garage after she'd opened the door electronically. Soon the ornate throne was hidden in a safe.

Penny sat back surveying her newly acquired lounge. The previous owner had agreed to leave all his furniture, as he was being transferred to New York, where his employer had provided an apartment in Manhattan.

So this is what it's like to be a rich South African, she thought. It was unlikely she'd be traced to this property soon, as her car swop and head start had, she hoped, thrown off any pursuer. But she was vulnerable, with a king's ransom in the safe. She'd arranged to meet her companions in a hotel in Cape Town, the Grand tomorrow at noon.

Tony drove as Septimus slept. They decided to make for

the main N2 through Bredasdorp. The road was a single carriageway, and there was not much traffic. Tony felt exhausted after the previous few days' adventures, but the landscape and lack of people calmed him down. He hummed 'The Battle Hymn of the Republic' and even began to feel optimistic, as if all troubles were over.

'Do you have to hum that awful tune?' said Septimus, 'I was dozing nicely when it jarred into my consciousness.'

'Sorry Sept, it gets a bit dull driving,' said Tony. 'Or it *was* dull, now I think that *bakkie* is following us.'

'So what do we do?' said Septimus.

'Well, I don't suggest we tear up the road at greater speed. Best we carry on then try to lose them when we get to Cape Town. It's impossible out here in the sticks.'

'As long as they don't do anything violent. Have you still got that gun Penny gave you?'

'Yes, but that's a last resort. I've never used it except for a bit of practice, and I don't believe in killing people.'

The *bakkie* - a type of small lorry much used in South African rural districts - kept a distance of about 300 meters behind.

'Do you think we should turn off somewhere and see if it follows?' said Septimus.

'No, I think that's a bad idea. What if we end up in a little *dorp* with just them and us? Very dangerous. Curiosity is not one of my vices. We'll have to wait and see. Don't panic, as the actress said to the Bishop.'

'He's still there,' said Septimus. 'I don't like it. I've noticed South African drivers usually tailgate you and overtake as soon as they can.'

'We need to keep our nerve,' said Tony. The crucial time will be when we join the N2. If he doesn't overtake us there then we can really be worried. Haven't we got Penny's number in that phone she left us?'

'I feel a bit of a wimp relying on a young woman for help,' said Septimus.

'Don't be ridiculous, she has more spunk and gumption than either of us, but let's wait for the turn off,' said Tony.

At last, the road junction that was the turn off to Cape Town loomed, and they signalled to follow the sign. The *bakkie* signalled too.

'Damn, he's following us. Better ring Penny,' said Septimus.

The first call was abortive and reached the answering message.

'At least text her, Septimus. Calls often don't get through,' said Tony.

Septimus obeyed.

'Think we're being followed, what should we do?'

The reply did not come for ten minutes.

'Where are you?'

'Just past the exit on the N2.'

'Drive on, help is at hand.'

That's a relief,' said Septimus, 'even if a bit brief. '

'Ask for more details,' said Tony, whose face was growing pinker from the effort, 'We need to know friend from foe.'

Yes, that's right,' said Septimus. I'll text her again.'

'How will we recognise the help?'

The reply came,

'Don't worry, you don't need to do anything.'

Septimus read the text out.

'Hmm,' said Tony, 'Penny's concocted a clever plan.'

Soon they saw a sign for road works. A small man with a flag waved them past a GO sign. Just as they passed he turned the sign round to STOP and pushed a barrier across the road.

'Look at that,' said Septimus, 'it's either Penny or your friend the Good Lord.'

'More likely Providence,' said Tony, 'I need to get ahead, as that'll probably only hold him up for a few minutes.'

Another text came through.

'Take the road to Caledon and stop there.'

They drove on and saw no further sign of the *bakkie* as they turned off as the main road went through Caledon.

'Go to the Spa Hotel,' came another text. Tony was able to do this and followed the signs to the hotel. After the dry scrub the sight of palm trees and green lawns took the pair aback.

'Best park out of sight if you can,' said Septimus. 'I'm not sure whether this dodging about is going to put these chaps off, but we should at least make some attempt at hiding.'

The hotel had an overflow car park, and Tony selected a spot behind a palm tree, so that anyone looking for their vehicle would at least have to search.

Another text came through,

'Go to the reception and ask for the manager. Say you were sent by Penny.'

They left their luggage and advanced to the reception. Tony followed the instructions to the letter and they waited in the lobby. They'd hardly sat down before a smiling brown man in a very sharp dark suit appeared.

'Penny's friends,' he said.' Please follow me.'

He led them down a corridor to a door marked 'OFFICE *KANTOOR*'.

Their new friend smiled as he gestured at some chairs next to a desk.

'Sit down gentlemen. I understand you need help.'

'We think we're being followed by some unpleasant men in a white *bakkie*. They may not have seen us come in here, but I expect they'll work it out soon, as this isn't a large town,' said Tony, mopping his wet forehead with his handkerchief. The hot Cape weather did not suit him.

The manager said,

'Let me introduce myself. My name is Ludio Williams, named after my grandfather. I believe Penny's aunt and he went way back. Would you like some tea or coffee?'

They were both parched and elected to have some of the local *rooibos* tea.

As they sipped their beverages, Ludio outlined his plan.

'The simplest way of evading your pursuers is to change cars. We have several guest cars and I'm sure the proprietors will not mind if I lend you one, particularly as you'll be leaving yours here. I'll arrange for a porter to transfer your luggage and as long as they don't actually see you get into it, then you should have a quiet journey to Cape Town.

I wish we had more time to talk. Your friend Penny's *tannie* and my *oupa* got up to some adventures in the war I believe, and she seems to be cut from the same cloth as her *tannie*.'

'So your name is Ludio too?' said Tony. 'We were told some of the story and I read Penny's aunt's diary. Your grandfather was a resourceful man.'

Ludio junior grinned.

'Yes he was. He was like a cat with nine lives. When *inkosikaas* Penny went back to England someone tried to kill him. Luckily his boss John found him and took him to hospital. He had been beaten up and had a fractured skull. He was sick for a long time and it was a year before he recovered fully. '

While this convocation was being held, Viljoen, a passenger in a *bakkie* a few miles away, cursed as he flung a *stompie*, the remnants of a cigarette, out of the *bakkie*'s window.

'Those fokkin *rooineks* have disappeared. We should have ignored that *kaffir* at the road works.'

'Ag, man,' said his companion Jan, we could have been flattened by a bleddie lorry and ended up as *konfyt.* '

Viljoen shrugged his shoulders in resignation. 'What you reckon they'll do?'

'No idea, not sure they even knew we were following.'

''They must have known man,' said Viljoen. You don't just stick behind people for miles and not overtake, or at least I don't.'

Jan, who was the calmer and more philosophical of the two, said,

'They must be well on their way to Cape Town and we'll never catch them. We should just ring Danie and tell him to watch at Houw Hoek.'

Viljoen, who never liked to give up anything, said,

'We could look in Caledon - they might have stopped.'

'Unlikely,' said Jan, 'but we might as well stop there for a coffee. I'm sick of driving already.'

Viljoen nodded.

The *bakkie* turned off the N2.

'Let's go to that spa place, they'll do a good coffee and we can park there,' said Jan.

The front car park was almost full, so they decided to park in the overflow car park. Viljoen shouted, 'Look, there, their car; it's parked next to that palm tree. We've struck lucky!'

'Be careful now Jan, we don't want them to see us. Let's go back round the front and squeeze our *bakkie* into that last space.'

The *bakkie* in place, the two men strolled into the front entrance of the hotel.

Jan addressed the receptionist,

'*Ekskies mevrou, goeie middag.* Is there anywhere we can have a cup of coffee?'

The receptionist replied,

'Of course, *meneer*, the lounge is through there.'

The two men sat down and surveyed the lounge. They had hoped they might espy the fugitive English pair there, but the only other occupants were a noisy family of five.

As the pursuers sipped their coffee, Tony and Septimus, guided by Ludio, unaware of their foes' presence, left the building through a back door, and ignoring the vehicle in which they'd arrived, climbed into a Mercedes station wagon. A porter had already transferred their luggage into it.

As they drove towards the exit, Tony said,

'Look, Sept, I'm sure that's the *bakkie* that was following us.'

'I doubt it,' said Septimus, 'this country is crawling with white *bakkie*s.'

They took the turning signposted 'Cape Town'.

Penny, meanwhile, had been busy. Apart from keeping her friends and herself alive, there was the problem of what to do with the Peacock Throne. She decided to visit an attorney for help.

Mr H was a small man with a fussy manner. He was an expert in maritime law.

Penny had looked him up on line.

After the usual identification formalities had been completed, Penny broached the subject. She told the story without giving away that her aunt and she had already obtained the treasure. She presented the facts as if they were going to search for it.

'I can only give you a general idea, Miss Duchesne. Without beating about the bush, there is the UNESCO 2001 Convention on the Protection of the Underwater Cultural Heritage. Various people need to be consulted in relation to wrecks. You need a licence to search. In essence, it is the practice of Customs to allow up to 50% of the treasure to go to the government and the rest to the finder subject to payment of duty and taxes.'

Penny's face was thoughtful.

'I've heard a lot about corruption. If you were put in charge of negotiations of this sort, would you be able to achieve a deal with people wanting to be bribed?'

'I think so, I know people in government but if the matter were to receive publicity, then the attention would act as a curb on someone's greed. Much like those Anglo Saxon hoards they find sometimes in England. There was court case in 1989 about the gold from the wreck of the Birkenhead. It's not simple.'

After paying the attorney's fees Penny made her way back to Bishopscourt. Her main desire was to get rid of the treasure without getting into any trouble. And not to be murdered. She had read that one could hire a killer in South Africa for as little as £600, and she knew that while she and her 'boys' were in the country they would never be safe. She wanted to do the 'right thing', however. Once the government had the loot it could be displayed in a museum and that would be that. Perhaps there would be a court case involving governments. It made her tired to think of it.

Penny was not a person who thought much of rules and regulations. She wanted rid of the treasure, but dreaded involvement in a long legal wrangle. She had been careful to be vague in her conversation with the lawyer. For all she knew, he might pass on any definite information to who knows whom.

In the meantime, Tony and Septimus had not yet reached Cape Town, and she feared for their safety.

The lawyer sat in his padded seat, thinking about the outrageously attractive woman who had just left. Everything he had told her was correct, but it seemed a pity, if she really had found something valuable, to waste it on the government.

He had contacts in Europe and America who would pay a lot for pieces of history, and who would know...

Penny's mobile phone rang; the number was Tony's.

'We're in Rondebosch, Penny. Where are you?'

'Leave the car, sweetie, and wait in the shopping mall. I'll be there in fifteen minutes. Stand outside the chemist.'

Penny rushed to her car and kept her promise.

'This is a posh pad, Penny,' said Septimus, 'must have set you back a bob or two.'

She said,

'Yes it did. Pour yourselves drinks and make yourselves comfortable. We need to have a Council of War.'

They sat down in the sitting room, which was elegantly furnished in a style that would have been a credit to a glossy magazine.

They recounted their adventures.

'I'm not sure you did the right thing going to that lawyer,' said Septimus. 'I've no doubt the information was correct, but where large sums of money are involved, I'd trust no one.'

'What else was I to do, darling?' said Penny. 'We'd agreed that we needed to be rid of the loot and giving it to the State seems the best way.'

'In theory it is the best idea,' said Septimus. 'But I was deluding myself that it could be done in a civilised way and we'd be shot of the whole affair. This country seems to be alive with people who mean us no good. I read in the local newspaper that you can have someone killed for a few hundred pounds. I think we're still alive only because no one knows where to find us. Who knows you live here, Penny?'

'No one darling, as far as I know. I bought the house in the name of an off shore company, using Jersey lawyers who in turn instructed local ones.'

'Hmm, thank goodness for that. But that only means

they'll have to look for you, and the lawyer you saw might spread the word.'

'Really?' said Penny, 'I thought everything was confidential.'

'It is, but it does depend on the individual. I may be needlessly suspicious, but it's better to be very careful. Money has a way of eroding principles.'

Penny walked over to the French windows.

'The view of Table Mountain is beautiful, but now I don't feel safe,' she said.

'What about this chap Ludio we met in Caledon,' said Tony. 'Can he help?'

Penny sat down on the designer settee, 'Maybe, maybe. I feel a bit stupid. My plan just seems to have put us in even more danger. We're now sitting on stuff even international criminals would be interested in. What was that? I thought I saw movement in the garden.'

23

Judge van Wiese was proud of his CBE 'for public services'. When the Honours List was published he told the reporter from the local newspaper that he was 'surprised and humbled'. Like so many, he had in fact lobbied for it for years.

The Order's ornate cross represented all he had been brought up to hate. It was at once a symbol of achievement and of the Empire which had oppressed his people, killing women and children in the notorious concentration camps during *Die Tweede Vryheid se Oorlog*, known to the British as the Anglo Boer War. His *ouma*'s tales of his childhood still repeated themselves again and again.

The judge gazed at the decoration in his display case, where it rubbed shoulders incongruously with various ornaments, including his grandfather's bandolier, worn throughout the old conflict.

His mind turned to more pressing matters. His agents in South Africa had made a mess of things. The dead woman's niece had made fools of them. They didn't know where she was and they'd even lost her two friends, who seemed to be incompetent amateurs.

He needed someone intelligent and reliable who knew the country. But who? Just then his phone rang,

'Van Wiese.'

'Good morning Your Honour, sorry to disturb your afternoon, it's Petrus van Rensburg. I was wondering if you could refer me to a reliable solicitor. I'm thinking of buying some property over here.'

'I can email you a couple of names,' said the judge. Suddenly inspiration came to him.

'Listen, I wonder if you're available for dinner one evening? I've something I'd like to discuss that might interest you.'

'Sure, I'm available Wednesday or Thursday.'

'Thursday at eight, here. You can stay the night. Ronald is an excellent cook.' The judge smiled as he put down the phone.

RONALD EXCELLED HIMSELF, and van Wiese treated his guest to one of the best French wines in his cellar.

As they chatted of this and that and the hour grew late, van Wiese leaned forward, the candelabra casting a mellow light that reflected on the shiny dome that was the top of his head.

'Your brother was murdered, you know.'

Petrus started. At last he was learning something.

'Do you have details?' he said. 'I know he was involved in the *Ossewabrandwag* and was on some kind of mission when he died.'

'*Ja, ja* he was doing very important work. He was a true patriot. It was while he was doing this work that he was brutally and treacherously murdered.'

The judge's face was grave.

'You know who did it?'

'Yes. It was his *rooinek* girlfriend. Shot him like a dog. Murdering bitch.'

'And what happened to her?'

The judge's voice was bitter.

'She lived very long and prosperously until recently, when justice caught up with her.'

'You mean she died violently too?' said Petrus

'Yes, as the saying goes, "what goes around comes around"'

'I see – she too was murdered?'

Van Wiese pursed his lips.

'Executed,' he said, 'but there's unfinished business. She had a niece.'

'So? Surely she had nothing to do with my brother's death.'

'The niece has prospered. She has also been carrying on activities against the interests of *Die Volk*. I can't reveal what at present.'

'Where do I come into all of this?' said Petrus.

'We need someone intelligent and reliable. The people I have mean well, but I'm beginning to realise they lack intelligence.'

Petrus sat silent for a moment, as the enormity of the proposal sunk in.

'I'm flattered, but I will need to think about it. It is tempting I admit.'

Van Wiese beamed.

'Would tomorrow be too soon? I want you to consider whether you are made of the same stuff as your brother and uncle? Are you committed to your people? Are you squeamish about taking life, for example?'

Petrus was silent. He knew very well he was not going to kill anyone, but could he afford to let this opportunity to gain vital information about his dead brother go? Also, if he gave a negative answer, would his own life be safe?

'In the right circumstances, if the cause is just. But you will forgive me, this is very sudden. I'm no psychopath.'

The judge smiled a wintry smile.

'A fair answer,' he said. 'I'm looking for a rational, balanced person who will think things through. I'm not a psychopath, either.'

So you say, thought Petrus.

The topic terminated as abruptly as it had begun, and switched to rugby, about which both had views.

After a fine English breakfast prepared by Ronald, Petrus departed with a promise to give his answer later in the day.

Sitting on the train to Victoria he reflected that he had no choice. Refuse and he was dead. He'd listened to what was in effect a confession to murder. The judge, in spite of his friendly manner, was a killer who would not risk his blabbing. Accept and he was entering a murky world, but at least he had a good chance of solving the conundrum of his late brother.

He tapped in the judge's number as the train left Clapham Junction.

'*Ek is jou man*,' he said.

'*Baie goed*, ' said the judge. Your instructions will be sent to you by encrypted email. Don't fail.'

24

Darkness comes suddenly in Africa. It was as if someone had said 'Lights out!' and the trio, exhausted, trooped off to separate bedrooms, of which there were six in the large house.

Tony had been hoping he'd become unconscious as soon as his head hit the pillow, but after half an hour of churning thoughts he gave up and stumbled down the stairs to the kitchen. He took a glass from the cupboard and homed in on the bottle of Cape brandy he'd seen in a cabinet in the lounge. It was a bad habit, he knew, but when troubled at the vicarage he'd used his friendly bottle of Calvados as a cure for insomnia. This South African stuff did not have a particularly smooth taste, but it would do.

The precious amber liquid shone in the light of the African curio lamp, and he settled down on a padded chair.

He felt the pleasant burning in his throat and stomach as he reflected on their adventures. Surely all would turn out all right? This burglar-alarmed well-protected house was safe, he trusted. Nevertheless, there was a tinge of anxiety, which needed the anaesthetic of his tincture to suppress. He began to feel quite calm after a few sips had taken effect. He thought of happier times. Perhaps Penny would soften once more towards him.

A banging on the front door jolted him out of his reverie.

Aware of the danger of violent burglars, he grabbed a poker from the fireplace and rushed to the door, peering through the spyglass.

He saw a lone figure and opened the door to a dishevelled female in a nightgown and with a wild expression in her eyes.

'Please, please, you must come, my husband's being attacked, I've pressed the panic button but they're not here yet. He's in there with them.'

Hearing the commotion, Penny and Septimus arrived, Penny toting her little pistol.

Penny said, 'Septimus, please stay here, Tony and I will go with this lady.'

The three of them walked around the front of the property as the burglar alarm belted out its raucous sound. They saw two figures in balaclavas hitting a man next to a large new 4 x 4.

'That's my husband please help him,' shouted the neighbour.

Penny raised her pistol and shot at the balaclava furthest from the husband. He yelled in pain, clutching his leg, and he stumbled off, accompanied by his startled companion. The three ran to the husband who was lying on the ground next to the car.

'Let them go,' said Penny. 'Let's see how your husband is.'

As she said this the husband a plump little man with shock of red hair, staggered to his feet.

'Marjorie, thank God you're safe. Who are these people?' He gestured towards Tony and Penny.

'Our kind neighbours,' said Marjorie. 'I thought you were going to be killed.'

The husband whose name turned out to be Harry, said, 'Thank God you're safe! I was nearly a goner; they were going to take me to an ATM machine and I wouldn't give them my pin number. I was worried that as soon as they knew it, they'd kill me and be off in the car.'

Ten minutes later the security vehicle arrived. By this time everyone was back inside.

Next morning there was a knock on the door of Penny's house. It was the formerly distraught neighbour, now a picture of smartness.

'Harry and I would like to thank you for your help last night. Without it I doubt he'd be alive. Would you and your friends like to come round to dinner this evening, say seven pm?'

Keen though Penny was on anonymity, she felt she would create far more problems by turning down the invitation. Part of camouflage is blending into the surroundings. There was a danger that she'd become known as the mysterious woman who knew how to use a gun.

'I'd be delighted. I will ask my friends, but I'm sure they'll be delighted too.'

The 'boys' were happy to go where Penny went. They were short of smart clothes, but a trip into Claremont shopping centre fixed that.

The front door bell trilled '*Sarie Marais*', familiar to Septimus as the regimental march of the Royal Marines.

The house was lavishly furnished, with African curios being prominent. A pair of Zulu assegais adorned the hall wall, in the manner of a Scottish baronial mansion.

'So glad you could come,' said Marjorie. Harry and I thought you'd find just us a bit dull, so we've invited another guest who's just returned from England, to give you someone else to talk to.'

As she entered the grandly furnished dining room, Penny

did a double take. Walking towards her, smiling, was the man who had shown her round the judge's mansion in Sussex.

'Petrus van Rensburg, glad to meet you,' he said. 'I've just returned from England myself. Haven't we met before?'

'Possibly,' said Penny, thinking on her feet. 'I did some work for the Historic Buildings Commission. Perhaps we met in the course of my work - I visited a number of houses.'

''Yes, yes, that must be it. I was staying with Judge van Wiese in England...'

Phew, thought Penny, but what's he doing here?

The conversation at dinner was lively. Septimus loved food and drink and could talk for England. Tony, unaware of the undercurrents, was his polite, restrained, vicarly self. Petrus was apparently a cousin of Marjorie's.

As luck would have it, he was seated next to Penny.

'Didn't we meet again, at the Savoy?' he said.

Aw shucks, thought Penny. He's on to me. 'Yes, I believe we did,' she said.

As the conversation meandered over this and that - the local drought, crime, including car hijacking, how terrible the government was - Penny felt herself warming to Petrus. He began to talk about the Afrikaner, his past and future. Penny was surprised to learn that he was glad his people's dominance had ended.

But could she trust him? She decided to probe.

'Your friend the judge, or is he your relative? Have you known him long?' she said.

Petrus found he liked Penny. He found it difficult to regard her as an enemy. He had no intention of revealing his homicidal instructions, which he'd never intended to carry out. However, it was necessary to play along.

'I don't know him well at all. In fact I'd only met him a week before we met.'

Penny dived straight in.

Are you what they call a *verligte* or a *verkrampte*?' she said. Loosely translated these words meant 'enlightened' or 'bigoted'.

Petrus laughed at Penny's boldness.

'Definitely a *verligte*, although I admit I've been moving in conservative circles recently.'

Penny grew confiding.

'My aunt was here during the War, you know, involved in some sort of hush-hush work.'

If Petrus had antennae, they would have vibrated. This was the sort of thing he desperately wanted to know and he had to admit, he found his auburn haired neighbour extremely attractive.

'Oh, really? Please tell me more.'

Penny paused, trying to gauge whether this seemingly pleasant and straightforward man was reeling her in. Should she reveal any more to this stranger? He was after all, associated with the dubious judge. Perhaps he knew it all already. She decided on limited disclosure.

'Auntie was, if not a Mata Hari, at least a code breaker of some sort. As with everybody, there's a human side. She fell in love with an Afrikaans chap.'

Petrus could barely restrain himself.

'And...' he said, leaning towards Penny. Lovely brown eyes, she thought.

'There was an accident of some sort, he died.'

'Accident, what sort of accident?' said Petrus.

'She was being pursued by some disreputable characters. She told me she thought he came to warn her and mistaking him for one of them in the dark, she shot him. She was heartbroken.'

'Heartbroken? Do you know the name of the man she shot?'

'Oh, Jan or Jannie van something. It's in a note she left in her bank which I found, but I can't remember the full name.'

'It wasn't van Rensburg, by any chance?' he said

'Could well have been,' said Penny

'She made vague allusions to it one evening when she'd had too much gin, but next morning told me she had been talking nonsense. It was the note that explained it all.

Now she's dead, and the events being so long ago, I don't suppose it matters much any more.'

'But it does matter,' he said. Some might have thought she killed this man intentionally.'

'I doubt that,' said Penny. 'She was no psychopath and her job was just code breaking. Also, she was very fond of him and as far as I know he hadn't done her wrong, as they say. I'm sure it was an accident as her note says. As they used to say, 'There is a war on' and I expect she feared for her life.'

'That may be,' he said. 'Well, it's been an interesting chat. Do you realise we're the only two left at the table? Perhaps we can meet again, soon. I do have to go now, but here's my card.'

He looked as if he was about to say more, but then stopped himself.

'I'll just thank Marjorie for the dinner, then I really must go.'

Penny found her acolytes in the lounge. Both were sampling some local wine with gusto, and Septimus was in the middle of a long story about his legal exploits, something to do with a vicar who'd robbed a bank. They stayed for another half an hour then made their way back to Penny's house, being careful to go through the elaborate rigmarole required by her burglar alarm system.

'You were getting friendly with that Afrikaans chap.' said Tony. 'Did he have anything interesting to say?'

''I do believe you're jealous, Tony,' said Septimus. 'If you weren't, I certainly was.'

'Now, now boys, enough of that, we're trying to stay alive and that man may well be a useful ally. He's an acquaintance of that nasty judge and I'm beginning to make sense of all the attention we've been getting in the past few months. I might also find who murdered my lovely aunt Theresa,' said Penny.

'So, what are we going to do?' said Tony. Penny leant over and squeezed his hand.

'Don't worry darling, I have the glimmerings of a plan. That chap has given me his card, so I'll be able to look him up and if necessary have it out with him.' After a stiff nightcap they went to bed.

As he relaxed in the lounge of the Netherlands Club, Petrus mulled over his conversation with Penny. It was a long time since he had met such an attractive woman. However, he put such thoughts to one side and considered what she'd said about her aunt and her lover, whom he was sure was his late brother. The story about his killing being an accident was very plausible. If the woman Theresa had meant to kill him, then she would hardly have lied about it to her niece. He had to continue the charade of cooperation with the judge. But his sympathy was now veering towards Penny, who had impressed him with her sincerity. He texted van Wiese, 'Found her. She has information, suggest I find out more.' The reply came, 'Gain her confidence and report.' Petrus had been hoping for such a response. He wanted to retain the trust of van Wiese, and also to satisfy his own curiosity.

25

'You seem very taken with that Afrikaans chap, Penny,' said Tony, as he sipped coffee in the sunny garden the following morning. 'He is rather a handsome specimen, isn't he?'

'Yes I was Tony,' said Penny, 'but no need to be jealous. As I said last night it was all in the cause of finding out more. He's turning up too often for it to be a coincidence. If he is an agent of the forces of darkness, then my careful cover is blown.'

'So what are we going to do?' said Septimus, who had walked over just as Penny had uttered her sentence of disquiet.

'Stay alive,' said Penny, 'Quite how I'm not sure. If the charming Petrus is in league with our enemies then something is going to happen pretty soon. The choice is whether to sit tight or to scarper. If we sit tight we have to be very careful. If we scarper then it's back to Blighty, but the problem will follow us.'

'I think we ought to see this through here,' said Tony.

'The good lord has looked after us hitherto and I have faith in him. He and our wits are all we've got, I reckon, Penny, and I'm relying on your brains to see a way through this.'

Penny made a face. 'I agree with you Tony, although I admit I am not the least bit religious. A plan is forming, as I told you last night. Petrus gave me his card. He's staying at the Dutch club, as Auntie used to call it. I'm going to suggest meeting him there.'

'Just you?' said Tony.

'Yes, I don't see why I should endanger you two, and you would definitely cramp my style.'

Petrus read the message from Penny with a slight frisson. So, his prey was walking straight into the web. Having met her three times, he was still not sure how he felt. She was a woman in a thousand and he was very drawn to her. Perhaps his late brother had felt the same way about her aunt. Although he had pretended to agree to van Wiese's proposition, he was a humane man, whereas he knew van Wiese was entirely different, a committed fanatic with a veneer of civilisation. A very convincing one too. Petrus was driven by curiosity rather than greed or revenge, which he could see were van Wiese's motives. Having met Penny he found it difficult to believe that her aunt had been a murderer, although in wartime the normal inherent reluctance to commit homicide was suspended in many. Perhaps he would find out more if he delved deeper. Their appointment was for lunch, and his reaction to seeing Penny walking up the grand staircase to the club dining room was to swallow a few times. Her bare shoulders were lightly tanned, and that combined with the richness of her auburn hair and eyes as green as any emerald were enough to make him want to... He put such thoughts aside as he shook her by the hand. He was no cheek kisser, particularly on slight acquaintance, regarding it as unduly familiar and a bit common. What a snob I am, he often thought. They sat the window overlooking the crowded street, and he opened the game:

'I had been hoping you'd call,' he said.

'Really?' said Penny.' I thought you might find it tiresome. We've met twice before, but in very different circumstances.'

'Three times I think,' he said. 'I'll cut to the chase. What are you really after? That visit to the judge's house - at the time I thought little of it, but now I feel there must be more. And you're staying in a fabulous house in Bishopscourt. And who on earth are your companions? There's something *baie snaaks* about the whole thing.'

Penny smiled. 'Yes, I suppose so, let's be honest, talking of "*snaaks*", van Wiese is a man of many layers. How well do you really know him?' Behind that façade lurks a man who I would have thought would hate the English, with good reason, yet he has a CBE and has acted as a judge in their legal system. He even has a pretty good imitation of an upper class English accent, one so affected by many at the English Bar. And what is your tie-up with him? If my pals and I are odd, what are you?'

'Touché. Suppose we're both frank with each other?' said Petrus.

Penny thought, now we're getting somewhere, I hope.

'Good idea.' she said, 'I think van Wiese is tied up with some very nasty people and may well be responsible for my aunt's death.'

Petrus was taken aback.' Really, I don't think...'

Penny broke in.

'Come on, don't play dumb. I wouldn't say this to you if I didn't think you're one of the good guys. I admit I have investigated your background and you're clean. The only thing you have in common with van Wiese is that you're an Afrikaner.

Otherwise I'm prepared to stake my life on your basic decency.'

Petrus blushed.

'Thank you, Penny. I'm relieved, you're right. I'm not a criminal. I guess you may be right about van Wiese.'

''So why are you in Cape Town and what's your interest in me?' Penny's green eyes seem to penetrate Petrus's mind in a quite unnerving way as he took this in. He was dealing with a formidable woman. He found that, in spite of his instructions, he had warmed to her.

'Penny, I'm trying to find out about my brother, former lover of your aunt, it seems, the one who was killed in the war. I'm sure van Wiese holds the key. I've played along with him just to find out more. He's dangerous. He's ordered me to kill you.'

'Ha,' said Penny, not perturbed. 'I thought it might be something like that. Well, I'm here. You know where I live. Hitmen are very cheap in this country. Have you hired one yet?'

She sat back in her chair and picked at the roll on her side plate.

'No of course not. I'm just not that sort of person at all. I think we should be allies.'

'An interesting idea:' said Penny. 'Dangerous for you though, wouldn't it be?' Petrus shrugged his shoulders.

'I was stupid enough to let my curiosity get the better of me. I think I'm a target whichever side I'm on. Van Wiese is a ruthless man.'

'True. How do you feel about meeting Tony and Septimus? They're involved because they know me. Good people and resourceful, in spite of their Woosterish ways.' she said.

Petrus replied,

'They're very English, aren't they? Well I'm on board.

Your presence here has no doubt been noted. I'll report I've made contact and am luring you into my trap.'

'I do hope you're not,' said Penny.' We are going to have to trust each other. By the way, I think I may be able to solve the problem you have with your brother's death, but that can wait for the moment.'

By this time, eating in the pauses in their conversation, they reached coffee. Petrus paid the bill. They exchanged WhatsApp identification and Penny left. She felt better. Petrus was attractive, but that was not important. In her relatively short life she had learned to judge people. She was not always right, but there was nothing inherently dubious about him. He'd been quite honest about his instructions to kill her, and she understood that he would have needed to pretend to accept van Wiese's orders, or he'd put his own life in danger.

What she'd said about cheap hitmen was quite true. The local university had even published a thesis on the subject. She felt safer knowing that Petrus had been entrusted with the task of eliminating her. Presumably that would mean others would not be doing the same, at least not for the moment. She drove her hired Lexus along de Waal Drive, which was flanked by the sprawl of the city and its multifarious housing and docks on the one side and the slopes of the mountain known as Devils Peak on the other. The wonder of Africa was there, alongside the other European part. The wildebeest and zebra grazed the mountain grass in desultory fashion, with white tick-birds standing on their backs looking for delicious insects. They do not care what humans do, she thought, and are oblivious to our elimination of their main predators over a hundred years ago. Lions had long ago been driven a thousand miles away now 'harvested' by ludicrous 'hunters' for money. Leopards had abandoned this mountain range for others and evolved, in this part of the country, into creatures half their former size.

Baboons had survived, tolerated mainly by the inhabitants, with outbursts of slaughter by a few who put money above nature. What unpleasant beings some of us are, she reflected. Thinking of unpleasant beings, her thoughts turned to van Wiese. He would not play the gentleman and give up. She, Tony and Septimus, and even their new ally were in danger.

26

V an Wiese retired from the Bench at 65. He was bored with the procession of criminals, tired of the same old speeches from Counsel, not quite so tired of being bowed and scraped to, but fed up with the panoply of justice. Besides, he had more interesting and important things to think about. Like revenge, money and he longed for home. I'm sick of cold winters and wet summers, he thought. His newly hired agent, the man van Rensburg, seemed no more successful than the thugs he'd hired previously. The woman Duchesne was still alive. Van Rensburg had even met her, for goodness sake. Time to take a personal hand. The house in Sussex had become a burden. At one time it had made him feel grand and important. For a while he had loved being part of the British Establishment. He'd entertained the former Prime Minister once. What a vain man he'd been.

Petrus met van Wiese at Cape Town Airport, and they drove in a large Mercedes limousine to an expensive hotel on the Waterfront.

'Why is the woman still alive? You're taking your time

about it. I could get the job done very cheaply. I chose you because I thought you were intelligent,' said van Wiese.

'Not for long, *Meneer* van Wiese. She is a British tourist and you will remember the fuss there was about the last one who was killed in this city,' said Petrus.

Van Wiese sighed, 'Yes you're right; it has to be an accident. Perhaps you can persuade her to go cage diving or bungee jumping?'

Petrus laughed.

'A motor accident would be easier. The signs are that she is a very cautious person. Also, she has two male friends with her. They all have to be dealt with.' As he was dropped off at the hotel van Wiese said,

'Tomorrow at noon, here.'

Petrus sat in the taxi, ruminating over the problem. It was going to be extremely difficult to avoid carrying out van Wiese's instructions. The man was determined to have his way. He had to think. Perhaps Penny would have a solution. She seemed a resourceful person.

That afternoon Van Wiese was surprised to receive a message that a Miss Duchesne wished to see him. They met in the lounge of his hotel, with a fine view of Table Bay, seagulls wheeling their way about the blue sky, making their distinctive cries, so loud they were audible inside the building.

'What can I do for you, Miss Duchesne,' said the former judge. 'I have agreed to meet you because, although we've never met, I'm always ready to talk to people. But first I want to know how you knew I was here.'

'It's easy,' said Penny, 'blame the Cape Times. In a backwater like this the visit of a South African boy done good in the English legal system is news - there is a short item on the front page announcing your arrival and saying how distinguished you are. It says you have recently retired and then goes on to say how well you did at one of the local schools and how many prizes you won at the local university. You're a marked man I'm afraid, Your Honour, or should I say plain 'Mr' as you've retired? As a devoted fan it was easy to persuade the reporter to tell me where you are staying. I told him I'm writing a book about South Africans who have distinguished themselves in the big wide world. Of course, you don't know me at all, at least face to face. I understand that you may have heard of my aunt, Miss Theresa Duchesne.'

'Ah yes, indeed I have,' said van Wiese. 'She was a murderer and an enemy of my people.' He glared at her as he spoke these words in his anglicised accent.

'That's harsh. I think you are quite wrong. My auntie wouldn't harm a fly. I think perhaps you have been misinformed,' said Penny.

'No, she shot a patriot, a van Rensburg, with whom she was having a relationship. It was cold blooded. She also caused a great deal of trouble to other patriots and stole what was rightfully theirs. If it had not been for her, some good men might not have died. I refer to the crew of a U-boat which was betrayed and sunk off our coast.'

The ex-Judge's voice trembled with suppressed anger. Boy, thought Penny, this chap's really got it bad.

'I know nothing about that, but she was a patriot herself, fighting for a just cause, you know. The one thing I'm dead certain of is that she was no murderer,' said Penny.

'Why have you come to see me?' said van Wiese.

'I know you have a grievance against me and I was hoping to resolve it in a reasonable way.'

'Grievance? I have no grievance. You are nothing to me. If, however, you have knowledge of the treasure stolen by your aunt and can deliver it back to its rightful owners, maybe we have something to talk about.'

'I do know something about certain items you want. But if you wish to find out more, I advise you to call off the weirdos who have been following me and friends of mine. For all I know, you had my aunt killed.' Penny spoke in a low but determined voice.

Van Wiese sat silent for a few minutes, then said, 'I'll think about it. How may I contact you?'

Penny handed him a card, got up and left. As she walked away, van Wiese gazed intensely after her. The thought of obtaining the lost treasure had whetted his appetite and his plans for elimination of Penny would have to wait.

At noon Petrus appeared. The meeting lasted five minutes. He was instructed to do nothing until he heard further. He was relieved the meeting was so short. He had been worried that his change of sympathy might be spotted. When he returned to his hotel he found a note from Penny.

'The boys want to meet you again. Suggest you take a train to Newlands. Leave a message at your hotel that you've gone to see your friends in Bishopscourt.'

Petrus wondered whether he'd been followed. He decided this was unlikely. Van Wiese, he hoped, knew nothing of his meetings with Penny and had no reason to suspect him of disloyalty

The four sat in the large lounge with a view of the back of Table Mountain, shimmering blue in the morning sun. Septimus opened the serious part of the proceedings,

'Penny tells us that you have been delegated to kill her, but she has persuaded to think you to think better of it.'

'That's true,' said Petrus, 'although I have never seriously had any intention doing any such thing. My motive has always been to find out about my brother who was killed in the war.'

Tony, who had been staring at Petrus, trying to assess him, spoke up,

'I have made a copy of Penny's aunt's diary. There is a fair

bit about your brother, something of a Lothario if I may
say so.'

'Do you mind if I read it?' said Petrus.

'Not at all,' said Penny,' I have a study you can use. Then
we needn't disturb you.' Penny showed him into a large
opulent room with a yellowwood desk. 'Help yourself,' she
said.

While Petrus was out of the room, they discussed him.

'Taking a bit of a risk don't you think, Penny?' said Tony.

'Yes,' she said,' but we have to find some way out of this
mess, so I'm surmising he's possibly a powerful ally, if we can
convince him of our bona fides. I've met a lot of chaps in my
time, and I think he's a good 'un.'

'Does he know about the treasure?' said Septimus.

'Not from me. Safer not to tell him. That grizzly old van
Wiese won't allow us to be killed while we're the only link to
the moolah, so it's vital to keep its whereabouts secret and
indeed, what it consists of.'

'There's nothing to stop their kidnapping and torturing
one of us,' said Tony.

'Sweetie, I don't think van W is likely to want his name
linked with anything that could become complicated and
sully his "good name". Now I've met him, I think he's evil but
a terrible snob. I'm sure he was playing a part in England and
part of him wants to continue with it.'

'Do you really consider our new friend is an asset?' said
Tony.

'Not sure, but better for us than against us. I'm hoping
auntie's diary is going to win him over.'

The sound of a closing door warned them that Petrus was
on his way.

'I've read it,' he said.

'What we need to know,' said Penny, 'is whether you're for
us or against us. I've met van Wiese and he is seriously bad.

The only reason I'm alive is that I know the whereabouts of something he wants.'

'And you're not telling me,' said Petrus.

'Not yet anyway, safer for you not to know, except that I really do have knowledge of something he wants badly,' said Penny. 'Do you think you were followed here?'

'Unlikely, van Wiese has no reason to distrust me.'

'How do you feel about the fact that my aunt says that she was ordered to kill your brother?'

'That's a difficult one, Penny. I'm reassured to some extent by the fact that she says in her diary the idea was anathema to her. Unfortunately, the diary stops and we don't know what she was thinking when the death happened. In any event van Wiese has put the plan to kill you on hold for the moment. I'm not sure why,' said Petrus.

'I might as well tell you. I went to see van Wiese yesterday and made clear that I knew what he was up to and the where-abouts of something that he wants, almost above everything.' Penny stared at Petrus to gauge his reaction. She was begin-ning to trust him and felt that he was beginning to trust her, but she sensed that the relationship was still very edgy. She wasn't sure how he would react.

'Penny, I am an average kind of guy and not a crook or fanatic. After meeting you and these two gentlemen I have more confidence in your veracity than I have ever had in the retired judge. There is something very sinister about him and the way he looks at one is pretty chilling. In my job as a lawyer I've met a lot of strange people and also a lot of decent ones. You, Tony and Septimus appear to be amongst those I'd call decent, so I'm going to back my judgement, and you may be sure I'm with you in this enterprise.'

'That's a relief,' said Penny. 'Now we have to plan how we are going to get ourselves out of the clutches of the afore-mentioned dishonourable judge. I don't want to give him the information he desires so badly. Yet I'm very much afraid for the safety of all four of us, because he will not stop until he succeeds.'

'I hope somebody gets a bright idea soon,' said Septimus, 'this chap is a persistent devil and he has the advantage having very few moral scruples. We, in contrast, are upright citizens - although we might bend the rules, we stop short of homicide.'

'Well put,' said Penny. I must admit to being stumped, presently. Petrus, do you have any ideas on how we can extricate ourselves from this dilemma?'

'Not a clue I'm afraid, Penny. I was rather hoping that, being a resourceful person, you would come up with something. At the moment our lives are precarious and I, personally, am a cat curiosity is likely to kill.'

'Does anyone know anybody in authority who might help us?' piped up Tony, who had been singularly silent hitherto.

'You must have contacts in the church here, sweetie,' said Penny. 'You clergy are like members of a mafia or at least a strong Old Boys Association or freemasons or something like that.'

'There is some truth in that" said Tony, 'but our story sounds so preposterous that I hesitate to approach any person in holy office with it. For a start, they'd ask how I got involved and why am I not in my parish doing good works and broadcasting improving sermons.'

'I can see that debating the matter is going to get us nowhere,' said Penny, sighing. 'I'm going to have to continue with my plan and just tell you what to do. I have some ideas and I trust they will bear fruit. In the words of that ghastly quiz show, I will "phone a friend."'

27

Van Wiese's phone rang,
'Call for you sir, a Miss Duchesne.'

'I'll take it thank you. Yes, Miss Duchesne, what can I do for you?' he said.

'Morning judge, I think I can do something for *you*. I'm prepared to give you what you want, on condition.'

'Condition? What condition? I don't think you're in a position to bargain' he said.

'Really?' said Penny. 'I think, in fact I know, I am.'

'Be in the lobby of this hotel at 3 pm this afternoon, he said.

'Very well,' said Penny. 'I'll be there.'

At 3 pm precisely Penny entered the hotel. She was dressed immaculately as usual, even if low-key. Even so, she drew admiring glances as she sat down in the lobby and waited for van Wiese, who took his time and was fifteen minutes late. Penny had expected this, as she knew he was an arrogant man with an inflated idea of his own masculine importance.

She had counted on his being rattled. She had had only a few hours to put her plans in place. She had not yet explained what she proposed to Tony and Septimus. They were apprehensive but they trusted her and her abilities. In her smart but modest attire she was not going to appear as anything but a person who had business to conduct. Van Wiese would be impervious to feminine wiles and besides, she didn't have any inclination to use them on such an odious man. The more she thought about him the more repellent he became.

'Well, Miss Duchesne, I hope you're here to give me what I want?' said the ex-judge.

'I hope so, Mr van Wiese, but there must be safeguards. It may help if I explain myself. What you want I regard as a problem to be disposed of. The value is nothing to me. I have quite sufficient for my needs and would prefer it if it all went to a museum or something. However, I appreciate that's probably the last thing you want. I expect you have schemes to finance. I don't want to know what they are. What I want is a guarantee of personal safety for me and my companions.'

'I see,' he said. 'I don't suppose we are far apart. I get what I want and your life and those of the others, in whom I have no interest, are safe.'

'How do I know I can trust you?' said Penny, who felt she was playing some ghastly game.

'You'll have to. I'm a man of proven integrity. A man in my position does not renege on deals.'

And the rest, thought Penny.

'I'm prepared to conduct you to where it all is. I suppose you know more or less what's there? I suggest you follow me and my companions and I'll show you.'

' So, you won't tell me now?' said the judge.

'No, I want this thing finished and to know it's finished,' she said.

'What are the arrangements - I presume you have something planned?'

'You're to come with us, alone and, as they say in the black-and-white films, "No funny business".'

'I might be putting myself in danger,' said the judge. 'How do I know I might not meet with a nasty accident?'

'That applies to both of us,' said Penny. 'I would've thought, based on previous experience, the risk is on my side. You have some dubious friends, for one so outwardly respectable.'

The judge grunted.

'How do we travel? I presume we have to travel somewhere?'

'I'm sure you know we're going to Cape Agulhas. Your heavies were all over us. I suggest we meet outside the lighthouse. We can keep in touch on cell phones. A week hence would be good, Thursday at noon.'

'I'll be there,' said van Wiese. His bland face was expressionless. It occurred to Penny that, with his rotund figure, he looked like a mobile egg. Penny left, taking a taxi to the railway station. From there she alighted at the next small station, Woodstock, and lost herself in the crowds of people. She had arranged to meet Tony and Septimus. A blue Toyota stopped at a pre-arranged set of traffic lights, 'robots' as they're called in South Africa. She jumped in. 'Thanks sweeties,' she said. 'I have no idea whether I'm being followed, but make for the de Waal Drive and we'll be able to see. Here let me set this satnav.'

After another hour of roundabout driving they arrived back at Bishopscourt. There was a message on the answering machine from Petrus. All he said was, 'I'll be at your place at seven.' He arrived at the appointed time.

'You look flustered, darling,' said Penny.

Petrus's face showed no reaction to the promotion to 'darling', He wanted to smile, but repressed the impulse as he was handed a gin and tonic.

'It looks like I'm riding shotgun,' he said. 'My boss wants me to go to Cape Agulhas, though not with him. I'm expected to get rid of you for him, once he's found what he wants, I reckon.'

'Hmm, not unexpected,' said Penny. 'Van Wiese is hardly the man to allow his enemies to stay alive. When and where?'

' Apart from the general area I don't know. He's waiting to see what you do. He really hates you by the way. Refers to you as "that whore"'

'Nice,' said Penny.

Tony spoke up. 'Really this man is an unpleasant character, to think he was sitting as a judge in our English courts! What a hypocrite, I remember those pompous remarks he made about that poor churchman we saw being sentenced by him.'

'Yes I know, Tony sweetie, but surely you realize the world is full of whited sepulchres? What about the vicar in Plymouth who robbed a bank Septimus was telling us about?'

Petrus sat bemused at this exchange. As a well brought up Afrikaner, he was quite shocked at van Wiese's turpitude, but, more worldly than Tony, he accepted it as a fact.

Penny took charge.

'Thanks for keeping us informed. I suggest you get in touch by cell phone. Although keep it to WhatsApp messages, as they're encrypted. You do realise that if van Wiese cottons onto your well-intentioned duplicity, your life won't be worth a cent of South African currency?'

'I know, Penny, but I don't see I have a choice. I'd better leave now. The less I'm seen about here the better, although I could always say I was visiting your neighbours, who are after all old friends of mine.'

With that Penny showed their new friend to the door.

'Well, Penny, it looks as if we're approaching some sort of climax to this business,' said Septimus. 'I must admit that six months ago all I was looking forward to was growing roses in Sussex and making a nuisance of myself at the local parish council meetings.'

'I'm sorry Septimus, sweetie. I hope I haven't ruined your life. I'm a dangerous person to know.'

Tony, who was listening from his perch on an antique African chair, tutted.

'What is so amusing, oh holy one?' said Penny.

'Every time I get involved with you we end up in some sort of jam. Septimus may seem to be whingeing, but he'd far rather be here where the action is, than pottering around some dull garden and exchanging platitudes with equally dull people at parish council meetings and similar malarkey.

"He hasn't said a word about his Morris dancing friend, I notice,' said Tony.

Penny sighed. 'Well boys it's back to the southern tip of Africa for us, unless either or both of you would rather stay here or beetle off to Blighty, as things have become rather hot.'

Simultaneously the two men said,

'We're staying.'

"You mean joining the fun, I take it,' said Penny.

'What are our orders, boss?' said Tony.

'We'd all better be armed. I hope there'll be no need for violence, but with people like van Wiese and his assortment of thugs, be prepared. I'm due to meet him on Thursday 15th at noon at the entrance to the Lighthouse. I shall be there on my own. You two, I suggest, drive separately to Arniston and keep your eyes open. That's all I can tell you at the moment because that's all I know.'

' Don't you have some sort of scheme?' said Septimus' '

'Perhaps,' said Penny. 'Now we only have a short time to get ready, and there are things I need to do. You two just hang about here.' With that she left the room. They heard the front door close and the sound of a car starting up and its sound receded.

28

It was unusually cold and windy as they drove towards Cape Agulhas in two cars. The uncharacteristic greyness affected their mood.

'I don't feel good about this,' said Septimus, as he cruised past miles of fynbos, seeing only Penny's 4x4 ahead and the occasional car coming in the opposite direction.

'The Lord will provide,' said Tony. 'Penny is a capable girl and she's bound to know what she's doing.'

'Wish she'd shared it with us,' said Septimus. 'All we know is that we need to hang about Arniston ready to be useful. I'd far rather she'd let us in on the detail of her plans, presuming she has some.'

'She will have, Sept. The turn off is about a mile ahead. That's where we lose her.'

As Penny disappeared towards Cape Agulhas she flashed them twice and they took a left turning, which promised to join the R316 to Arniston.

'I feel very alone, now she's gone,' said Tony.

'Cheer up Tone, you've still got me,' said Septimus.

'Yes,' said Tony, 'but you're a bit like me, a novice in this business. I've taken careful note of where we're going. It's nearly eleven. Penny says she is meeting the dreaded Judge Jeffreys at noon.

'Van Wiese,' said Septimus. 'Oh, I see, you were joking.'

'Yes, I do sometimes,' said Tony, 'lightens the mood. Now Penny's given us very precise instructions. We are to park in the town and walk over to where the cave is. I hope we can find it.'

Upon arriving they walked in the direction indicated by Tony's phone, in which he had entered the coordinates supplied by Penny. 'What do you suppose she has in mind?' said Tony.

'I expect something pretty clever. She's such a resourceful girl. You're in love with her, aren't you?' said Septimus. Tony's face went even redder than usual.

'I've asked myself that question occasionally, but have always shied away from the answer. She's so attractive and intelligent. I've often wondered why she has the slightest interest in me. Anyhow, romance between us certainly isn't blossoming at the moment. She's been treating me like an old pal, a sort of faithful but not very bright dog.'

'Yes, I suppose that's how she treats both of us,' said Septimus. 'She's pretty and alluring, all the same, even if something of a will-o'-the-wisp.'

'What's that Sept?' said Tony.' There's a chap over there walking towards our goal. He's still quite far away but even at this distance he has a thuggy sort of look.'

'I see him, hefty like the rugby players you see on TV. We'd better be careful to maintain a jaunty, innocent air, as if out for an afternoon stroll,' said Septimus.

'Is your gun loaded?'

'Yes,' said Tony, but the safety catch is on. 'You?'

'Roger,' said Septimus. 'You may remember I was in the Territorials? We practised with these things every weekend. I still go regularly to the local shooting range. We're no longer allowed pistols, but I reckon I can still do it. It's you I'm worried about; you're as likely to shoot your foot or me as any villain. I suggest you keep your pistol where it is.'

'Indeed, Sept, it's more of a comfort than anything. That chap is still marching towards our goal.'

The two men found their routes converging with the stranger and stopped, pretending to examine wild flowers, of which there were many. Soon he disappeared from view.

'We could be walking into a very dangerous sitch, as Penny would say,' said Tony.

'I know,' said Septimus. 'I suggest we proceed very cautiously and try to be as invisible as the terrain will allow.'

Luckily they came across a number of large rocks and tried to keep behind them as much as possible.

'Do you remember where we found the cave entrance?' said Septimus. 'I've a feeling it's very near.'

'I have coordinates remember,' said Tony. 'We're getting close. Don't think we've been spotted.'

Van Wiese's man watched the two dodging through the rocks. He muttered into his cell phone:

'Two men acting suspiciously, Petrus. I saw them earlier. What shall I do?'

'Just keep an eye on them,' said Petrus, who found himself van Wiese's second-in-command of this operation.

'We have things under control. I expect they're just tourists.'

'Okay,' said the man, 'but I'll keep my eyes on them. They're behaving very strangely.' Petrus sighed. It must be Tony and Septimus.

Van Wiese had told him to keep out of sight near the Lighthouse and he'd seen Penny arrive and walk off with van Wiese. His instructions were to follow Penny until van Wiese called for him. He trudged after the pair and, as mile succeeded mile, he wondered whether Penny was leading van Wiese to nowhere in particular. He was worried about the thug who was watching Tony and Septimus, although he was nominally in charge of him. Perhaps the ex-judge was playing a double game, and he would be killed along with Penny.

Penny arrived at the Lighthouse on the dot of twelve o'clock. Within a minute Van Wiese, who came out of the lighthouse door, joined her.

'I'm glad to see you value time,' he said.

'Let's get on with it,' said Penny. 'You'll need to follow me along the sea shore.'

'Very well,' said van Wiese. 'I trust you'll keep your word.'

Penny didn't grace this barb with an answer, and began walking in the direction of Arniston in silence. The portly Van Wiese's years of sitting in courtrooms and drinking only the best wines and gourmet meals began to tell after a mile.

'How much further?' he asked.

'A mile or two, and no more,' said Penny. 'Of course if you can't make it ...'

'I can make it,' said van Wiese, his face red with unaccustomed effort.

After a further hour of walking Penny said,

'We're nearly there. I'll show you where it is. No doubt you'll be able to make arrangements to collect it later.'

'Humph,' said van Wiese.' I warn you young lady, if this is a farce you'll pay for it.' Penny look round with contempt.

'I really wouldn't bother, van Wiese, my time is precious. Ah, here we are.'

They had reached the mouth of the cave. The tide was out and to the casual observer there was nothing to see but seaweed hanging down in multiple blue-green fronds.

'You expect me to go in there?' said van Wiese.

'That's where it is, whether you go in or not is up to you.'

'Very well, I'll have to accept what you say. You go first.'

Penny pushed the seaweed aside and entered the cave flashing a torch. Soon they came to where the sacks of treasure were stashed. Van Wiese opened one and trained his own torch on the glinting assortment of jewels and gold. He was silent for a moment, transfixed, before saying,

'It really is here. I admit I only half believed you. I'll need to arrange for this to be moved.'

'Well goodbye, judge. You have what you want,' said Penny, turning to go out of the cave.

Van Wiese said,

'I'm sorry Miss Duchesne, but I can't let you walk away now.'

Penny saw a glint of metal in his right hand and dived to the floor just in time as a shot rang out. She crawled away as his torch flashed this way and that. He shot again but missed. Then there was a thump and silence.

'You can get up now, Miss,' said a voice with a distinctive Cape Town accent. 'I'll tie him up.'

'Thanks, Ludio. That was close. I hadn't expected him to do something quite so quickly. I was frightened you might not be here. We'd better watch out, there may well be some of van Wiese's friends about. What are we going to do with him? Not kill him, that's for sure,' said Penny.'

'Don't worry, I have plans for him, he won't be causing you any more trouble,' said Ludio. Something in the calmness of his voice gave Penny confidence.

'I'd better see what's happened to Tony and Septimus and I'll leave you here,' said Penny. 'I'm not going out of the sea entrance. I'll crawl up the back way we found last time I was here.'

Petrus had been watching Penny and van Wiese walk along the seashore for several miles. It was his brief to come to his boss's aid when they reached wherever she was heading, but he had lost sight of them. He'd met one of van

Wiese's thugs, a Johannes de Bruyn, who'd called him earlier. If necessary they were to dispose of Penny's body after he'd shot her. De Bruyn was a beefy man in his thirties whom he adjudged well able to perform adequately in any physical confrontation.

After Penny and van Wiese had disappeared from view there was a loud bang and Petrus said,

'This is our cue, let's get down there.' De Bruyn followed him. They walked down to the beach, Petrus picking a spot ten meters from where they had last seen Penny and van Wiese. But they had trouble finding the cave entrance. All they could see was a cliff overhung with green and brown seaweed.

'Ag man, where the hell have they gone? I'm fucking sure it was here they were,' said de Bruyn.'

'It's true, but this is where I saw them. Let's wait awhile and see if they turn up,' said Petrus

'It's bleddy windy man, I hope It's soon,' said de Bruyn. Petrus assumed Penny knew what she was doing and hoped his companion wouldn't look too hard. De Bruyn made him feel uncomfortable and he wondered how many years he'd spent in prison. He had that look about him.

'Look,' said de Bruyn, there are the two *okes* I saw up there looking down at us.' Petrus recognized Tony and Septimus.

'They're probably just walkers. Ignore them and act casual,' he said. Let's walk further along and then double back.'

This they did, and Tony and Septimus disappeared from view. There was what sounded like a clap of thunder and it began to rain. There was another bang.

'Listen man,' said de Bruyn, 'I'm not staying outside here in this, let's go to my *bakkie* – It's parked up there.'

Petrus nodded. He wondered what had happened to van Wiese but didn't really care. The rain was pelting down and a flash of lightning followed by what was definitely a clap of thunder caused Petrus to say,

'Let's get out of here.'

Penny crawled to the surface to be greeted by heavy rain and sounds of thunder. She saw Tony and Septimus running to take shelter under a tree.

'You idiots,' she said, that's the most dangerous place you could go. I've a car waiting. Follow me.'

The three ran in single file, Septimus puffing like the unfit man he was, but the slim Tony kept up easily.

'Look, isn't that Petrus with a heavy in that *bakkie*?' said Tony once they reached Penny's car, which she'd somehow managed to spirit into Arniston.

'Yes it is,' said Penny. 'Sorry to have kept you two in the dark, but I have other allies. You're by way of backup.'

'What's happened to His Honour?' said Septimus.

'Still in the cave, I imagine,' said Penny. 'Ludio Mark Two is looking after him. The judge had no intention of keeping our agreement. I'm glad I had Ludio's help. The only problem is what to do with van Wiese. I really don't care about the loot down there, but I need to keep him off our backs. Ludio will get some insurance though, I hope. He's going to see if he can record van Wiese admitting he had auntie killed. I expect he'll resist, but underneath the bravado I suspect he's a coward. Don't expect it will be admissible in court, but even an investigation will be curtains for that precious reputation of his.'

'I thought that only happened in TV dramas,' said Septimus.

'That's what gave me the idea,' said Penny. 'Let's get out of here.'

They drove off at speed. Petrus saw them pass and chuckled. She's safe, he thought. What's happened to the blessed van Wiese? He and his companion sat in the vehicle for an hour, the rain thudding against the roof of the *bakkie*. Suddenly the weather changed and sunshine lit up the sea in front of them.

'Hadn't we better go and look for the boss?' said De Bruyn.

'I think we should, let's go back to the beach,' said Petrus. They walked back to where they'd last seen Penny and van Wiese, but after about 20 minutes going up and down trying to find where they'd gone, Petrus said,

'He must've left. We should go back to Agulhas.'

'Okay man, we can't stay here forever – we've done our best,' said De Bruyn. 'That van Wiese, he's a hard one. I hope he's not going to *donder* us for leaving him.'

'That is a possibility, but what can we do?' said Petrus. ' We are not endowed with magical powers.' De Bruyn looked puzzled for a moment. Polysyllabic words were not his strength. He grinned.

'*Ag* you mean we couldn't know?' he said.

'Yes, that's it,' Petrus said.

They drove in silence on the road back to Cape Town. As they approached Bredasdorp they saw a car at the side of the road. Three people were standing alongside and it was tilted, they guessed by a jack. A flat tyre. They were going to pass on by, glad that it was not their problem, when De Bruyn said,

'Hang on man, that woman looks familiar. She's the one we were chasing a few days ago, and those *okes*, I'd recognize them anywhere. I reckon this is our chance to do the boss a good turn. He won't be so angry when he sees we've got rid of his enemies.'

Petrus did a double take. He had no wish to be involved in a scrap, least of all with people he now regarded as friends. De Bruyn slammed on the brakes and leaped out of the *bakkie*, brandishing a pistol.

'You there, hands up,' he shouted. The apparition startled

the three distressed motorists, but the shot that whistled past them cause them to obey. Panting, De Bruyn walked up to them.

'I know you - get into our *bakkie*.' They walked towards the *bakkie* and surprised and relieved to see Petrus there, looking as surprised as they were. 'Come on, into the back,' said De Bruyn.

'It's not safe,' said Tony.

'Shut up you arsehole,' said De Bruyn 'It's good enough for you.' They clambered into the back of the *bakkie*. It smelt of manure but a gun pointing at you is gun pointing at you, so they did as they were told.

'Let's go,' said de Bruyn, 'We'll drive back to Agulhas and show the boss what we've got.'

Petrus was not a man of action and he didn't have the confidence to shoot De Bruyn there and then. Once they got going he was afraid that if he did anything sudden, they'd all be killed.

'Shit,' said Penny. 'This is bad luck boys. Our only hope is that our friend Petrus will turn out to be just that and do something to that ape.'

The noise of the wind made conversation difficult and the sky began to darken. The lights of Agulhas showed on the horizon and they drove into the little town. De Bruyn went up a side street and into the driveway of a large house. He got out of the *bakkie* and said, '*Uit*,' to his prisoners. He turned to Petrus.

'We have a cellar here where we can keep them till we see the boss.' Petrus nodded. The three prisoners trooped out of the *bakkie* and into the house. De Bruyn opened an internal door and pushed them one by one downstairs into the cellar. He pushed the door and the Yale lock clicked.

'Why the hell didn't Petrus do something?' said Septimus. 'Some friend.'

The cellar was musty and dark. As they began to get their bearings they moved around, knocking over various things which they didn't recognise.

'This is a fine kettle of fish,' said Septimus.

'Yes, I admit I was waiting for Petrus to help. I didn't want to endanger our lives in that *bakkie*. Now I don't give much for them - if that thug is feeling homicidal we're toast,' said Penny.

Tony sighed.

'We've been in scrapes before, Penny. I expect Petrus will not have abandoned us.'

Hour succeeded hour.

'It's getting bloody cold,' said Septimus. 'I wish I had my long johns and vest.'

Penny laughed. 'It is cold in this country sometimes - do you have any matches?'

'Yes,' said Septimus. 'As you've noticed, I smoke a pipe, which is in an abandoned car somewhere between Bredasdorp and Cape Town. What do you propose to do?'

'That thug didn't search us,' she said. 'Do you have your wallet upon you? I need a credit card,'

'A miracle,' said Tony 'I have a card here in my wallet - what do you propose to do with it?'

'If Septimus would be kind enough to strike a match, then I can look at the lock and see what can be done,' said Penny.

Septimus struck a match and Penny inserted the card in the small gap between the edge of the door and the jamb. There was a tiny click and she pulled the door open. 'Simple,' she said, 'I don't know why it took me so long to think of that. Internal doors are pretty rudimentary. Now keep very quiet. I don't want us shot immediately we show our faces.'

The men crept up the stairs behind Penny and into a dark passageway. They could see a light underneath the door at one end. Penny approached it and put an ear to it.

'I can hear some awful row on the TV, I think we should wait,' she said.

'What about rushing them?' whispered Septimus. Penny shook her head.

'I expect the thug will come to check on us. Three of us should be able to jump him.'

Suddenly the sound of the TV ceased.

'Brace yourselves,' said Penny.

The door opened and the figure that came through found itself overwhelmed by three bodies, the smallest one with a tight grip around the neck.' 'Search him,' said Penny.

'I can't find anything,' said Tony. The body on the floor groaned.

'I was just coming to let you out,' said Petrus from his prone position. 'De Bruyn has gone off somewhere. Do you mind turning on the light? It's just next to the door.' Light revealed the dishevelled Petrus. After a few minutes they were all sat in the room with the TV.

'When is the thug returning?' said Penny.

'Tomorrow I think,' said Petrus. 'He's taken the *bakkie*, but I have my own car nearby. I suggest we drive to Cape Town and you can tell me what's been going on. Van Wiese is nowhere to be seen.'

'He's taken care of for the moment,' said Penny, 'but we don't want to stay another second in this place. You took your time by the way.'

Van Wiese, trussed up in the corner of the cave, glared at Ludio as two companions loaded the treasure onto pallets. He couldn't talk because they'd gagged him. Ludio was amused at van Wiese's discomfiture.

'*Ag baas*, don't worry, you're safe. We have a better use for this stuff than you.'

Van Wiese's mind churned with thoughts of the revenge he was going to exact on Penny and all her friends. Where were his men? He hoped to see the burly figure of De Bruyn at any moment. He'd deal with these *skollies*. And Petrus? The man was intelligent but clearly not a man of action. He'd been outmaneuvered utterly. Still, when he got out...There was a flash of light, then another. He was being photographed!

'This is insurance *baas*, by the way,' said Ludio. 'Miss Duchesne says any publicity about this will kill your reputation. By the way, if you don't want to be left here you will need to tell me how you killed her aunt.'

Van Wiese's eyes blazed with anger. If this... man thought he could bully him, he was mistaken. Soon all the treasure was gone, loaded up after dark on a *bakkie* and disguised as farm produce. Van Wiese was alone. Surely his men would find him? It began to get cold and he could feel the dampness of the air. The sound of the nearby sea became monotonous. He fell asleep. The relief was only temporary – he kept waking up, hoping to find himself out of there, anywhere, a hotel room, his house in Sussex, somewhere warm. After hours he saw the torch. Ludio was back.

'Now baas, I'd like to let you go, but I can't you see. I know you have lots of friends, and they'll kill me if I do. I have a bargain to make with you. It's simple – you tell me how you killed Theresa in England and I'll let you go. I'll even give you a drink of water. You must be thirsty by now.'

Van Wiese was not a robust man. Years of the best wine and food had made him soft, physically. Right now, he'd have confessed to killing President Kennedy to get out. He nodded his head. His confession would be worthless in a court of law. He was under duress. So, his gag untied, he told the story. First of all he was brief, but Ludio wanted names, dates, details on how instructions were given, secrets that he kept his head – how he'd gone after Penny, how he'd had Tony watched as a means of getting to Penny. He revealed names of his agents in England how he hated all English people and wanted to avenge the harm done to the *Ossewabrandwag* by Theresa. Ludio listened and recorded everything. It took hours. Occasionally he gave Van Wiese a sip of water.

'I've told you everything, now let me go!' he said.

'I'm going to die here. I have a heart condition and I need my blood pressure pills.'

'*Ag man*, I'm sorry about that. Now the deal is this - we deliver you to your hotel in Cape Town. This recording is going to be copied. It will be in several places. If you're causing trouble, if anyone I know is harmed, and I mean Miss Duchesne and her friends or any of my friends, that recording will go to the newspapers in England and also to the police. There is enough information there for them to convict you of murder and other offences. Even If they can't use the recording itself. If you get arrested that's your good name gone forever. And no loss if I may say so.'

Defeat showed in van Wiese's eyes as the torch shone on him, and he nodded. Later, when it was dark outside, he was bundled into the back of a large Mercedes. Gagged once again, he felt the indignity of his position. Ludio belonged to a race he'd always secretly despised in spite of the politically correct attitude he'd always displayed in England. To be bested by a 'coloured' man was something he found hard to take. He felt quite ill, too, and he feared for his health. At 66 he was mentally sharp, but he relied a great deal on his private medical plan to keep himself going. It was this fear that had made him surrender to Ludio's demands so easily. When faced with death or disgrace, disgrace was preferable. All his careful plans had come to nothing, but he would get revenge in his own way in his own time.

EPILOGUE

It was Sunday morning. Tony had preached on the theme of 'Lay not up for yourselves treasures upon earth'.

Septimus and Penny, neither of them religiously inclined, but rather leaning towards agnosticism, had attended the service, curious to see their friend in action.

'I did like some of the music,' said Penny, back at the vicarage, 'but I thought that tall bod in the front row spoiled the last hymn by singing so loudly and out of tune. He was even worse than Septimus.'

'Hold on,' said Septimus, 'I accept I rarely enter a church, and failed to get into the choir at school, but I'm not *that* bad.'

'You tried, Septimus,' said Tony. 'Penny, I will say, has a delightful contralto.'

'Thank you darling,' said Penny, 'and you sing in a fine tenor.'

'Enough of this mutual congratulation,' said Septimus. 'I suggest we go to the pub. There's a reasonable one in Bletchingley. It's not far, but far enough for none of Tony's parishioners to see him quaffing on the Lord's Day.'

. . .

ENJOYING the pub's log fire, Septimus browsed through the Sunday paper.

His companions looked up as he said,

'Goodness me, Front Page News.' He pointed to a headline,

'ANCIENT ARTEFACT RETURNED'

'It says here that someone left a parcel at the Indian High Commission in Aldwych. Nobody noticed it until they were closing for the day. Doesn't say much for their security. They were alarmed and called out the Bomb Squad. Luckily they didn't blow it up because it's turned out to be the Peacock Throne of the Mogul Emperors, lost for centuries. The reporter says they examined CCTV footage and a dark haired woman was spotted near it, but she disappeared somewhere along the Strand.'

'Well, whatever next,' said Penny.

THE END

HISTORICAL NOTES

From the invasion of the Cape in the early 19th century by The British, there was always conflict with the mixture of Dutch, French and German immigrants who became known as the Afrikaners.

In 1836 many Afrikaners sought out land to the north of Southern Africa to escape what they saw as onerous government by the British. There they encountered indigenous black Africans, with whom again they were in conflict.

The discovery of gold on the Rand in 1886 brought numerous immigrants from Britain, who soon formed a powerful community. The Jameson Raid in 1898 set the conflict alight. The Boers, as the Afrikaners were known, feared they would be overwhelmed by the mainly British miners and once again become a British Colony.

The Anglo Boer War (*Tweede Vryheidsoorlog* in Afrikaans) lasted from 1899 to 1902. Eventually, by dint of vastly superior numbers and resources, the British won.

The last years of the war involved guerrilla warfare on the part of the Boers.

To counter this the wives and children of the Boers were

herded into concentration camps. The sanitation was poor and there were many deaths from disease. This became a lasting grievance amongst Afrikaners.

Some Afrikaners reconciled with the British, notably Botha and Smuts.

The Second World War was seen as an opportunity by many Afrikaners to break free from Britain.

South Africa decided, by a narrow majority, to join on Britain's side.

The *Ossewabrandwag* was an Afrikaner nationalist organisation dedicated to independence, as they saw it. Many acts of sabotage were carried out by their supporters.

German submarines did attack shipping off the southern coast, from the Cape right up to Mozambique. Many British soldiers were stationed in South Africa. Some Afrikaners supported the British and some did their best to further the Nazi cause.

In those days the indigenous people were treated as though all they were good for was manual labour and they had few political rights. It was only in 1995 that they achieved their rightful place in government.

This is not a political book, but the attitudes of the wartime characters reflect those current at the time.

As South African born in *apartheid* days I was only too aware of these attitudes. My schoolteachers, parents and many of my friends were hostile to the regime, some being heavily involved in the 'struggle'. However this is not a political book, but an adventure story and attitudes are shown so as to reflect the motivation of various characters.

ABOUT THE AUTHOR

Digby Fletcher was born and brought up in South Africa. At the age of 21 he moved to England and qualified as a solicitor, practising in many different courts. He spent ten years as a Duty Solicitor representing criminals and alleged criminals.

He is married to Jenny, who writes crime novels. His interests are rugby, reading, history, travel, tennis, opera and nature. He has five children, including stepchildren.

if you enjoyed this, then read Holy Disorder by the same author. A free first chapter is available on my website www.digbycreative.net

'

'

GLOSSARY OF AFRIKAANS WORDS

aangename - pleasant ('aangename kennis' - pleased to meet you)

ag - ugh, oh

allemagtig - almighty (expression)

asseblief - please

baie - very

bakkie - small pickup truck

beweging - movement

bietjie - bit

donder - literally 'thunder' colloquially 'hit hard'

dominee - clergyman

dorp - village

die - the

distrik - district

daar - there

dankie - thank you

ek - I

geheime - secret

glas - glass

gogga - insect

goed - good

hê - have

inkosikaas - chieftainess (Zulu)

is - is, are

jy - you informal)

jou - your

kennis - knowledge

kerk - church

konfyt - jam

kaart - ticket

knobkerrie - club

lawaai - noise

mag - may

meisie - girl

meneer - Mr

mevrou - Mrs

moenie - don't(followed by 'nie')

net - only

nie - no

nog - another

OB - abbreviation of Ossewabrandwag

oke - fellow (see okie)

okie - fellow (see ou)

oom - uncle

oorlog - war

ou - fellow

ouma - grandmother

oupa - grandfather

ossewa - oxwagon

Ossewabrandwag - 'Oxwagon sentinel'- Afrikaner nationalist organisation

papiere - papers

praat - talk

rooinek - 'redneck', nickname for the British

Sarie Marais - Boer War song

seun = son

skelm - rascal

skollie - thug, criminal

snaaks - strange

stompie - butt of a cigarette

tannie - auntie

tweede - second

uit - out

van - of

verkrampte - narrow minded

verligte - enlightened

verslag - report

vir - for

vryheid - freedom

waar - where

waarom - why

wag - wait

ALSO BY D M FLETCHER

Holy Disorder

Made in the USA
Monee, IL
06 May 2022

96011175R00167